WHEN THE MIRROR CRACKS

MAY MCGOLDRICK

JAN COFFEY

Janet O'Donnell

MM BOOKS

For our Children

PROLOGUE

YOU'LL NEVER LEAVE. Death awaits you here. Believe me, fate is dogging your every step. It is the wavering reflection on the tile in front of you. It is the shadow on the pillar that you pass. If you listen, you will hear it breathing behind you. Your gaze passes over me but you no longer recognize me. I'm the one whose life you threw away.

How far you've flown to come back to me, to come back within my reach. You are a dead woman.

You have found a perverse sense of accomplishment in destroying the lives of others. No more. Happiness and contentment will turn to ash. Your shriveled heart will be ripped from your chest and roasted in the flames of hell.

You made me suffer, and I'll make sure that you will suffer. You made me lose those closest to me. You will lose those closest to you.

You left me with a future that was no more than a dark, starless night. You assumed I would die, but I am not dead. All this time I have been waiting here for your return, and I will have my rightful vengeance.

I'll forgive you then...when you are dead.

PART I

I am not from the East
or the West, not out of the ocean or up
from the ground, not natural or ethereal, not
composed of elements at all. I do not exist,
am not an entity in this world or in the next,
did not descend from Adam and Eve or any
origin story. My place is placeless, a trace
of the traceless. Neither body nor soul.

—Rumi

1

CHRISTINA

THE BLACK PICKUP truck comes out of nowhere, and headlights explode in a spray of glass. As the car spins, my head snaps to the side, and I'm slammed hard against the steering wheel. No. No. The baby. *Please stop. Make the car stop.* Suspended in a world out of control, I try to make some sense out of what is happening.

Like a rag doll, I'm flying from side to side, hitting the door hard before getting jerked forward. The belt tightens around my hips.

My child. Is the belt enough to protect the baby cocooned in my womb?

Jamming my arms against the steering wheel, I try to force my distended belly away from it, create some space, and shield my baby. I press back against the seat as hard as I can until the spinning stops.

"We're okay, sweetheart. We're okay." She has to be scared. I'm scared. My heart beat drums in my ears, muffling the desperate cries of the woman in my car. It takes a moment to realize the voice belongs to me.

Bright lights flash in the passenger side just before the next avalanche of disaster arrives. Someone T-bones me. The windows shatter, showering my face and body with pebbles of glass, and the car rolls over. *God, no. Don't let her die. Please. Save her. Don't let her die.* The airbag bursts open and hits me with a blinding blow to the face and chest, smashing my arms against me.

Everything comes to a halt—time, the ugly screech and grind of brakes, the car horns. We survived...or are we dead? It's surreal. In my mind, I'm not even in the car. I'm a detached onlooker, gazing down at a mangled vehicle with a pregnant woman inside.

Save them. Please save them. I need to get them out. My feet don't move. My body refuses to follow directions. I blink and I'm back inside the car, hanging, suspended by the seatbelt that's digging into my neck. The only sound is the creak of the roof as the car rocks on the pavement...and my own gasping breaths. Shards and pebbles of glass are everywhere, and there's blood on the deflated airbag.

You're okay. We're okay. Shouldn't I be feeling pain? I was coming from Jax's funeral. Maybe I'm as dead as Jax.

The smell of tires and gasoline burns my nose. The coppery taste in my mouth is blood, and I spit it out.

Footsteps approach and someone is asking muffled, unintelligible questions. Turning my head toward the sound, my throat struggles to push the words free.

"I'm pregnant. Eight months pregnant. Save *her*."

A hand touches my shoulder. There's so much blood all around, and I can't focus on the face of the person talking. We couldn't have survived the accident. Hope withers and shrivels my heart.

"One casket. My baby should be buried with me in one casket."

"You'll be fine."

Sirens and flashing lights approach. The car is a twisted pile of metal and broken glass. No one inside could have survived the accident.

"No cremation."

Disembodied voices join the first one. Words become clearer.

"We've got you."

I close my eyes. I want to believe them. *They've got us.* I keep repeating the words in my head, wishing for my unborn child to hear them. Four weeks until our due date, but the doctor had said she could come anytime. *She's perfect. All should go well.*

All had gone well, until today. Moments from the past eight months flood my mind. Hearing her first heart beat, the hiccups that make my entire stomach jump. The feeling of her toes digging into my ribs. The kicks. The constant kicks to remind me that she's there, taking care of me as I watch over her.

Kick me now. Please kick me. Tell me you're okay.

They have me out of the car. All the EMTs are talking at once as they lift me onto a gurney. The glass crunches under the rolling wheels, and then I'm in the ambulance.

Sharp cramps hit me. My underwear is soaked. I know what's happening. "First pregnancy. I'm in labor." They would want to know. My voice is scratchy and sounds like it's coming from the bottom of a well. "Save her. If it's her or me, save *her*. Please."

"We've got you. Both of you."

I'm a broken record, saying the same things again and again, but I feel myself fading in and out. Someone is asking me whom to call. Did they say *husband,* or did I imagine it?

"No...no husband. Kyle doesn't want her."

I force my eyes open and look into the blurred face of a woman moving beside the gurney. The ceiling lights behind her head are blinding. We're already in the hospital, but I don't remember getting here.

"My mother," I say to her. "Call my mother."

HOT BILE BURNS like acid in my chest, and my eyes pop open as I sit up. I'm not in a hospital, but for a moment I'm not sure where I am.

I look around, trying to focus, but the memory of the accident is still right there in front of me, refusing to let go.

The sky is bright outside the open windows of the strange room, and the black screen of a TV stares back at me from the wall. My suitcase sits open on the floor next to a portable crib.

Then it all comes back to me. I'm in Istanbul. The flight from Los Angeles arrived late yesterday afternoon. Fourteen hours on the plane and a ten-hour time difference, and I was exhausted, but my brain refused to shut down. Sometime during the night, I dug out the bottle of melatonin pills. I can't remember if I slept afterward or not. I must have.

7

Nausea climbs into my throat and, running into the bathroom, I bend over the toilet, heaving and retching. Where I have been, what I have done, where I am going to and what I must do are a blur. I'm traveling through time on a speeding train. There are no stops. No chance for me to catch my breath. No going back.

You have a beautiful girl.

My head is swimming with the lights and humming sounds of the hospital as I sit back on my heels.

She's eight pounds, one ounce, and twenty-two inches.

My fingers trace the perfect nose, the clump of dark wet hair, the round cheeks.

My body is cold and clammy with sweat, and I pull myself up to lean against the tub. I take deep breaths, trying to settle my stomach.

Smells waft in through the small window over the tub, and I breathe in the aroma of Turkish coffee and spiced, fresh bread. I can't remember when I last ate. Maybe that's the problem.

When I stand up, I feel wobbly and hold onto the edge of the sink until the wave of light-headedness passes.

I turn on the shower and watch the water run down the marble tiles. Another memory flashes back. A nurse is holding my arm, helping me take the few steps from the bed to the shower. The sound of my mother's voice comes from the chair by the window. *Do this on your own, Christina. She'll be right there at the door if you need her.*

Every millisecond of the accident plagues me night and day. The crash, the spinning, the tumbling over and over. It all comes back to me every time I get behind the wheel, every time I see a black pickup truck on the road. In the hospital, they had the hardest time finding my veins, and still they took blood every morning. Bruises take shape on my arm, and I blink to make them disappear. A thick fog clouds my mind, and I blame it on the sleeping pills. I don't like taking them, not even the over-the-counter types.

My stomach is tied in a knot. I step into the shower enclosure, and the water pricks my skin like a thousand needles. Do I want it hot or cold? I can't decide, so I stand there as water beats down on me, and the swirls and patterns in the tiles blur.

Focusing on my job always takes my mind off the rest of my life, so

I think of Externus, Jax and my mother's company. That's why I'm in Istanbul. The company is for sale, and we need to come to terms with a buyer and close the deal. I try to recall dates and schedules, but it's so exhausting. Leaning my head against the tile, I want to shut down every troubling door of my life, but my brain keeps pulling me back to that horrible night. I can't drag myself clear of that mangled car and the hospital.

The baby's cry rips through the fog, and I force my head off the tile.

My vision is blurred, but my body reacts immediately. It knows what to do. Instinct kicks in. I shut off the water and grab my robe. My feet are wet, and I slip on the bathroom floor and nearly go down but catch myself somehow.

The baby is wailing between gasping coughs. She's getting sick. The flight from LA to Istanbul was too long. She's too young to travel. I shouldn't have brought her.

I hurry into the bedroom and go directly to the crib. "Hush, Autumn. I'm here, my baby love."

The morning light streaming through the window blinds me. Gauzy curtains lift in the breeze. Another flash of a memory materializes, and voices fill my head.

You can't pick her up every time she cries, Christina.

She's my daughter, Mother. And I'm not you.

I bend over the crib and stop dead. I stare, trying to make sense of this. A roaring sound is building in my ears. The crib is empty, the sheets stretched tightly over a mattress.

"No. No. No. Where are you?"

I whirl and spring toward the mess I made of my own bed last night, tearing off the blankets and the pillows.

"Autumn! Autumn!" My cries echo off the walls.

But I *heard* her cry. Where is she? Someone took her. Someone picked her up and took her. My eyes are everywhere, searching the empty room. On the door, the security bar is still latched. Panic floods through me. My hotel room is on the third floor, and it's a long drop to the grassy courtyard below. No one could have come in or gone out that way.

My body is shaking, and tears sting my eyes. I'm hysterical when I punch the button for the front desk. Thankfully, a woman answers in English.

"Call the police. Get a manager up here. Please. Help me. I was in the shower. My baby is missing. Help me. She's gone. Someone took her."

The woman's tone immediately becomes urgent. She fires directions at others in Turkish, and garbled voices come through the phone.

"The manager is coming up to you right now, Miss Hall. I'll call the police. We'll find her."

The handset slips out of my fingers, and I watch it bounce on the floor. My knees are locked. I can't move, and my head is about to split open.

Again, headlights and the crash. I'm back in the hospital, and Kyle is furious. *She's mine. My daughter, too. I should have been the first one you called.* I can't argue, so I turn my head away.

"Autumn...sweetheart." I choke out the words. "Where are you, my love?"

There's a loud knock at the door, and voices call from the hallway. I don't feel the floor under my feet as I move to the door and open it.

"We've called the police, Miss Hall. Guards are standing at every door. No one will leave the hotel..."

I don't want to hear what they're doing. I only want Autumn back.

Bodies bump past each other. I back up to get out of their way and sink into a chair. I rock back and forth, trying to understand what's happening, but I can't think. Their voices are so loud, and they're bombarding me with questions in Turkish and English.

"My child. Gone. She was right there. I was in the shower. I heard her crying. I came out of the bathroom. She was gone." I say it again and again. "I didn't leave the room during the night...No....I'm a good mother."

I don't see her come in, but I recognize the familiar touch. It's a poke, actually. I lift my head and feel relief push against the anguish tearing me up inside.

"She's gone, Mother. Autumn's gone." My voice breaks, and I hiccup while struggling to speak. "They took her. Help me find her."

My mother pulls up a chair and sits facing me. "Christina, breathe."

Shaking my head, I rock back and forth, unable to catch my breath. "I'm going to throw up."

"Not in front of all these people. Go into the bathroom."

Hot and cold, trauma has me shaking. "I can't move. She's *missing!*"

"Think, Christina." This time her tone is sharp enough to shatter glass.

Turning abruptly to the manager, Elizabeth speaks to him in Turkish. A long pause fills the room. Then, heads nod and eyes dart toward me. There's more whispering and, one by one, they file out.

"Where are they going?"

"I told you to order room service last night. But you haven't eaten, have you?" It isn't a question. Elizabeth closes the door and sits down again.

"What did you say to them? Why did you send them out? Where is Autumn? What has happened to my baby?"

She takes my hand and brushes away a wet clump of hair draping over my eye. "You should have kept on these people about the crib when you checked in. I should have said something to them myself. That was thoughtless."

The crib? I glance at the crib and at my suitcase. My clothes are spilling out of it. But there are no diapers, no baby clothes, no stroller.

"Tell me about the cry you heard in the shower," she asks softly. "Did you hear Autumn cry, Christina?"

The panic drains slowly out of me. But as reality reasserts itself, a sharp pain stabs me in the chest.

"No. There was no cry." I take a deep breath. "There was no baby. I lost her. I lost Autumn...after the accident."

2

CHRISTINA

THAT FIRST DAY, the doctors called the outcome of the accident a miracle.

Autumn, born a couple of hours after we arrived at the hospital, showed no sign of stress from the trauma. Her Apgar score was eight. As I held her in my arms, the pain from the whiplash and cuts and bruises, and the haze of concussion I'd suffered during the accident, disappeared. She studied me and I watched her, her small hand clutching my finger, her trust unconditional. The happiness flowing through me was unlike anything I'd ever experienced. In my mind, the circumstances that led me to keeping the baby after learning I was pregnant were justified, regardless of Kyle's reaction or feelings.

My life was finally whole. Autumn engulfed my heart; she was in my arms. She was a piece of me, all of me. I had brought her into this world, and she was everything I'd wished for, dreamed of.

"I'm recommending a minimum seven-day hospital stay before sending you home, considering everything," the internist explained to me the following day.

Whatever they wanted to do, any test they wished to run, was fine with me. I was happy so long as they allowed Autumn to stay in my room.

It was on the third day that my condition raised concerns. My headaches were lingering, and the doctor ordered a CT scan.

"You'll only be away from her for an hour," a soft-spoken nurse assured me before wheeling me away.

Autumn's crib was rolled into the nursery. During the test, a tight fist closed around my heart, as if in warning, letting me know something wasn't right. When I came back, my daughter's crib was empty.

"The pediatrician ordered to have her moved into the ICU." The same nurse escorted me to where Autumn had been taken.

Maybe they were doing another test, I thought. I tried to build a bridge of hope, thinking I could cross it, bring my baby back. But with every passing hour, with each test they ran, the supports to that bridge weakened and cracked and finally collapsed. It was then that I was told the structure was flawed to start with.

A day later, Autumn died.

Tears burn my eyes. This morning is another reminder that some sorrows never leave. The loss of my daughter will be with me forever.

The doctors had an official term for what happened to Autumn— traumatic brain injury. It had occurred during the accident. There was no way to have known it.

"You should call the front desk and explain."

Elizabeth's words are a slap, cutting into my thoughts of the past.

"Mother, please. Not now." I keep my tone mild, but she knows what I've been through.

"You had good reason for acting that way. And it was their fault for leaving a crib in this room."

"It doesn't matter whose fault it was. It's over."

I bury my head into my hands. Over the past two months, I've been trying to rebuild my life. Piece by piece. The fact is, something broke inside of me when my daughter died, and I can't quite get a firm grip on my grief. Feelings of guilt dog my waking hours and haunt the restless nights.

The pickup truck changed lanes. No alcohol or drugs were involved, but I should have been more attentive. I should have been quicker to react. I should have...

Too many *should haves* rattle around in my brain.

There is no quick fix, no going to sleep and waking up and forgetting what happened. The empty crib in the hotel room this morning transported me back to the hospital nursery. My first thoughts then were that someone had stolen my baby. It was after speaking with the nurse that I learned the floor pediatrician didn't like something she'd seen while examining Autumn.

"We're booked in this hotel for ten days. I don't want them to think less of you. At least, call them and explain what happened. Tell them you're in mourning."

My nerves are getting stretched thinner with every word she speaks. "I don't care what they think of me."

"But I do," she persists. "You're jet-lagged. You didn't know where you were."

I'm a fucking guest at this hotel. A paying customer. I don't need anyone's understanding or sympathy. But I know there's no point in arguing with Elizabeth when she sets her mind to something. She's doing this for my sake. To protect me. Her way of showing love is to take charge of my life.

I run my hands over my face and stand up, looking for my cell phone.

"Losing a baby is a very traumatic thing," she says. "I had three miscarriages before I got pregnant with you."

I've heard Elizabeth repeat this too many times since leaving the hospital. It's as if she thinks my knowing what she went through can somehow diminish *my* pain. I need to distract her as much as I need to distract myself.

My cell phone is charging next to the bed. I fire a text to Kyle to remind him about sending the updated schedule for today. He's been in Osaka attending a gaming convention, but he's flying into Istanbul tomorrow night. The two of us have been assigned by my mother to oversee the sale of Externus. Kyle has been in charge of sales and marketing, and I'm the business strategy person. We're the bookends holding the small company together until we can hand it over to the next owner.

Elizabeth Hall and Jax York married six years ago and two years later started the active-media gaming company. Since then, it's been a five-person operation. Using a pool of freelance programmers, Externus has thrived. Now, with Jax gone, my mother is the sole proprietor. And she's ready to sell.

"Time marches on, Christina. You're young. There'll be lots more babies in the future for you two."

There's no point in arguing with her. Kyle and I work together and live together. We were an item when I got pregnant. Thinking back, there were conversations he and I should have had long before I slid that First Response test in front of him. It should have been obvious to me that he wasn't ready to be a father. True, he didn't immediately pack up and move out, but I guessed it was only a matter of time before we went our separate ways.

"Before it happens next time, though, see if you can get him to put a ring on your finger."

Elizabeth's words make me feel cheap. There's plenty I'd like to say to her, starting with a reminder that she was an unmarried mother too. But staying silent wins out. I've come to terms with my mistakes. I should have communicated with Kyle. And even though my mother did the same thing, my holding back with him was still wrong.

While I wait to hear back from Kyle, I sit on the edge of the bed and page through my Instagram account. My thumb hovers over the pictures I posted while I couldn't sleep last night. The aerial view of Istanbul while the plane circled. The photo I took coming out of the international arrival gate at the new airport. The driver who met us was holding a sign reading *Hall*. I enlarge the photo and look at the woman wearing a brown headscarf and standing next to the driver. They have the same pose, the same expectant expression. They're both waiting for *us*.

Elizabeth continues. "When they were leaving, I said a few words to the manager about taking the crib away. I assume housekeeping will take care of it."

My attention stays focused on the woman in the picture. The raincoat covers her from chin to knee. Her face is washed out, sick pale. High cheekbones dominate her thin face. A surgical mask is draped around her neck, the kind people who are worried about germs in public places wear.

"She looks like she's just seen a ghost. I hope she connects with her people."

"Who are you talking about?"

I get up and hand my mother the phone. "Her. The woman at the airport. We saw her coming out from Customs. She looks sick. I hope she connects with her people."

Elizabeth zooms out of the photo and stares intently at the driver and the woman standing side-by-side.

"I liked the driver. We should use that company again. I know we're going to be busy with meetings, but I hope we'll have a chance for some sightseeing. This is your first time in Istanbul. There's so much of the city I want to show you."

I leave the phone with my mother and go to the window, pulling open the curtains. The hundred-year-old hotel we're staying in was originally built as an Ottoman jail. But with all the marbled hallways and plush furnishings, I doubt any former prisoner would recognize the place. And I do want to get out and feel the true pulse of the city, if possible.

"Who is she?" Elizabeth asks, coming to stand beside me. She's still going through Instagram pictures. "Is she on my company's payroll?"

Elizabeth isn't on my page; she's on Kyle's. The post is from last night, and the picture shows the front of the Externus booth at the convention.

"They look pretty cozy, standing that close."

I try to ignore the wave of jealousy rolling through me. Kyle's finger-combed blond hair stands out amid the sea of dark-haired people in the picture. The woman beside him has jet-black hair that hangs nearly to her waist. She has a practiced smile, and confidence oozes out of her. She's a woman accustomed to being stared at and admired.

I've seen her picture before on his account. He posted it the last time he was in Japan four months ago.

"Those legs," Elizabeth says admiringly. "Everyone needs a short black dress like hers. What size do you think she wears? Maybe a two?"

"I wouldn't know." I reach for my phone, but she holds it away from me.

"Did you bring the black dress I bought you at Bloomingdale's last year?"

"No. I'm twenty pounds heavier than this time last year. It doesn't fit me."

"Maybe you should think about going on a diet. It's been two months already."

My weight was an issue with her even before the pregnancy. That's another conversation I don't want to have right now.

Relief comes through the text notification popping on the screen, and I snatch my phone back before walking away. "Kyle says we have no meetings today or tomorrow. The first one is scheduled for Wednesday morning."

"He'll be here for it?"

"He'll be here." I pick up my suitcase and put it on the bed, sorting my clothes to put in the dresser drawers.

Cozy. I think about Elizabeth's not so subtle insinuation that Kyle has something going on with that woman in the picture. Our relationship has definitely been on the rocks since I announced my news. But with the baby on the way, I'd hoped...I'd hoped...what, that he'd suddenly decide he's ready to be a father? That he'd forgive me for not being forthcoming about wanting a baby badly enough to leave him out of the equation?

"What do you want to do today?"

Elizabeth's voice puts an end to the thoughts of my fractured relationship. I need to get out and move around. Maybe it's the history of this place as a prison, but the walls are closing in on me.

"Maybe take a walk in the neighborhood. I should get some work done too."

"No, we're going to a *hamam*. Massage. Pampering. There's nothing like it. You could definitely use it, especially today."

Elizabeth picks up the phone, and I listen to her speaking Turkish to the concierge, making arrangements. It amazes me that after so many years, she is still fluent. My mother knows her languages. In any given situation, she can break into German, French, Farsi, or Spanish. She credits it to being an Army brat, traveling everywhere. That and her years working as an interpreter overseas. Four of those years were spent in Turkey, during which I was born.

She did her best to encourage me in languages as I grew up. After-school programs. Native-speaking tutors. But some broken high school Spanish is the best I can do.

"I asked for a good place where locals go. She's booking us at a traditional *hamam* near the Spice Bazaar."

"Give me a few minutes to put myself together." I disappear inside the bathroom to dress.

I pause in front of the mirror and cringe. My face is all puffed up. My hazel eyes are slits, barely visible. I shudder at my hair. It's frizzy and totally out of control. I think of all the people who paraded through my room an hour ago.

I pull on my clothes and gather my hair into a ponytail. By the time I come out, Elizabeth has a bag packed for me. As we're walking out, my eyes are once again drawn to the crib. It was here in the room when we arrived last night. A mistake, or a misunderstanding, by the hotel staff. The dates of the travel, the length of stay, the hotel where we're staying were all decided by Jax months ago. He and Elizabeth had planned to come on this trip themselves. The two were to be joined by Kyle later when the acquisition details were finalized. I wasn't supposed to be part of this trip because of the baby.

"The Spice Bazaar isn't too far away from where we're going. Maybe we can walk through it afterwards."

"Lead the way. Take me were you want. You are the expert."

Passing through the lobby, I don't look at the people behind the desk. I can feel their eyes on me. Elizabeth walks beside me, chatting with everyone as if half of the hotel staff wasn't upstairs this morning, searching for my imaginary infant. I think of what she said as far as explaining. I should have thanked them, at least. But I was still too numb. And it's my nature to always react to whatever Elizabeth says. All part of a long story of our mother-daughter drama.

Outside, the doorman signals to a cab that immediately pulls up in front. The sun is shining. The leaves on a pair of trees across the narrow cobblestone lane are starting to turn.

Just as the taxi starts, I see her. She's standing at the corner, by the door of the Seven Hills Restaurant. Sunglasses cover her eyes. The surgical mask hanging around her neck. A group of tourists are lined up, waiting to go in the restaurant, but she's not with them. She's watching us.

"There she is," I say to my mother.

"Who?"

"That hijabi woman. I showed you her picture."

"Where?" Elizabeth is distracted, counting her Turkish liras.

I look out the back window. Her face is turned to our cab as we move slowly down the street.

"Next to the restaurant. The woman in the brown headscarf and raincoat."

"We're in a city of eighteen million people." She counts the coins.

"I'm talking about one face, one person. She looks familiar. Are you sure you don't know her?"

Elizabeth finally turns around and follows the direction of my gaze. "I don't see anyone I recognize."

I pull out my phone and search through the photos for the picture at the airport.

"Her." I point. "The woman who was standing at the gate."

Elizabeth half glances at my phone and dismisses the whole topic. She's more interested in talking to our driver in Turkish. They go back and forth, and both are smiling.

She catches me watching her and decides to take on the role of tour guide.

"This city has been the center of the world, connecting the East and the West, for thousands of years. Persians, Greeks, Romans, Arabs, Crusaders, Ottoman Turks. They all came and conquered. One civilization building on top of the last. And our hotel is in the heart of it all."

The car maneuvers through the traffic, and she's pointing at buildings. Hagia Sophia. Across a huge plaza, the Blue Mosque. Tourists and locals crowd the sidewalks and open spaces. Buses are lined up along the streets. Signs direct people where to queue up. Tour leaders carrying signs snake their groups along, pointing out what they should see, diverting attention away from beggars and refugees. Like a young girl with a dirty face, dressed in a ratty T-shirt and pants. She holds a cardboard sign toward my window as the cab stops for a red light. It reads in scrawled English, *Syrian. Hungry. Help.*

My fingers move for my purse. Elizabeth clamps her hand on mine, stopping me.

"Don't do it. The money doesn't go to them. Don't enable their handlers."

The car moves into the intersection and turns down a side street. The look in the child's dark eyes stays with me, and my shoulders stiffen. They told me all babies are born with blue eyes. Autumn's were blue too, a dark blue, the same as the color as the sky just before dawn. What color eyes would my own baby have eventually had? I'll never know.

The headache is back. This car and these streets are closing in.

We take another sharp turn into a busier street, and I clutch at the worn leather seat of the cab. My fingers slide off.

Today, I opened a door to thoughts of Autumn, and I can't close it.

My baby cried all the time. But as soon as I picked her up, she'd nestle against my bare skin, listening to my beating heart, and then she'd sleep.

I remember counting her fingers, breathing in the smell of her skin, feeling the silky softness of her light brown hair.

Kyle came and stayed late at the hospital the first night we were there. He brought me a giant vase of flowers and did a great job of pretending that he was happy. But Autumn cried the entire time he held her, as if she knew this father-daughter thing wasn't permanent.

For the rest of my stay, he came late or his visits were short. He had to work. With Jax dead and me in the hospital, someone had to take the reins of the company. It's sad that he wasn't there when our daughter was born, and he wasn't there when she died.

"*Burası*," my mother says.

The driver cuts in front of a moving bus, blocking traffic as he pulls to the curb. As we get out, Elizabeth says something. The young man says something back. They're all smiles. She even calls back to the driver of the bus, and we get a friendly wave.

Inside the *hamam*, cushions line the walls of a carpeted waiting room. In one corner, a low table holds a samovar and glasses for tea. By the reception desk, a potted jasmine plant fills the air with its sweet, exotic fragrance. Seeing it makes me think of the little balcony of my apartment, where jasmine grows wild with the star like flowers. A tall, fit woman greets us in broken English. I've worked with enough Russian programmers to recognize her accent. She looks visibly relieved when Elizabeth answers in Turkish.

While my mother is deciding on what package we're signing up for, I look back out through the smoked glass door onto the busy street.

She's there across the way, by a raised flower bed. The sunglasses are pushed up on top of her head, and she's wearing the same head-scarf and raincoat. She's staring at the building.

I walk toward the door and flatten my hands against the glass. "She's back."

Elizabeth enjoys practicing her Turkish and is talking a mile a minute to the front desk person.

"She followed us here," I say louder.

"Is an eighty-minute massage enough?"

I glance over my shoulder at my mother. "I think I'm going out there to speak to her."

She finally comes over. "Who are you talking about?"

The street is crowded with locals going in every direction. From what I've seen, Istanbul is a city of both tank tops and hijabs, and everything in between.

"The same one we saw on the sidewalk. I think she's following us. Are you sure you don't know her?"

"I don't see anyone I know. You probably are confusing one head-scarf for another."

She's disappeared. My mother doesn't say it, but from her tone it's clear she thinks I might be imagining the young woman altogether. I know I'm not.

"She was there a minute ago."

She pats me on the shoulder. "Eighty-minute massage?"

"Whatever works for you."

My feet are dragging as I move away from the door. The Russian woman hands us each a thin red-and-white plaid towel and terry cloth slippers. As we follow her, she points down different hallways, explaining where everything is. Marble floors, marble walls, the ceilings are white too. This place feels as sterile as the hospital I was taken to after the accident.

"The *hamams* are separate for men and women." Elizabeth translates. "The big pool and the steam room and sauna are over there. They do the massages in that direction. The central *hamam* is through that door."

I haven't really been thinking about what we're doing, and it's quickly sinking in. This is not just a massage, but a *hamam,* a *public* bath.

Ahead of us, two middle-aged women come out of the pool area, chatting away. They smile and walk into the locker room. They're naked. The elder is pear shaped with a birthmark the size of a quarter on her ass. A red-and-white towel is draped over her arm. The younger is thin and flat chested and wearing her towel around her hair like a turban.

I stare at the towel the receptionist handed me and curse under my breath, hoping that Elizabeth stuffed a bathing suit in my bag.

In the locker room, another naked woman is blow-drying her hair in front of a wall of mirrors. I try not to stare. I don't want to make eye contact. They're perfectly at ease with their bodies, but I'm not. I look for any space that will offer a little privacy. There's none, except for the toilet stalls around the corner.

Clearly, this is the norm, and I'm the aberration. Turkish women have a very different attitude than Americans about their bodies. In this culture, modesty has little in common with Western women's inhibitions. Or *my* inhibitions.

The receptionist speaks to my mother again.

Elizabeth translates for me. "She only has one masseuse available this morning. We'll have to go back-to-back. Do you want to take the first appointment?"

"No. You go first."

I'm relieved to have answered right, as she doesn't put up an argument and walks to the wall of lockers.

I need a little time to adjust to this. My expectations of going to a *hamam* were plush white robes and a masseuse behind closed doors. Probably that's exactly the experience our hotel has for tourists, like they never left America.

I have hang-ups about my body, and my mother knows it and likes to rub it in. She's seventy-four and petite and fit, and as toned as a forty-year-old Pilates instructor. Far different from her, I'm big boned. I was never a size zero, two, four, or six. I might have worn size-eight jeans when I was twelve years old, but not after that. The pregnancy only added on the pounds.

I stuff my bag into the nearest locker and disappear inside a bathroom stall. The door reaches to the floor, and it gives me a small semblance of privacy.

The sound of water running in a sink beyond the door makes me think of Autumn. I had given her a sponge bath at the hospital. Her eyes were wide open the whole time, watching me. She had a cleft on her chin, round cheeks, an angel kiss between her eyebrows.

The tears come, and I can't stop them. *Don't.* I can't fall apart. I won't. Not twice in one day. I can deal with this. I *have* to deal with this. I have a job to do in Istanbul.

There's a tap on the door of the stall. "How are you doing, sweetheart?"

She has a sixth sense. I use my shirt to wipe my face and flush the toilet to muffle my voice.

"Good. I'll be out soon."

"Where are you going first?"

"*Hamam.*"

"I can wait and show you the way before I go in for my massage."

"I'll find it. I remember the way."

She's silent for a few moments, but finally I hear her getting into a conversation with the women in the locker room. They laugh at something she says. Still fully clothed, I sit on the toilet and wait.

Think about work. Think about work.

It's so much easier thinking of business. Elizabeth has promised Kyle and me a bonus once we close the deal on Externus. We'll both undoubtedly lose our jobs, but we've never spoken about what happens after. I have no idea what he's planning to do with his money or what he'll do for work. I know what I'm going to do. I decided it months ago, even before I lost Autumn.

The hairdryer stops, and Elizabeth's conversation ends. I wonder if the women think it's strange that I've barricaded myself in this stall.

"Are you sure there's nothing I can do for you?" My mother is outside the door again.

"I'm fine. Really. I'm coming out." I hear her footsteps drift away.

The changing room is silent now that she's gone. I wait a minute more before stepping out. The women are all gone. But there's a young girl reaching into my locker.

"What are you doing?"

She jumps back, wide-eyed, and waves a folded paper at me. "*Korkma. O bana verdi.*"

I don't know what she's saying. I look inside the locker. My purse is still zipped. The duffel bag with my things is sitting next to it. Neither looks touched. I think of all the warnings everyone says about pickpockets and beggars. But she doesn't seem to be either. And she isn't running away. She continues to wave the paper in front of me.

"*O bana verdi. Amerikalı için.*"

"I don't speak Turkish."

"*Amerikalı mısın?*"

"Yes."

"*Bu seninki.*" She shoves the paper into my hand and goes out, looking like she's just done me a favor.

I unfold the note and stare at the words. The writing is in English. *Welcome back, Christina.*

3

ZARI

THEN

SHE'S MINE. Mine. You can't take my daughter away from me. I won't let you.

Tears bathed Zari's face. They wouldn't let up. She'd come to Istanbul, to this hotel, prepared with the words she had to say, with what she was willing to do. But she had no chance.

The journey here was a nightmare, the hours careening along the razor edge of panic and despair. The bus from Ankara broke down in a long tunnel that cut through the green mountains. The honking, blaring sounds of car and truck horns were deafening, echoing in the steaming concrete tube that entombed them. Zari thought she would die in that darkness. The five-hour journey turned into eight, and the rain beat on the bus roof, falling in sheets as they crossed the Golden Horn into Istanbul's old city.

The trip was torture, but this was worse. She was too late.

She paused on a landing of the hotel's back stairwell. The walls around her were pressing the air from her lungs. But in reality, it wasn't Zari who was struggling to breathe. It was the baby in her arms.

"I'm not going to let you die, little one."

Giving up was not the Kurdish way. Back in Qalat Dizah in Kurdistan, before the bombs murdered her people, before the army tanks and bulldozers leveled her city, Zari grew up memorizing Ferdowsi's *Shahnameh*, the Book of Kings. Character and perseverance were ingrained in her from childhood.

She always saw herself as the intelligent and independent Sindokht. As Farangis, who raised an army to avenge her husband's death. She was the brave Rudabeh, mother of Rostam, the greatest of all heroes. And when Zari was forced to leave behind her country and everyone she loved, she was Manizheh going into exile. The blood that flowed in their veins flowed in hers.

Memories of those heroic women from their history came to her now. They embodied wisdom, devotion, and courage. They shaped civilizations. They were mothers who fought for their families, for their people.

But today, she had no chance to be like them. She had no chance to raise her voice or fight. Zari's body trembled. She'd come here as quickly as she could, but she was too late. Every shred of hope she'd been clinging to was gone now. Her life was shattered.

The Kurds have no friends but the mountains. It was so true. Here in Istanbul, she was alone. She had absolutely no one to help her. No one to fight with her, to stand at her side. She was nothing but a refugee, just one of the million forced to walk away from their war-torn homeland.

But Zari hadn't walked away. She ran. With the shriek and blast of artillery shells all around her, she'd ran as quickly as she could. Cradling her swollen belly with both hands, she'd escaped the city she called home.

Joining one weary, tattered group and then another, she'd dragged herself through the rugged passes. The moon glistened on the snows of the rocky peaks as she traveled north and west into Turkey. She could still feel the bitter night-cold in her bones. And beside the trails, she'd seen the remains of fellow Kurds, mostly the old and the injured, who had not survived the arduous trek. But when they passed by the small, swaddled bundles—too numerous to count—she'd averted her eyes and whispered soothing words to the one in her womb.

Now, here in the hotel in Istanbul, Zari tried to pry open the fingers squeezing the blood from her heart.

The child flailed one arm, unable to get even a whisper of air into her lungs. The cough was getting worse by the hour.

"Breathe, my love. Breathe."

The congestion was as thick as mud. From dawn to dusk and more, twenty-four hours a day, Zari had fed her, changed her, played with her, loved her. If she could only breathe for her.

She was no doctor, but she knew that any one of these moments could be the last. A final, exhausted try. And then surrender.

A coughing fit and the baby gasped.

"Please do it. Don't give up, *kızım*."

Kızım. My daughter.

Panic prickled down her spine. Placing the child on her thin shoulder, Zari clapped her repeatedly on the back as she descended the steps. Suddenly, a hard cough and the child drew a raspy, wheezing breath. And then she shrieked.

She hurried down, knowing the reprieve was momentary.

At the bottom of the stairwell, the door to the service alley swung open. A uniformed hotel security guard stepped forward, blocking their path. Wariness darkened his features.

"Wait." He stared at the scarf on her head, at the heavy bag slung from her shoulder. She averted her eyes. "You're not a guest, and you don't work here. What are you doing inside the hotel?"

The guard spoke Turkish. Zari understood the language well enough, but she couldn't risk speaking it. Her native tongues were Sorani, Farsi, Arabic. None of which she could speak now, for he'd recognize that she was a Kurd and a refugee. Since arriving in this country, she'd learned and spoken mostly English. She had to. That's what she decided to use now. "I came to see a friend who is staying here. I *thought* she was staying here."

"A tourist?"

"A tourist."

"From where?"

Zari clutched the child tighter in her arms.

"America. But I was wrong." Before he could ask the name, she motioned to the door behind the guard's shoulders. "I'm leaving now."

"Your baby?" He looked suspiciously from Zari's worn, wet clothes to the child's new coat and shoes.

"Yes. Tiam. Tiam Rahman. She is mine."

"You are not a Turk. Show me your papers."

The skin on Zari's neck prickled with worry. She was illegal.

"Papers." He extended his hand.

She could play the confused, submissive woman. It had worked before, when a policeman stopped to question her on a dark highway outside of Kayseri. Perhaps this one would let her pass, but she was so tired of it all. Tired of these men. Just then, a horrible gut-wrenching cough erupted from the child in her arms, filling the stairwell. It sounded like the baby's lungs were being ripped apart. He stepped back involuntarily.

"Papers."

The child flailed her arms, trying to breathe. The blood of those women of the old stories caught fire in Zari's veins. Fierce, maternal anger rang out in her voice. "I cannot stop for you. I must get her to a hospital. Get out of my way."

Pushing past the security guard, Zari rushed out the door and turned down the alleyway toward the street, praying he wouldn't follow.

4

ZARI

Zari ran along the streets, praying she would find help in time. The baby was struggling to breathe.

The city was new to her, but when she found a pharmacy on a side street, she pushed past pedestrians and went in. One of the clerks approached her immediately.

"I need to find a hospital," Zari said.

The woman eyed the wheezing child with concern. "Of course. There's a clinic on the next street, but you'd be better off at the hospital by the Grand Bazaar."

"Where is that?"

"Do you know the city at all?"

She shook her head. "I have just arrived."

"Follow the tram tracks up the hill. The hospital costs money, but your child will be better off in their hands."

By the time Zari reached the sliding doors of the emergency room entrance, she thought her own chest would burst. The nurse who took them in, checked the child's vitals, and wrote down the information, however, was calm and reassuring.

The doctor who came in greeted Zari in Turkish. After examining the baby, he straightened up, draped his stethoscope around his neck, and turned to her.

"The congestion in the chest is heavy. She's having more than an asthma attack. I suspect pneumonia." He gave orders to the nurse, who hurried off, leaving the two of them.

Zari leaned over the crib, trying to soothe the agitated child. "Can you help her?"

"How long has she been like this?"

"Two days, maybe more. We've been on the road. But this is the worst." The child's lips were blue. "Can you get her to breathe now?"

"Any vomiting or diarrhea?"

"Both today."

"How long has she had the fever?"

"Since this morning."

"I have to admit her." He looked toward the door where the nurse had disappeared. "We have a new respirator in the ICU that can get air into her lungs. I'll start her on medication."

They knew Zari was an outsider. Still, no asking for papers. No demand for money up front. No turning her away because her shoes were worn and she covered her hair with a headscarf. No ignoring her because she spoke Turkish poorly. No strange looks.

At least, not by the nurse or this doctor.

"Has she had antibiotics before?"

"Yes. Last week. And the month before. She gets like this. Can't breathe. Bronchitis and pneumonia. She's sick a lot."

"Hospitalized?"

"Yes."

"What hospital? Who is your doctor?" He took a pad and a pen from his pocket. "I'll need to contact him about previous treatment and medication."

Zari felt her heart rise into her throat. "I...we have no doctor here. We're visiting a friend."

"Give me the name, and I'll search the hospital directory of your city."

No directory would have their name. She shook her head and reached for the child's hand. Cold, fragile fingers wrapped around hers.

He glanced at the satchel hanging from her shoulder. It was worn and contained all the belongings she'd had time to pack. Zari didn't know what she would do if he insisted on answers.

"Does it matter?" she blurted out desperately. "She has no allergies. The last time, they kept her in the hospital five days. She could breathe when she came home."

Understanding flickered across his eyes. She wouldn't be the only sick refugee who would show up at the hospital doors. The biggest fear for most of them was getting arrested. They'd be sent back. But there was nothing in Kurdistan for her to go back to.

"This is not a state hospital. Treatment here is not free. Once she is stabilized, we can send her to—"

"No. I have money."

He stared at her, doubt clouding his face.

"If you could just help her breathe, I can pay." She scrambled to slide the bag from her shoulder.

"Not now. They'll settle it with you tomorrow at the front desk."

A set of double doors opened, and the nurse returned.

"They're ready in ICU, doctor."

The physician pulled Tiam's chart from the hook at the end of the crib. When he looked back at her, she read compassion in his eyes.

"We'll help with her breathing tonight. In the morning, we'll have to do some tests."

"Can I wait here? Stay with her?"

"No. You need to go to your friend's tonight. Your daughter will be in good hands. Tomorrow, we can do the x-rays and run any other tests that are needed. Come back in the morning."

A weak cry from the crib drew Zari's attention. Tiam. Zari had chosen that name herself. She'd decided on it while delivering her child in a roadside village with strange women offering shelter and showering her with kindness. *Tiam* meant "my eyes." And how appropriate, she thought, as she looked down into the innocent eyes.

"I'll be here early, my love. I promise." Tears welled up, and Zari's vision blurred. She blinked them back and leaned over to kiss the child's forehead. "And you promise to get better. Please, little one. Live for me.'

The crib was wheeled away, and a sharp feeling of loss cut into

Zari's chest as she followed them to the swinging doors of the ICU. There, an attendant wearing a cap and surgical mask took charge. The doctor went in with them.

The nurse put a hand on Zari's arm. "You do have a place to stay tonight?"

She was in her forties perhaps, or even older. Lines etched her brow. Zari guessed she was not a woman given to smiling.

"I do."

"Do you have a husband?"

Another wave of sadness washed over her. "Yes."

"Is he in Istanbul?"

"No, we came alone."

"*Do* you have papers?"

Zari's face burned. She met the dark brown eyes. Silence filled the space around them. She recited a *dua* to herself. *Oh Allah, open to me the doors of Your mercy.*

"You don't." The nurse answered for her. She looked up and down the hall. No one else was around. "You're a good mother. I can tell."

The words stabbed at her heart, but she fought back the sob rising in her chest. She *was* a good mother. She loved her daughter.

"I am Emine. Where are you from?"

"Kurdistan."

"My mother was from Kurdistan."

Her prayer was answered.

"Zari. I was born and raised in Qalat Dizah."

Emine nodded, and the sad look in her eyes told Zari that she understood. Fifty thousand people were dead or had been driven out of Qalat Dizah. Months after the attack, it was still being mentioned in the news. But the Kurdish people's struggle was nothing new. In conflict after conflict, decade after decade, they'd had to escape into the mountains as entire cities and villages were leveled.

Her own place of birth was now forbidden to her. Four thousand towns and villages in Iraq were forbidden to the people who once lived in them.

An orderly called to Emine from down the hall. She was needed.

"Find me tomorrow morning. I'll go with you to hospital registration. I'll help with the forms."

Zari wanted to throw her arms around the older woman. She wanted to thank her a thousand times, but Emine turned and hurried down the hall.

Tears of relief threatened to fall. At least tomorrow was taken care of.

The clock above the doorway of the ICU showed it was nearly eight. She wondered how early the registration office in this hospital opened.

Whatever time it was, she would be here. She wouldn't have far to go.

Zari padded silently to the end of the corridor and went through a fire door. Going down the dimly lit stairs to the basement, she tried another set of doors. Locked. Sinking into the cool cement corner of the stairwell, she pulled her satchel onto her lap and wrapped her arms around it.

The air was stale and damp. She listened to the distant sounds. From beyond the basement doors, there came the low, muffled hum of ventilation machinery. The faint ululation of an ambulance siren reached her. A door opened far above, and the scuff of footsteps descending made Zari hold her breath until another door opened and closed. Silence surrounded her.

This would have to do for the night. It was safer than the street. She had nowhere else to go. No friend here in Istanbul. She had nothing but a sick child who needed her.

Zari thought wearily of the stories that had given her strength so many times in the past. Those great mothers who suffered epic losses but forged onward. Once again, courage stirred in her blood.

In this hospital, a little girl was fighting for every breath. She was not giving up. And neither would Zari. She would not abandon that child. Her child now.

Never.

5

ZARI

"THIS IS *NOT* A STATE HOSPITAL," the clerk told Zari curtly, picking up her cigarette from an ashtray. She took a deep drag and waved it at her. Words came out with a plume of smoke. "The doctor says he might have to keep her for a week. There are tests he needs to run. You must pay ahead."

Zari guessed that Turks didn't need to pay ahead. Well-dressed people didn't need to pay ahead. Maybe if she had papers or references, she wouldn't need to pay ahead. Back in Ankara she never had to pay ahead. But right now, she had no choice.

She knew the difference between private and state hospitals. She'd been to both. She was too familiar with the crowded waiting rooms and the futility of trying to get someone's attention. The doctors were overwhelmed. The nurses overworked. Unless you were bleeding to death, no one would pay any attention to you. Yesterday, Zari was afraid Tiam would die before she got help for the child. She was glad she'd brought her here.

"Will you pay, or should we arrange a transfer?"

The woman stubbed out the cigarette and frowned. Zari was aware of two filing clerks pausing from their work beyond the registration counter. They were listening to the conversation.

"I'll pay."

The clerk glanced at her skeptically and then turned to her computer. A knot grew in Zari's throat as she waited. She didn't know if she had enough money. She hoped she did.

Letters and numbers were punched in. A few minutes later, a printer whirred and spit out a piece of paper. The woman pushed it across the counter.

"Can you pay this much? I'm giving you the minimum of what the patient's stay will cost for a week."

Zari looked at the sum. It was a great deal of money. She picked up her satchel from the floor and reached for the envelope with all her savings. As she counted carefully, she realized the two filing clerks had sidled over. They seemed to be counting the bills with her.

She didn't have enough. Close, but not enough.

Zari laid the stack of liras on the counter, praying silently that the registration clerk would be merciful.

The counting became a group project as the two young clerks hovered over the woman's shoulder, adding comments here and there when bills stuck together or there was chance of error.

Zari was accustomed to the watchful eyes. This was the way with Turks, but Kurdish people were the same. One person's business was everyone's business. In the home or at work, it was the same. For the most part, no one meant any harm. Their intentions were rooted in kindness, in a desire to help. That is, when Zari lived in Kurdistan, and they'd looked on her as one of them. Here though, she was an outsider and a refugee.

Three times, the money was counted. "You're four thousand five hundred liras short."

"I'll get it for you. Today."

The filing clerks had opinions and readily voiced them.

"That's a lot of money."

"How are you getting that much today?"

The registration person waved them back to work and sipped from the glass of tea she'd forgotten sitting by her ashtray.

"The hospital's admission requirements are specific. I can't let your daughter stay."

"Wait. I can get the money." Zari pushed up her sleeve and untied the scarf around her dowry bracelet. Eight gold coins on a chain jingled as she exposed them. A gift from her husband at their wedding.

Her husband. Yahya. The bracelet was the last thing of value she had from him.

In Kurdish tribal ways, their marriage was unconventional. Yahya and Zari weren't first or second cousins. Nor did they grow up in the same neighborhood, or know a friend of a friend. Their union hadn't been decided on since childhood.

They met at college in Qalat Dizah, and right away they knew. Zari would never forget the day Yahya's mother and sisters arrived at her mother's home. She'd never met his family. Her own mother knew in advance about the visit, so two elders were already there.

She knew the traditions. The visitors would explain to her mother the reason for coming. Zari was the only child of a widowed woman. She wanted this marriage, and her mother had promised to accept the offer. But she couldn't do so immediately. So many ritual formalities needed to be observed. Minutes dragged, and it felt like hours before she was asked to bring some water for the guests. The purpose of serving them was to give the guests a chance to inspect her. She was on display. Her height. Her curves. The arch of her eyebrow. Her smile. Did she blush when they stared at her? Would she talk back to her future mother-in-law?

From that one meeting, they'd judge her character and suitability. According to Kurdish ways, she was supposed to stand there until the guests finished drinking the water. If they were impressed, they'd arrange a second visit and bring the intended groom.

Her *khastegari* or formal courtship, however, only consisted of that first visit. Yahya's family was agreeable, so they had tea and sweets, and Zari phoned Yahya.

"*Diya te min qebûl dike.*" Your mother approves.

He came over, tall and handsome in his best clothes, and they all stayed for dinner. Before the guests left, the wedding date and arrangements were settled.

She turned the bracelet on her wrist so they could see. It was her dowry. The one costly thing that she hadn't parted with since fleeing her old life.

But what was the value of gold or even a cherished memory compared with the life of an innocent child?

"I'll go to the bazaar today. I'll sell this and bring the rest of the money back. Keep Tiam here. She has to be cared for. Please."

The registration clerk shook out another cigarette. Her eyes flicked toward a shadow that materialized beside Zari.

Emine, the nurse who had helped her last night, was back. They'd seen each other briefly this morning, and she'd promised to come and help her with the forms.

The clerk waved off the two behind her who'd crept close again and tapped the form with her pen. "Fill these."

Emine took the paperwork and handed Zari the pen. "Cover your gold."

She rattled off an address and showed her what sections needed to be filled in and what she should say. When they were done, Emine herself handed the form to the woman behind the counter. It was an expression of solidarity.

Draping the satchel over her shoulder, Zari directed a grateful look at her new friend. In spite of the heartache she was feeling about her loss and her anxiety about the bleakness of the future, the nurse's kindness and support warmed her and gave her a glimmer of hope.

"Will you take me to see Tiam now?"

They started down a long hallway.

"You gave her all of your money." Emine motioned to the sleeve covering the gold. "And I'm guessing that bracelet is the last thing you have? Are you sure you want to do this?"

"Absolutely. You can save her. Can't you?"

"She's breathing. But the doctor is ordering a dozen tests. By the time they're done, you'll owe them more than what you can get for your gold."

"Then I'll sweep the floor at the mosques. Wash the hospital stairwells. I'll rely on people's generosity. When they see how hard I work, maybe they'll toss me a few coins."

"Where *is* your husband?" Emine tone was sharp, clearly not liking Zari's suggestions.

"Gone. Disappeared. I don't know if he's dead or alive."

"You must know something. You must have some way of finding him. The father must shoulder his responsibility."

"I'm from Kurdistan. *Iraqi* Kurdistan." Zari's anger was restrained, but just barely. "Do you know what's happened to thousands upon thousands of us? Do you know why so many like me are here? Homeless? Desperate?"

Emine sighed and turned her face away. "I know."

It hurt to swallow, to breathe. Zari forced her voice to remain gentle. She didn't want to come across as a threat to anyone. Her past was hers alone. Her misfortunes belonged to no one else.

"You worked before coming here," Emine said finally.

"Yes, in Ankara."

"Did they give you any references?"

When she thought of all that had been taken from her, anger rushed through her, making her blood boil in her veins. "I worked for foreigners. They left."

If Emine thought it strange that Zari wouldn't have references, she didn't show it.

"And you speak English?"

Zari nodded. "I can read and write in English too. And I had one year of college. That was in Qalat Dizah."

They paused by the doors to the ICU. "You visit with your daughter. I need to make a call to a friend to see if he'll give you an interview."

"An interview for a job? A paying job?"

"His family owns a pharmacy. He's always looking for someone trustworthy to deliver prescriptions to tourists in the hotels. But they have to speak English."

Zari's heart filled with gratitude. "You're a good woman. A charitable woman."

"You don't know me. I have two married sons and my mother, and they all live with me. And I'm the only one working. There's nothing extra to give away."

"The Prophet said, your smile for your sister is a charity. Guiding a person who is lost is a charity. Seeing for a blind woman is a charity. Removing a rock from the path of people is a charity."

The pinched corners of Emine's mouth softened for the first time. "A hadith. My mother is big on reciting them."

6

CHRISTINA

"SHE'S THE TEA GIRL," my mother says, trying to dismiss the incident of the note as unimportant. "The towel girl. She runs around the spa and fetches whatever anyone needs."

"Why would she leave me a note?"

"She thought you were a repeat customer. That's what they do."

"How would she know my name?"

"The receptionist had our names from the concierge before we got here."

"Did *you* get a note?"

"No, but you're making too much of this. It was a nice gesture. That's how Turks are. They love their tourists."

The masseuse is looking at me like I have two heads.

"Forget about it," my mother suggests. "Relax and enjoy the experience."

I can't help but wonder why everything had to happen today. I don't believe in coincidences. I don't believe in fate. Everything that happens to us is a response to something that went before, to who we are, to our actions. Jax had been overweight. He spent too many hours in front of a computer and not enough time taking care of his health. So his heart stopped.

Welcome back, Christina. My mother might not be worried about it, but the note still bothers me.

After Jax's funeral, I had so much on my mind. He was my mother's husband, my boss. With his death I lost a dear friend. The night of the accident, if I'd been paying closer attention, I might have reacted to the truck changing lanes and veering toward me. Four cars ended up being involved. Autumn was the sole fatality. Even as I think of it now, the gaping hole in my heart is wrenched open even wider.

And then there's that picture of Kyle and the woman in Japan. My relationship with him has been languishing in no-man's-land since the day Autumn died, partly because we refuse to talk about what happened. We still live together, so technically we're still a couple. But I know he's moved on emotionally, and so have I.

On the way back from the *hamam*, I ask Elizabeth to watch for the woman in the brown headscarf. She pretends to look. The streets are brimming with people and cars, but there's no sign of her.

We have an early supper in the hotel. My mother comes up with me afterward and immediately turns on all the lights. A couple of steps into the room, I stop and I stare at the empty space where the crib was this morning. Four circular shapes mark where the legs pressed into the rug. Those indentations will disappear, but my heart and mind are permanently marked with my love for my lost child.

Elizabeth turns to me and realizes what I'm staring at. "You have to move past this. You were doing really well before we got here."

I don't tell her, but the truth is I've only *pretended* to be doing well. The way to preserve my sanity is to make everyone around me believe I am perfectly fine. This morning was an aberration.

My mother walks to the TV and picks up the remote. "How about we order tea and watch some Turkish soap operas?"

"Turkish soap operas?"

"They're a big deal here. Back in the states too, actually. I was talking to the masseuse about them today."

Coming to Turkey is a stroll down memory lane for her. I was born in Ankara, an hour's flight away from Istanbul, but we never came back to this country together until now.

Welcome back, Christina.

"We should have asked at the reception desk about the note."

"Why can't you let it go?"

"What if the note *wasn't* from the spa? What if someone from outside came in and handed it to them?"

"Like who? This is your first time in Istanbul. Who knows you?"

"My point exactly. That's why I'm curious."

"You're a mess." She leaves the remote on the dresser and pokes the jacket I just tossed on the back of the chair. "Talk about a mess. How much effort does it make to hang this thing?"

I grab the jacket from the back of chair before she hangs it up for me.

"Did you bring any moisturizers? Your skin looks dry."

Glancing in the mirror, I see nothing wrong with my skin.

"They have a massive gym downstairs. Maybe you should go down there and check it out."

One moment, she wants to be my friend and the next she's trying to reform me, improve me, make me become a better version of myself. At the very least, a version that she'd be happy with. I could understand her sentiment when I was fourteen, but at the age of thirty-two?

The same goes with her displays of affection. On any given day, I still don't know if she'll shower me with love or be openly critical of me. I've known for a long time that our relationship is an emotional minefield. But maybe that's the way it is with most mothers and daughters.

"Do you mind going and watching TV in your own room?"

"You're throwing me out?"

"No, I'm asking you to go so I can work." I hang the jacket in the closet. "You've paid me to come on this trip and make sure the sale of your company goes through. Now let me."

She respects me as a professional more than as a daughter. Both she and Jax had a lot of confidence in my abilities. I was recruited to work for Externus two years ago. Close quarters, considering the size of the company. But the job took precedence, and it worked out. My education and experience as a software engineer and small business strategist had paid off.

"Fine, I'm going, but don't forget the gym is open twenty-four hours."

Never a conversation without an insult. I'm relieved when she finally goes.

All the lights are on, and the windows are open. The curtain moves in the breeze. The geraniums on the outside windowsills are blood red. A crimson rose in a crystal vase and a plate of Turkish sweets sit on a side table. I pick up the note beside them.

The note is from the hotel management, hoping I enjoy my stay. They're pretending this morning didn't happen.

I check the time on my phone. It's a few minutes after nine in Istanbul. Three in the morning next day in Osaka. I need to speak to Kyle about the schedule and what's left to do on my end for the acquisition. He's very efficient, great at the job, and has probably sent me some emails about it already. First, I open Instagram and post a couple of the pictures I took of the mosque in the neighborhood of the *hamam*.

My phone rings. Speak of the devil. It's Kyle.

"What are you doing up so late?" I ask as a way of greeting. "Or are you up early?"

"Staying up late."

I wonder if he had company. Maybe she's still there in the room with him. I've spent too much time dissecting our relationship since Autumn has been gone. Did we change? Were we ever really in love? Did the earth move when we first met, when we first made love?

We both went to Cal Poly, him three years ahead of me, but didn't meet until Elizabeth and Jax started Externus. He was one of the first hires. His parents are from the East Coast and divorced. Boarding schools since fifth grade.

Maybe the earth did tilt a little when we first hooked up. That was two years ago, right after I started there. Kyle is tall and handsome. He's got that blue-eyed, blond-haired, cover model look. He turns heads when he crosses a room. And he's smart. And charming, when he sets his mind to it. He was the perfect salesperson for the company. And me? I was always just me. Not too tall, not too short. Heavy in the chest and hips. And my face? My nose is too long, my mouth too wide. My eyes are the best part of my face. But how far does that take you?

If I'm lacking in the self-confidence department, it's partly due to a lifetime of being reminded by my mother that we live in Los Angeles, the home of the best plastic surgeons in the country.

Kyle must have found something attractive about me though. It was his suggestion that we move in together.

The silence is deafening on the line. Neither of us is speaking. A wall-like hedge has grown between us. The seeds were planted the day I told him I was pregnant. He never said anything cruel though, like suggesting that I get rid of it, or that he didn't want any part of it.

Getting pregnant was my doing. I could have lied and said it was an accident, but it wasn't. I wanted a child more than I cared about my relationship with Kyle. And his role in raising her was way down on the list of priorities.

Like mother, like daughter. Elizabeth has never told me the name of the man who got her pregnant. Whether it was a one-night stand or not, I don't know. Even mentioning the topic has been a sure way to start an argument. She was forty-three years old when she gave birth. Her last chance at starting a family. I suppose I was thinking the same thing. Except in my case, Kyle is no stranger, and I was only thirty-two.

The divide between us keeps getting wider. I don't know why he hasn't moved out of our apartment. Maybe he's waiting for me to go.

I pluck a petal from the rose on the table and rub it between my fingers.

"How's the conference?" I ask him.

"Good. How was your day with Elizabeth?"

"She took me to a Turkish *hamam*." I consider telling him about the unexpected note in the locker room, but I don't.

"Is that all?"

Something about his tone tells me I haven't answered his question. "Would you like to know what I had for lunch?"

"That would be a start."

"First, tell me what *you've* been up to."

"I just got here. It's been all work."

Our flights left LAX a couple of hours apart yesterday.

"Who have you met with? Anyone I know?"

"We're not talking about me. I called because I'm worried about you."

Massaging a kink in my neck, I stare at the ornate ceiling. I think of the picture Elizabeth showed me on his Instagram account. Do I really want to bring it up? I decide that I don't.

"Why are you worried about me?" I ask finally.

"Christina, we're a team."

"I know we're a team."

"So why did I have to hear about today from your mother?"

I don't have to ask what he's talking about. This is about the crib. My throat tightens. I don't want to dig up the memory or think about what happened or how I felt.

"When did she call you?"

"It doesn't matter. You should have called me yourself this morning after the episode."

Episode makes me think of TV dramas. Elizabeth and Kyle have a close relationship, probably because of Externus. She thinks the world of him. She believes he's the best thing that ever happened to the company and to me personally. She loves Kyle and doesn't want to lose him. But after the company is sold, keeping him means he has to stay with me.

"When did she call you?" I don't wait for him to answer. "Or maybe I should ask how *many* times she's called you."

"Once. She left me a voicemail. Thought I should know about it. She's worried about you. I'm worried about you."

"So now you know."

"What happened?"

"I don't know. It was a combination of things. Exhaustion, I think. I woke up in a new place, jet-lagged. I was confused for a few minutes. Nothing to worry about. I've been perfectly fine since this morning."

I want to shift the conversation away from me.

"Tell me what to expect this week. Any surprises with the buyers?"

Before they started Externus, Jax and Elizabeth both used to work for the same Silicon Valley company. He was a programmer; she worked in accounting. Jax saw a need for a company to serve as a distribution platform for independent video game designers.

The gaming business is bigger than Hollywood, with higher revenues than the music and movie industries combined. With a focus on independent game designers, Externus's revenues were a sliver of the big guns. But since distributing two well-received, first-person shooter games this past year, the company's value has skyrocketed. Jax and Elizabeth were ready to sell.

Earlier this year, there was an offer from one of the big fish in Japan, but Jax refused. Their intent was to buy and dissolve us. Instead, Jax put out feelers to a number of small-to-medium-sized gaming companies.

This week, Istanbul will serve as neutral ground for a limited auction of Externus involving three potential buyers from France, Sweden, and Russia.

"Other than a reshuffle of the schedule, I don't foresee any problems. I emailed you what I have. But before I get there, why don't you get into Jax's emails and make sure there are no surprises."

When I hang up with Kyle, the clock on top of the antique wardrobe says it's only nine-thirty. Taking my laptop, I head out.

I take the stairs to the rooftop lounge. The A'ya Terrace has clusters of chairs and benches, cream colored with tastefully patterned throw pillows. The only people I see are two businessmen chatting at the far end. A white-jacketed server tells me that the bar is closed, but I'm welcome to sit anywhere. He also offers to get me refreshments from the kitchen if I so wish it. Politely, I send him away.

The night is cool, but I grabbed a sweater on my way out. For a moment, the breath hitches in my chest as I stare at the brilliantly lit Hagia Sophia, guarded by its four minarets. The significance of the four-thousand-year history of this city is a testament to human survival. I have a thing or two to learn from it.

I take a seat facing the ancient mosque and open the laptop. A few minutes later, I'm poking through company files. My inbox shows the emails Kyle sent me. This sale is as important to me as it is to Elizabeth and Kyle. Each of us stands to make enough to reshape our futures.

The hair on my neck prickles, and I turn in the seat, wondering if someone is watching me. The same two men as before are there, but no one is paying any attention to me.

I turn to the computer, and my heart aches when I glance at some of Jax's last messages. He died too early. At the age of sixty-eight, he had no reason to suspect he wouldn't be around for at least a couple more decades. But he was a planner and he did think ahead. He was big on goals and on research. He always had contingency plans. This week is no different.

One of Kyle's emails asks about the company's attorney and whether I'd seen the notes on the draft of the acquisition contracts. I have faith that everything is ready to go, but I log out of my account and log into Jax's company email. The contracts that Kyle wrote about are easy to find. Two months ago, right before Jax died, the lawyer added some notes and questions on the terms. I check Jax's sent mail to see if the issues were ever addressed. There's a draft email, but he never had a chance to send it back. Of the emails that he did send during that last week, one with an attachment stands out. The subject line is *Baghdad*.

Curious, I open it. It was sent to an email address that I don't recognize. The message simply says, *All of them too.*

My phone vibrates. I ignore it, realizing it's Elizabeth.

A shadow moves on top of the stairs. The figure of a large man passes under the lights.

I click on the attachment. It's a PDF of a news article from two years ago. Certain names are underlined. The article concerns an Iraqi-born billionaire named as a defendant in a $4 billion lawsuit filed in Baghdad on behalf of survivors of Saddam Hussein's chemical weapons attack in Iraqi Kurdistan on March 16, 1988. The Halabja Massacre. Planes and artillery pounded the city and environs with Sarin and mustard gas. Over five thousand Kurdish civilians killed. More than ten thousand injured. The complaint names five co-defendants, alleging that these men were co-conspirators in the assault.

I'm surprised by the cryptic message and the article. Jax never got involved in politics. He was an engineer and a businessman. He was no politician or historian. I'm curious what this is about. I read on.

47

The Halabja Massacre was and remains the largest poison gas/chemical weapon attack launched against civilians since World War II. The assault was part of a highly organized, three-year, genocidal campaign called Anfal, during which the Saddam Hussein Regime murdered as many as 180,000 Kurdish civilians, destroyed approximately 4,000 Kurdish villages, and depopulated entire areas of the Kurdish region of northern Iraq.

I read the article again. Perplexed, I search for other emails to or from that address. Nothing. I sit back against the cushions. One connection I have with what I'm reading is the date. I was born in 1988.

I think about logging into Jax's personal email to see if there's more to this story. I don't have his password, but that wouldn't be too hard to figure out.

Before I do, the call to prayer rings out in the crisp night air, forcing me to pay attention. I love hearing the *adhan.* Five times a day, Muslims in the city halt what they're doing and pray for a few moments.

I check the time. Ten minutes past ten.

On this rooftop terrace, I can hear it coming from several mosques across this section of the city. The blending of the men's voices is beautiful and haunting. It stirs my emotions. *Adhan* means *'to listen'.* I shut the laptop and close my eyes. I drift away from my troubles and listen.

The call ends, and the city sounds edge to the forefront. It seems as if they fall silent for only a moment out of respect. I open my eyes. The two businessmen are gone, and the server is nowhere in sight. I'm alone on the rooftop, except that again I have a sensation of being watched. A line of sweat runs down my spine and chills my skin.

I turn in the seat and see her. The woman in the brown headscarf is here. She is standing twenty feet away from me. My heart drums in my chest.

Shadows from torches on the rooftop create dark stripes across her face. I have to speak to her.

I get up, but my mother's voice stops me and I turn away.

"I've been searching for you everywhere. I called you, but it went to voicemail. I stopped by your room, but you didn't answer the door. I asked the front desk if you'd left the hotel, but they didn't know. I was sick with worry."

"We said goodnight."

Elizabeth glances around her as if searching for an excuse. "I couldn't sleep. I figured I'd come and hang out with you. By the way, did you talk to Kyle at all tonight?"

"Never mind Kyle. She's here."

"Who's here?"

"The woman at the airport. The one outside of the hotel. The one on the street by the *hamam*."

"Where is she?"

When I look around, she's gone.

7

CHRISTINA

I'M DRESSED and working on my laptop before the call to pre-dawn Fajr prayer comes in through my open window.

What did people do before the Internet? Without it, how would we know essential things like the "fact" that using a cotton swab can lead to infection and erosion of your skull?

After Autumn's death, my gynecologist suggested that I see a therapist. What I had gone through was traumatic, and she made me understand that emotionally I needed help. In many ways I was relieved; my life seemed to be coming apart. I didn't tell Elizabeth or Kyle about the sessions. Neither one of them completely understood what I was facing.

What I've learned through therapy since is that grief and depression have similar symptoms. In my case, sadness ebbs and flows, but it never goes away. When I told my doctor I was coming to Istanbul only two months after my daughter was gone, she gave me a prescription for antidepressants. But I didn't fill it. I was still in a kind of denial.

What happened yesterday, however, makes me think I should be prepared. I don't want to do anything that will jeopardize this trip and the role I need to play. I do a quick Google search, and the results ease my mind a little.

Most medicines that require prescriptions in Europe or the US are freely available over the counter in Turkey. Just enter any pharmacy and ask for it by name. Bring your prescription if you have it.

Elizabeth doesn't know anything about the prescription either. I plan to keep it that way. The front desk people are extremely helpful. They don't roll their eyes when I ask for the nearest pharmacy. Nothing is said or hinted about yesterday whatsoever.

The place they send me to is toward the Grand Bazaar. They assure me someone at the pharmacy will be able to speak English.

The old Ottoman jail-turned-hotel we're staying at is growing on me. Maybe it's the staff's helpfulness or the dozen places in the gardens or the rooftop terrace, where one can escape to work or hide.

I start along the cobblestone streets through the heart of Sultanahmet, this part of old Istanbul. I'm not in a huge hurry. The sun is rising, its golden glow spreading upward, above the buildings. The area immediately around the hotel is shadowy and quiet. Only a few cars and delivery vans are on the narrow streets, and fewer people are on the narrower sidewalks. Two laborers pass me, pulling hand trucks loaded with boxes.

I pause before an alley between two ancient stone buildings. All along the dark passageway, people are huddled against the walls. Dull gray and brown blankets are their sole possessions. I live in Los Angeles where homelessness is an epidemic. An ache swells in my chest. I know each of them has a story. They had lives before, homes before, families before, children and parents before. They once loved, wanted, dreamed. But they're lost now, looking for any temporary refuge they can find in this city. In any city.

Close to me, the weathered face of a woman looks up. Beside her, a young girl also lifts her head. She could be the same child I saw yesterday only a few blocks from here. The battered cardboard sign says the same thing. *Syrian. Hungry. Help.* The large dark eyes are immediately alert. I feel queasy, thinking about the dangers of living on the street.

How can they survive like this? But what choice do they have?

They take the money I give them, and I turn away, feeling

ashamed. What I do isn't enough. But I have to keep going, for a lot of reasons.

Only a couple of blocks away from the hotel, the Hagia Sophia again comes into view. Across a wide plaza, the Blue Mosque, with its domes and minarets, glistens in the morning sunlight. I can see more lost souls scattered across the open space, sitting on benches or against low walls.

It's too early for the assault of tourists. A smattering of souvenir and food vendors are wheeling their hand trucks in and setting up, just as they have for generations. The smell of sesame-covered bread wafts from a red cart. Everywhere, stray dogs are sleeping on the paving stones and on grassy areas protected by short, white border fences. I pass and they raise their heads hopefully, tails thumping, looking for a handout.

At the corner, a signpost with a dozen arrows pointing toward different cities in the world looms over me. *London 2502 km. Lyon 2015 km. Athena, Moskva, Mecca, Tehran, Baki, Pekin,* and others.

It reminds me of another time. I got not one but three copies of the Dr. Seuss book *Oh, the Places You'll Go!* as gifts at a baby shower for Autumn. I remember thinking then that the universe was telling me something. I guess it was.

I stop, take a picture of the sign, and post it.

Elizabeth says I traveled to five continents when I was little. I don't remember any of it.

During the early days of our relationship, Kyle and I talked a lot about going places. At least, I talked and he listened. But we never did anything about it. To him, getting on a plane and flying nine hours here, twelve hours there, sixteen hours somewhere else, is just part of his normal work week. His idea of a vacation is doing nothing and going nowhere. Backpacking through Moscow, Athens, Mecca, Tehran, Baku, Beijing isn't him, either. Maybe someday I'll go on that journey myself.

That's when I see her, and my heart immediately speeds up. She's moving slowly up a slight incline on the street. She's coming directly toward me, toward the hotel. The surgical mask is covering her mouth and nose. Today, she's wearing a navy blue headscarf and a matching raincoat. A large purse hangs from her shoulder, and she has yet to see me.

A teenager brushes past her, staggering her for a moment. She pauses and presses a hand against the vendor's cart, struggling to take a breath. A thin, ragged child approaches and holds out a hand. She takes a coin from her pocket and places it in his palm.

We're a couple of steps apart when she finally sees me. Her eyes widen. I pause and we both stare. People are moving around us.

"Do we know each other?"

She's frozen in time and slowly she pulls down the mask. "We do."

"How?"

She casts a glance over my shoulder and then looks back into my eyes. "I am you. And you are me."

PART II

Joseph, the lost, will return to Canaan; grieve not.
This house of sorrow will become a rose garden again; grieve not.
Oh grieving heart, you will mend, do not despair.
This scattered mind of yours will return to calm; grieve not.
When the spring of life sets again in the meadows,
A crown of flowers you will bear, singing bird; grieve not.
— Ḥafeẓ

8

ZARI

THEN

DISTANT LIGHTNING FLASHED OVER ANKARA, and Zari held the child's half-folded jumper to her chest as she looked out the kitchen window. The skies were gray above the tall, modern buildings of the neighborhood, and the thunder rolled in, low and ominous.

"Maman?" Tiam appeared in the doorway, clutching a doll to her chest.

"It's all right, little one. Go and play. I'm right here."

The toddler ran off, and Zari glanced out the window again, drawn back to another time, another summer storm.

Lightning had lit the sky over Qalat Dizah the July night when two middle-aged brothers from a village far to the east stumbled into the masjid. The men had been traveling on foot all night and day. Zari learned what happened the next morning from her neighbor, who had stopped at the door to see if she needed anything before heading to the market.

"Three days ago, trucks carrying Saddam's men rolled into their town," the woman told her. "The soldiers broke down doors, raided homes, collected every man between the age of fifteen and fifty."

Stories similar to this had been circulating for months, but no one had arrived in their town. The danger had never seemed quite so real. Zari's stomach clenched with fear for her own husband.

The night before, she and Yahya had lain wrapped in each other's arms. With her head on his chest, she'd listened to the solid, steady beat of his heart as he slept. She'd breathed in the scent of jasmine from the white and yellow star-shaped flowers he'd placed on her pillow. Before he slept, they'd talked about where they would put the crib when the baby was born, about whether they should think about finding a house with a second bedroom.

Now, all those plans slipped away on the summer breeze.

"Those arrested were taken in trucks to a makeshift detention center," her neighbor continued. "The soldiers made them get out and stand in a fenced-in parking lot. The younger men—the ones who might carry a rifle for Kurdistan—were shoved at gunpoint into a warehouse. They were beaten and tortured in there. The men said they could hear the screams through the broken windows."

"How did they get away?"

"I don't know, but somehow they escaped."

Her neighbor told her that one of the elders of the masjid arranged for a message to be sent to their family. That morning, they would be driven through the mountains to a town near the Turkish border.

"I only pray they never come for our men," the woman had said, pressing Zari's hand before going off down the lane.

What she heard that day was nothing compared to what followed. A month passed before two others—a woman and her daughter-in-law—arrived at the house of Zari's mother with their own account of horror.

"All the men of our town were taken by soldiers. My husband and son among them." The older one's face took on a wild look as she remembered. "We followed the trucks on foot. They didn't go far. Just a few kilometers from our town, we saw dust rising in the distance. Tracks led through the fields. We went up a hill and saw them."

Zari spread her palms over her stomach, wishing she could stop her unborn child from hearing these terrors.

"A bulldozer with a backhoe waited at the end of a long trench. Piles of dirt lined the hole. Our men were forced to stand shoulder to shoulder. The soldiers fired their guns, and our people, men we have known our whole lives—my doctor, our imam, the teachers from the school, every one of them—tumbled forward, filling the trenches. I saw my husband and my son fall together."

Tears streamed down Zari's cheeks. They sat silently for a long time. There was nothing she could say, nothing to do to console them.

"Afterwards, the soldiers climbed into the trucks and went away, and the bulldozer covered the bodies of our loved ones."

By September, every Kurdish militia group had been pushed back into the mountains. The stories of mass arrests and executions came from every direction. Iraqi troops were spotted approaching Qalat Dizah.

She would never forget the night before Yahya left.

They sat against the wall in their garden. The sun was resting on the mountain peaks to the west, and the neighbors were spraying the lane with water from their hoses. The smell rising with the steam from the packed dirt mingled with the scent of jasmine.

"You have to go." Zari pleaded.

He said nothing at first but watched the sun set, lighting the sky with streaks of gold.

"How can I leave you and our baby?"

"Nothing is happening to the women. Other men in town have gone. Into the mountains. To Turkey even. When the baby comes, I'll follow you."

He took her hand in his. "How can I leave you?"

"You have to. I can't lose you."

That night, a few hours before dawn, the Iraqi army's trucks rolled into Qalat Dizah.

The city immediately erupted with the sound of bullhorns and screaming and sporadic shooting. The shouts of soldiers could be heard, coming closer. They were going from house to house.

Zari pushed Yahya and begged and argued. Finally, when a truck stopped at the bottom of the lane, he gave in. Even then, he tarried, holding her in his arms.

"I promise you," he whispered, his voice hoarse with emotion. "I'll send word to you as soon as I reach Turkey. If things are not better here, I'll get a job there. I'll make a life for us."

"And I'll join you," Zari swore, "with our baby."

The night was giving way to the graying dawn as she watched Yahya standing at the top of the lane, stamping his feet defiantly on the packed dirt. Death was coming for him, and still he remained. He bitterly resented going. This was his home, his life. He didn't want to leave his wife, his unborn child.

A few weeks later, she received his first letter. He'd made it to a crowded tent encampment at Ibrahim Khalil at the border of Turkey. Zari read the words again and again. She read it to her mother and to his mother. She shared the news with *jinên pîr*, the old women puffing at their pipes on the doorsteps along the lane.

Eventually, Yahya made his way to Ankara. He had no papers. No family. No one to offer a roof over his head. No one to share a meal with at the *sofreh*. His science degree from the university meant nothing. He was a refugee. An outsider. Finally, he was able to find a job as a handyman in an apartment complex. Very little money, but he received a private room of his own in the building's basement.

Yahya was safe, but as winter dragged on, Zari's body and heart grew heavier.

"First-time pregnancy jitters," the doctor called it, tucking her stethoscope into her lab coat.

It was only ten days before *Norooz*, the celebration of spring. Zari had gone to the new hospital in the outskirts of the city when cramping and pain came on fiercely and suddenly.

"Everything appears to be fine. But to be safe, we'll keep you overnight."

That night, the sound of explosions awakened Zari. Planes and jets screamed overhead. When the bombs and the shells began to fall on the city, chaos erupted. From the window, she saw fires burning in the distance. By morning, the hospital was inundated with the injured.

Zari left the hospital, determined to go home and find her family. The streets were packed with cars and trucks bringing the wounded or trying to escape the city. The noise was deafening, competing with the sounds of artillery. Death itself had come to Qalat Dizah.

She stepped into the crowded street, and an ambulance driver, an older woman, caved in to her pleas and agreed to take her into the city. With Zari sitting beside her and siren blaring, she edged through the madness.

"Saddam has issued new orders," she said grimly. "All of Kurdistan is now designated as a forbidden area. The soldiers are to kill any human being or animal they find here."

They pushed against a river of people trying to flee. Panicked faces surrounded them.

By the time she reached her mother's house, it was empty. So, too, was the house of Yahya's family. The phones were dead.

A shell screamed low over the rooftops and exploded only a few streets over, close enough to make the house shake.

Zari left and stumbled through smoke-filled lanes. The streets were now nearly empty, and eventually she reached her own home. She glanced around her, trying to decide what to take.

But what does one choose with only minutes to decide?

Ten things? Five things? Did she have the luxury of time to be sentimental or practical? Could she pause to reflect what her life would be like if she never again sat on the chair that once belonged to her father? If she never gathered warmth from the quilt sewn so affectionately by the women in Yahya's family? The clock on the wall. The rug under her feet. The rows of jars filled with jams and *torshi*, the relishes lovingly prepared by her mother. Her wedding picture went into the bag; And so did her dowry gold. She had no car. No friends left to call.

As she slogged toward the end of town, the peaks of the Qandil Mountains, imposing and magnificent, loomed ahead. Even as she walked, Zari knew that the life she had been born into, and blessed with, ended that day. But she no longer thought about herself, for she wasn't alone. She carried a life in her womb.

Lightning flashed again over the buildings of Ankara, drawing Zari back to the present.

Even after all that had happened, she continued praying that her family had survived. Fifty thousand fled her city during those attacks, making their way toward Khabat, Bazyan, Kawergosk, Daratoo, Jadida. Refugee camps. In the weeks that followed, Qalat Dizah was completely flattened by bombs and tanks and bulldozers. Her history was eradicated. Soldiers killed every living thing left behind. Her history was eradicated. There was nothing to go back to.

Tiam was born on a cold night in a roadside village. The heavy snow on the ground denied that spring had arrived. Strange women took Zari into a nearby home and cared for her. For the week that she stayed with them, she was not a Kurd, not a refugee, not a stranger trespassing in their village. Zari was their sister. Their daughter.

A month later, when she finally arrived in Ankara, she found that Yahya was gone. Disappeared. No one knew where he'd gone or what happened to him. She was on her own, a mother struggling to survive.

The sound of children's laughter cut through her memories.

"My Tiam," she murmured, returning to the kitchen table and the unfolded laundry. "You saved me and I saved you."

The childish laughter suddenly became angry cries, and Zari went to the doorway.

"Mine."

"No."

Two sets of hands were playing tug-of-war. Two stubborn children, both wanting the same doll. One pulled a little harder, and the other fell backward, crying. Zari crossed the room.

"No, Tiam. No, honey. That's too rough."

She gathered the other child into her arms and sat down, wiping the tears with the edge of her scarf. The toddler was already wheezing. The bronchitis was back, and Zari considered calling the doctor. Tiam looked on, her eyes round.

"*My* maman." She tried to push her friend off Zari's lap and take her place. "Down. *My* maman."

"I am your maman, Tiam. But you have to be nice to her. Christina is sick."

PART III

The sun's light looks a little different
on this wall than it does on that wall,
and a lot different on this other one,
but it's still the same light.
We have borrowed these clothes,
these time and place personalities,
from a light, and when we praise,
we're pouring them back in.
— Rumi

9

ELIZABETH

NOW

Istanbul was always a place of evocative smells. New leather in the shops at the Grand Bazaar. Turkish coffee and warm *simit* from the red carts and the bakeries. The intoxicating blend of exotic spices and herbs at the *Mısır Çarşısı*. Freshly prepared apple tea in sidewalk cafes. The cool, salty smell of the Bosphorus. Grilled fish sandwiches on the pier by the Galata Bridge.

A part of Elizabeth looked forward to walking through the streets and experiencing all these things once again. Istanbul was the gateway to so many memories. It was at the city's airport that she arrived in Turkey for the first time. And thirty years ago, it was from here that she left for what she thought would be the last time.

She rolled onto her side in the bed and stretched. The window was open, and she watched the gauzy curtains rise and fall. The breeze brought to life moments from the past...

"Tebrikler. Congratulations. You have a daughter."

The doctor immediately disappeared from her bedside. She'd delivered the baby after ten hours of labor and two hours of pushing. He'd warned her of the risks. Because of her age and her medical history, it might be safer to opt for a C-section. But Elizabeth wanted to try. She wanted to experience it all. She guessed this would be her last pregnancy.

Why didn't they give her the baby to hold? She lifted herself on her elbows and watched the doctor and the nurses working frantically on a tiny infant lying on a table across the room. The baby was silent and motionless.

"What's wrong with her?"

No one answered.

"Why isn't she crying?" Her heart raced and panic set in. This couldn't be happening to her. During her first three pregnancies, she'd lost the babies in the first trimester. But this time, her child held on, and Elizabeth did everything she was told to do to go full term.

"You have to save her. Do something."

A weak cry emerged from the infant. Elizabeth sank back against the pillows unable to control the tears. They said it was only seconds, but to her it felt like an hour before Christina took that first breath. Eventually, a blanket-wrapped bundle was placed in her arms.

"She's two kilos, three hundred grams," someone told her. "A tiny one."

Elizabeth converted the numbers in her head. The baby was around five pounds. The scrunched-up face was red and blotchy, and her skin flaky. But no baby looked beautiful when it first emerged from the womb. She had ten fingers, a little nose. A rose bud for lips.

"She's perfect." She placed a kiss on the infant's forehead. "Why does she taste salty?"

ELIZABETH THREW the covers aside and sat on the edge of the bed. She touched her cheek and then gazed at the wetness on her fingers. Damn the tears. She hated crying. She thought she had been done with them long ago. But the trouble was that she was in Turkey. Years ago, she'd sworn to herself she'd never come back here. To top it off, this was September, her nemesis of a month.

It was in September that her father hanged himself in the basement of their house in Northeast Philadelphia while her mother was making him lunch. Elizabeth was twenty-two and starting her last year of college. Years later, her mother told her that she ate the sandwich before she called for the ambulance. She couldn't see it going to waste.

Another year, another September. Elizabeth was twenty-nine and working in London when she got the call that her mother had been hit by a cab and killed while crossing a street.

And Christina was born in September.

Her eyes burned. She impatiently grabbed a tissue from the box next to the bed and wiped her cheeks.

It was illogical to blame a single month for the rawness of her emotions. The fault belonged to the sleeping pill she'd taken last night. She was feeling the aftereffects of it.

In order to age well, one needed good, long-term self-care habits. And she had them. Exercise, a good diet, and sleep. Years ago, when she first started traveling for work, she'd learned that popping a pill helped her avoid jet lag.

She rolled her neck. Everything had aftereffects. Every action had a reaction.

Elizabeth reached for her cell phone. It wasn't on the bedside table, but the charger wire dangled from the plug.

Strange, she thought, looking around the floor by the bed. There was no sign of it.

She tried to remember the last time that she used it. She called Christina last night from here. When the call went to voicemail, she'd gone up and found her on the rooftop terrace lounge. A few minutes later, each of them had gone to her own room.

She got out of bed, looked under the covers, and peered under the bed. Nothing.

Elizabeth was a creature of habit. Order was second nature to her because of her father and her military upbringing. She always plugged in her phone before she went to bed. She was certain she'd done it last night too.

She crossed the room to the desk. Her keycard was there, but no phone. She checked in her purse. Glancing around the suite, she felt a tingling sensation run down her spine. The door to the hallway was closed, but the metal bar of the security latch was unfastened. Something was definitely wrong. She'd fastened it. She *always* fastened it.

From where she was standing, it looked like the bathroom was empty, but the closet door was open. She knew she'd closed it last night. Her clothes hung like dutiful soldiers in a line. One of her empty suitcases lay on its side on the floor.

The sound of a door slamming somewhere close by sent a jolt through her. It came from down the hall. Suddenly, cold fear whispered across the nape of her neck. She glanced again at the security latch. Someone had been in here last night. But why steal her cell phone?

A hotel phone sat on the far side of the bed. There was another in the sitting area. But to get to one of them, she'd have to move. Her legs were stiff. She shuffled like a damaged robot to the phone by the bed.

She called her daughter's room. Christina was holding on to a spare key to this room. Maybe she came in here for something during night. But that would mean Elizabeth *had* forgotten to latch the door. The room phone rang and rang. She hung up without leaving a message and tried her daughter's cell phone next. Getting no answer, she called the front desk.

"Good morning, Mrs. Hall," the hotel operator responded brightly. "How can I help you?"

Elizabeth struggled to find the right words.

Her gaze lit on the open closet. From this angle she could see the door of the small safe was open. She carried the phone across the room. The safe was empty.

Her wallet, passport, and jewelry—everything she'd locked in there last night—were gone.

"Is there something wrong, Mrs. Hall?" the woman persisted.

Her voice trembled. "Yes. Robbery. *Soyuldum.* Someone broke into my room last night."

10

CHRISTINA

NOW

A TEENAGE GIRL bumps me and runs past the hijabi woman. A battered pickup truck loaded with vegetables is blaring out advertising through a speaker mounted on top. I'm not about to be distracted by anything though.

I am you. And you are me.

To go through life with the feeling of an inner isolation, to look around me and realize I don't belong, has been part of my very existence. I was the child with my nose pressed against the window watching my classmates play outside. The one who didn't look like her own mother. The one who asked a lot of questions but rarely believed the answers she was given.

"She has such *exotic* look. Where is she from?" I'd hear women ask Elizabeth in a whisper.

"Nowhere. Here. She's mine."

I grew up hating when people referred to me as *exotic* or *different* or *unusual*. Or ask, *Where are you from?* It all meant the same thing: you're an outsider. I didn't belong. All those moments were clues that the story I grew up believing about my life was a lie. I wasn't me.

I am you. And you are me.

You'd think hearing something like those words would shake the ground under my feet, tilt the axis of my life.

69

I want to talk to her. I have questions to ask, but I don't do it. Not yet. She isn't looking at me. She isn't saying anything more. She's focusing on someone or something behind me.

I turn and see Elizabeth pushing through the crowd toward us. I glance back to make sure the other woman is still here. She hasn't moved. Her eyes are glued to my mother. I feel like I'm part of an audience, watching a Greek tragedy unfold.

Whatever my expectations are of what's about to happen between these two, they don't happen. There's something wrong with Elizabeth. She looks pale. Her classic bob hairstyle is mussed, as if she forgot to look in the mirror before she ran out the door. Dark glasses cover her eyes. No lipstick. No earrings. She's wearing workout clothes. One of the laces on her trainers isn't tied. She *never* goes out in public looking like this. She wouldn't go to her Pilates class looking this messy. Out and about in the heart of Istanbul? No. Never.

"What's wrong? Are you okay?"

The day Jax had his stroke, Kyle and I went to the hospital as soon as Elizabeth called. She met us in the waiting room. She looked more put together *that* day.

"I'm fine. Fine." She pushes the glasses on top of her head. "Let me catch my breath."

"Take your time."

She clutches my arm and holds tight.

"Take your time."

For my entire life, I'm used to seeing her composed and in complete control. But something is up right now.

"Can I get you something? Do you want to sit down?"

She shakes her head. "Who were you just talking to?"

I'm guessing the woman behind me is gone. I look around and she has disappeared. Before I get to explain anything though, Elizabeth cries out and pulls me sharply toward her as a man on a motorcycle buzzes past us on the sidewalk.

He zips back onto the road and disappears between the line of cars and vans. Rush hour has started. He hadn't slowed down at all.

The pedestrian traffic is picking up. People bump us as they go by.

Elizabeth tugs on my arm and moves us back near a wall topped with a wrought iron fence.

"What are you doing out here on your own?" she asks.

"I need to get something at the store." Her face has taken on an ashen hue. "What's wrong, Mother?"

"The woman you were speaking to. What did she want?"

A car or truck backfires somewhere close by, and she flattens her back against the wall. This is not like her at all.

"Talk to me. You're getting me worried. I've never seen you like this."

"Did you get her name?"

"No."

"What does she want?" she asks again. She still has a white-knuckled grip on my arm.

"Nothing."

"What did she say?"

I am you. And you are me. I'm not about to say those words. Not now. Not when my mother is so wound up. So I lie. "She spoke Turkish. I didn't understand her."

"You don't know your way around. You shouldn't be—"

"Stop worrying about me. Tell me what happened? What's wrong? What happened to you?"

She searches the faces around us. "I was robbed. My passport. My jewelry. My wallet. All of it is gone."

My heart sinks. It's a horrible feeling knowing someone was in your space, touching your things, taking what's yours.

"How? When?"

"Last night, I think. I put everything in the room safe. They might have broken in when I came up to the rooftop lounge to check on you."

The familiar old door of resentment slides open between us. Her words hurt more than she realizes.

She didn't come up there to check on me. She was up there because she was bored. Right now, I'm wondering if she's blaming me for getting robbed. It wouldn't be the first time.

"How could you not see that car coming?"

71

"If you'd stayed at the funeral parlor, like I told you, instead of running out..."

"You should have had yourself and the baby transferred to UCLA Hospital as soon as Autumn was born."

Elizabeth has always been big on playing the blame game, regardless of how old I was, no matter the circumstances.

Blinking back the unpleasant thoughts, I focus on what happened to her last night. "When did you realize your stuff was gone?"

"This morning. I woke up and the safe was empty. My social security card, my license, my credit cards. The money I left in there. They even took my phone."

"Did you call the front desk?" They must love us. A missing baby yesterday, and today a robbery.

"Of course. They're being extremely helpful. I also talked to hotel security, and they wrote up a report. They'll file it with the police."

"You need to call to cancel your credit cards."

"I've already done it."

I search for the right thing to say. As a programmer, I know identities get stolen by the minute, and the hackers don't need the physical credit cards. She has travel insurance. The loss of money and jewelry won't break her.

"Everything is replaceable. You're safe, that's all that matters."

"The passport is the problem."

"How do you replace it?"

"I have to go to the police station and get a physical copy of the report. Then I take it to the American Consulate. With any luck, they'll issue me a temporary ID right away. That'll be good enough to travel with until I get back to California."

"Do you want me come with you to the police station?"

She looks around us again. "What are you doing now?"

"I want to go to a store for something. After that, I was planning to go back to the hotel and work. Kyle sent me a bunch of documents I need to go through before the first meeting. Still, I can come with you."

She thinks for a second and then shakes her head. "You don't speak Turkish. You'll be no help to me at the police station. I'll handle it."

Her words and her tone clearly convey that I'm a disappointment because I don't speak Turkish. Nonetheless, I feel bad for her, and I stop my defensiveness from ramping up.

I reach inside my bag, take out an envelope with a stack of liras, and hand it to her. "You said your money was stolen too. I'll get more at an ATM."

She slips the envelope into her pocket. "Go right back to the hotel after running your errand. I don't want to worry about you."

Elizabeth walks away and crosses the street. As I watch her go, I spot the hijabi woman. I wonder if we're going to have the conversation that was interrupted. But she's not interested in me right now. She's crossed the street too, and is walking in the same direction as my mother.

11

ELIZABETH

NOW

ELIZABETH STOPPED to look back at her daughter. Christina had already disappeared into the throng of pedestrians.

She tried to decide if she'd been short with her. Since the loss of the baby, she'd consciously tried to be more sensitive, more patient. Even before the accident, Christina had become fragile, prone to bouts of being argumentative, disagreeable. In many ways, she'd regressed to the difficult child and teenager she used to be.

Elizabeth knew they were both at fault for those problem years. The downside of being a single parent was that it was way too easy to take your frustration out on your child. She'd done that too often. The one closest to you, the one you loved most, was always the target. Go home and kick the dog.

Christina had dished out plenty of attitude at times, but for the most part she took the criticism because Elizabeth wanted to be a good mother. Besides, what other choice did she have? What choice had Elizabeth had before she left her parent's home?

Growing up, she'd changed schools eight times by the time she graduated from high school. Every one or two years, her father was moved to another military base, uprooting the family. Leaving neighbors and familiar places behind was part of the routine. Her mother didn't bother to make friends. She didn't join clubs. As a result, no one invited them over. Neighbors' kids didn't come to play.

Elizabeth learned early in life that there was no point in forming close connections. Caring for someone only brought hurt. At least, that's what her mother told her.

As she got older, she decided that boys were good for sex and fun, and that was enough for her. She wasn't interested in emotional attachments. More importantly, she wouldn't allow any man to raise a hand against her.

Her father was a hard man with a violent temper. A volatile undercurrent of anger seethed right beneath the surface, and it was always there. Like lightning, he could change, lash out. He could go from good-natured teasing to clutching her mother by the throat in a heart beat.

His baiting and his badgering extended to Elizabeth as she got older.

"Where the hell were you? What were you doing? Who were those boys?"

It didn't matter what she said. He wasn't looking for the truth or for any real answers. He already knew what he planned to do before the stream of questions began.

"You're a *whore*, just like your mother." Then the belt would come out.

A child is a liability for an abused spouse. After rushing her out of the room or out of the house, Elizabeth's mother took beatings for her, time after time.

No wonder she ate that sandwich after he finally hanged himself in the basement. If Elizabeth had been home, she would have poured her mother a glass of sherry to go with it.

Because of that upbringing, she *never* relied on a man. She could take care of herself. She controlled her own life.

Still, since discovering the theft this morning, a twinge of worry kept poking at her that perhaps what happened was somehow related to the years she'd lived in Turkey. Those were the most vulnerable years of her life.

She tried to dismiss the possibility. The theft in her room was a nuisance, she told herself. That was all it was.

But the thought kept nagging at her.

A hotel manager and the head of security had showed up at her door this morning after she called the front desk. Her answers to their questions were brief and to the point.

The security director would make certain a police report was filed, and the manager had been sincerely apologetic.

"We'll move you to another room without delay, ma'am."

She felt for the money Christina had given her, and then signaled for a taxi. Immediately, one pulled to the curb.

"*Nereye gidiyorsun?*" Where was she going?

Elizabeth took the piece of paper with the address that hotel security had given her for the police station out of her pocket. He'd said it might take a few hours at least before the police could have an official report of the theft ready for her to pick up. But she knew there was paperwork she needed from the embassy.

"*Amerikan Konsolosluğu.*" She started to give the address of the consulate, but he cut her off.

"*O kapalı. Yeni bir konsolosluk var.*"

A new consulate? Elizabeth didn't know they'd closed the old one.

Out of habit, she reached for her cell phone and remembered that it had been stolen too. The man rattled off the location of the new one. It was in a northern suburb of the city.

The car jerked forward and moved into the crawling morning traffic. This would take forever, she thought. They were going to pass by the Grand Bazaar on the way out of the neighborhood, and she searched for Christina. There was no sign of her, but all the faces Elizabeth looked at on the sidewalk appeared hostile. They were not just people rushing to work or tourists trying to find some old monument to photograph. From every direction, hard gazes were fixed on her window.

The men had her father's look. His eyes before the storm was unleashed. This was what happened when she thought of her upbringing. Some memories never went away. A chill slid upward along her spine, prickling between her shoulder blades. She willed the past away and tried to focus on today.

Her head was clear now. Regardless of what she'd said to Christina, her things must have been taken while she slept. She specifically remembered closing the safe before crawling into bed and turning off the lights.

The security director had suggested that someone might have crawled in through the bathroom window and left through the door. Her cell phone had definitely been next to the bed. That meant that the intruder stood next to the bed. He could have hurt her.

Once again, the past edged into her thoughts. This time, it wasn't her father that scared her. It was someone *she'd* wronged. A man.

"Why are you doing this to me?" she murmured to herself.

Elizabeth knew why. She was in Istanbul. She scanned the sidewalks looking for *him*. She had no trouble remembering his face. But what would he look like now? Years changed people. *She'd* aged.

Could that be him, pretending to be talking to a vendor? Or that man at the corner, standing with his hand in his jacket pocket? Would he break into her room and steal her things?

She pinched the top of her nose, trying to stop the foolish thoughts. As far as she knew, he was long dead. But what if he wasn't?

There was nothing worse than the unknown. She wished the traffic would clear up and the cab would go faster.

To replace a passport, you needed a police report and some kind of documentation or proof that you were who you claimed to be. She guessed those restrictions were much tighter now, considering the state of affairs in the world. And she had neither of those documents.

But she realized that it wasn't so much the forms or the temporary ID that had her traveling to the American Consulate this morning. It was fear. She needed help. Perhaps someone at the consulate could help her search for the answers she was after.

The line of traffic stopped yet again, and people crossed the street, weaving between the cars. She jumped when someone slapped the rear end of the cab with a hand. The driver cursed and gestured out the window.

A tram went by, carrying a blur of faces. She wished she were on it. Anything to move faster and get out of here.

A tall man on the sidewalk was taking pictures. Elizabeth automatically recoiled from the window, pushing back into the seat.

"American?" the driver asked.

She'd forgotten about him.

"*Amerikalı mısın?*" he repeated in Turkish.

"*Evet.*"

"I must ask. How do you know the language? Your Turkish is good."

She studied the driver's short white beard and kufi and stared at the ID mounted on the front dash. She guessed Egyptian or Moroccan. "How do you know *English* so well?"

He smiled, showing a mouthful of stained teeth. A smoker, like so many in this part of the world. Coffee and tea and cigarettes. That hadn't changed.

"I learned. It is for my job. Tourists pay well when they know I understand. They trust me. I give them my card. They call me when they are in Istanbul. And they give my name to their friend. And you?"

"I know a number of languages. Turkish is one."

With only a cursory glance at the road, he took a sharp turn and raced up a narrow alleyway. At the next corner, he went the wrong way along a one-way street before turning again. In the old days, taking a cab in Istanbul was an adventure. The drivers would normally take the longest route between Point A and Point B and let the meter tick away. Some things hadn't changed, but she didn't have much choice today. So long as she arrived at her destination in one piece, she would be happy.

"Why do you learn Turkish? No one speaks it, except for here."

Elizabeth held onto the grab handle as he weaved through an intersection to the sound of shouts and blaring car horns. Why did he have to drive like a maniac?

"Languages are like puzzles. I like to solve them."

"How many you speak?"

She shrugged. "*Bilmiyorum. Çok.*" I don't know. Many.

Elizabeth had no interest in making this guy her best friend. Or in distracting him with conversation. And considering the way he drove, she wouldn't be taking his card or recommending him to anyone else.

The man's gaze wasn't on the narrow road. It was fixed on the rearview mirror, staring at her. "CIA?"

"No," she snapped. Elizabeth cursed inwardly. That's all she needed, a cab driver thinking she was something she wasn't. She could end up in a room in some basement, tied to a chair. Or at the bottom of the Bosphorus.

"Maybe you answer too fast."

"I'm a little old for that kind of work," she scoffed. "Don't you think?"

He turned right around and looked at her. "Maybe yes. Maybe no."

"Hey!" she said, putting a hand out and pointing.

A woman pushing a cart filled with bags was about to cross. He hit the horn and sped past.

"Watch the road."

He was unfazed. "Do they teach all these languages in America?"

"Anyone can take classes."

"*Ama aksan yok.* No accent."

There once was a time when she would have taken his comment as a great compliment to her. But no more. She stayed silent.

"How old *are* you?"

He was getting too personal. She didn't like it. A right turn and a sharp left, and the driver continued along the narrow side streets through increasingly sketchy neighborhoods.

"When did you live in Turkey?"

This was turning into an interrogation. "I didn't say I lived in Turkey."

"Did you?"

"No," she lied.

"CIA."

"You have a big mouth and a bigger imagination."

"You say you're not expat. Lots of expats here. And CIA always lies. You lie. You say you did not live here. I say you did."

Her jaw hurt from grinding her teeth.

"I didn't live here."

"I think you know the word *haram*."

"I do know the word."

Haram. Sinful. Forbidden. For chrissake.

Elizabeth was an atheist. All those beliefs drilled into her about God and religion faded years ago. They held very little relevance in her life now. Jax was a believer. Not so much a churchgoer, but a believer. When he died, she could have had some priest say a few words at his funeral. She didn't.

Maybe she should have done more than just pour his ashes in the Pacific.

"Lying is *haram*."

"That's what I hear."

"You know *Jahannam*?"

"I've heard of it."

"It is the place you go after you die. The place of punishment for liars."

"Okay. That's enough." On a day like today—especially on a day like today—she didn't need to hear about her shortcomings as an infidel. "Stop right here. *Dur. İniyorum.* Now."

He shrugged and yanked the wheel. The cab screeched to a stop. Elizabeth glanced at the meter and threw some liras on the front seat before getting out.

"You want my card?"

She said nothing and slammed the door. As he did a U-turn and raced back toward the city, she stared at the gloomy cinderblock apartment buildings looming above her. Clothing and linens hung drying from porch railings.

"Where in God's name am I?" she murmured.

He'd dropped her on a back street in a tough, rundown neighborhood. Dogs eyed her warily from the edges of cracked sidewalks littered with garbage. Walls of buildings were covered with spray-painted graffiti praising the PKK.

The PKK. The Kurdish resistance. This was a Kurdish neighborhood. Perfect.

Only a few people were walking on this street, and they stared at her as she hurried by them. She was certain that if she had two heads, she couldn't have been more obviously a stranger. Half a block ahead, a dozen men were loitering around the open doors of an auto repair shop, smoking and laughing. They'd already spotted her.

There was no way she was going to walk by them. But she couldn't very well turn around. God, how did she get herself into this?

Her steps slowed as she passed a vacant lot filled with piles of brick and trash. A narrow alley on the far side of the lot led to the next street, where Elizabeth could see traffic and shops. To reach it, though, she'd need to pass through the alley.

She had no choice.

Elizabeth picked her way through the lot, climbing over piles of rubbish until she found herself on a path, of sorts. Ahead of her, a temporary structure of scarred wood and hard plastic lined one side of the alley. Battered pieces of corrugated metal served as a roof. A few ratty sheets partly covered the open spaces. A toothless old man sat wrapped in a dirty blanket, muttering out loud to no one.

Kurdish refugees.

Elizabeth averted her eyes, feeling her stomach clench. She didn't want to see these outcasts, a byproduct of the ongoing struggle for power and oil and control. Not now. Not today.

A little girl was crouched against the shack farther on, lecturing a puppy tethered to a plastic cord by her feet. The dog barked as Elizabeth approached. The child lifted her face to her. The eyes were that startling blue-green color common among the Kurds. But she was pale and thin. Sickly looking.

Elizabeth tried to pass by the opposite wall. The dog continued barking, trying to protect his charge.

"Where is *Maman*?" the girl cried out to her in Kurdish.

Elizabeth shook her head, pretending she didn't speak the language.

"Your fault."

There was no way to get through.

"You are *Shaitan*." A child was calling her the devil. "*You* did it. You sent her away."

MAY MCGOLDRICK & JAN COFFEY

Elizabeth stumbled against the wall, trying to find a way around the child.

The girl jumped up, blocking her path. "Bring her back. I want my *maman*."

"I don't know where your mother has gone," she answered in Turkish.

"There is no food. Everyone is gone."

The dog was barking nonstop, competing fiercely with the child who was practically shrieking now. "You left me. You want me to die. We will all die, and then you will be happy."

The words stabbed her. Elizabeth tried to get by her, but the Kurdish girl reached out and grabbed her sleeve.

"Don't leave me. Don't go." Tears ran down dirty cheeks. This close, Elizabeth could see she was clearly feverish. Hallucinating. "Hungry. I want *Maman*."

Elizabeth jerked her arm free and pulled a few liras from the envelope Christina gave her. Backing away, she threw the money on the ground, turned in panic, and ran blindly toward the end of the alley.

When she reached the busy street, she nearly collided with an older woman in a headscarf. Stepping in the line of traffic, she threw herself at a passing cab.

Once inside, she locked the door and tried to calm herself enough to give the driver directions.

"American Consulate," she said in English.

The cab pulled away from the curb, and Elizabeth looked back. The child was standing at the entrance to the alley, sobbing and staring after her, the puppy at her feet.

Elizabeth touched her wet cheeks. She didn't even know she was crying.

She was still shaken when she arrived at the US Consulate forty minutes later. The Turkish policemen guarding the outer gate watched her as she entered. Hearing her business, they waved her to another window by an entrance building. On the hill beyond, the white consulate building gleamed in the morning sun.

A young man in his mid-twenties smiled placidly and listened to

Elizabeth before producing forms to fill out. Placing them in a drawer beneath the window, he slid the papers to her.

"I need to see someone inside."

"You can make an appointment and come back."

"No. I have to speak to them today."

"Yes, ma'am. Is this a life-and-death emergency?"

Elizabeth paused, trying to retain her composure. "Not exactly. But I'd still like to speak to one of the officer's inside."

"But it isn't a life-and-death emergency?" he repeated.

She leaned closer to the thick glass separating them. "Yes. It is."

The young man sent out another paper. "Here is a telephone number to call. And instructions."

"I don't have a phone. It was stolen."

"You're welcome to use one of those." He pointed to three phones on a wall to the right of the security window.

Elizabeth stalked to the phones and yanked the headset off the hook. A woman's voice greeted her.

"Good morning, ma'am. I understand this is a life-and-death emergency?"

"No, but maybe. It could be. I need to talk to the head security officer on duty."

Lowering her voice, Elizabeth rattled off several names, a series of numbers, and some dates.

"Input these items into your system. Then inform your superior that I'm waiting."

12

CHRISTINA

NOW

THE PHARMACY ISN'T on the map on my phone. The instructions I was given brought me to this neighborhood around the Grand Bazaar. Along the street, steel doors on rollers are sliding up as shops open for business. The front desk at the hotel told me the merchants in the bazaar itself open anywhere between eight thirty and ten.

Not that I'm in any mood for shopping.

Now that I've had a little time to think things through, I'm worried about my mother. She's a staunch believer in keeping a stiff upper lip. The fact that she came searching for me, the anxious way she acted and looked, makes me think she's in worse shape than she's letting on.

I should have gone with her to the police station. It's true, I don't speak the language, but I could have been there to provide moral support. She would have done the same thing for me. More, actually. She'd have taken over.

I check my phone. I've been getting a bunch of calls from random numbers I don't recognize. I try Elizabeth's number. Her cell rings and rings and then kicks over to her voicemail. I remember what she said about her phone being stolen too.

The robbery complicates things. On top of everything, she'll need some kind of identification for the acquisition meetings. It's not the end of the world, but the notary will require it when she signs the papers and sells the company. I hope the passport replacement goes through fast.

"Where are you from, my lady?"

I look up. I'm standing in front of a carpet store. The man stretches out a tulip-shaped glass filled with tea toward me. We haven't even done business, and he's being hospitable.

I shake my head politely about the tea. "Is there a pharmacy on this street?"

"You must be here to buy a carpet, yes?" He points at the colorful rugs stacked higher than either of us. Various patterns cover every wall, from pillowcases to floor sizes. With the exception of a narrow walkway to get to the cash register, every inch of the small shop is packed with them.

I shake my head, and the clerk at the lantern shop next door calls out to me. "*Eczane?*"

I assume he's trying to sell me something too. I smile at the hundreds of lamps hanging from the ceiling of his stall. The bright colors glow like magic. Each lamp is a mosaic of color, a kaleidoscope of tinted glass. They each have a unique look. I imagine that they are conveying a secret message. Together, they blend brilliantly.

"Pharmacy? *Eczane.*"

The young man is being helpful. He understood what I was asking.

"On this street?"

He says a few things in Turkish and points down the narrow side street. He motions that I must go left and then right. "Osman. Kemal Osman. *Eczane.*"

I'm not too sure, but I think he's giving me the name of someone who works there. Or is it the name of the pharmacy?

Thanking him, I start to walk away. But before I go, he pushes a card for his shop into my hand. He's quick to say—in practiced English—that they ship their lamps everywhere. And as we part, he sends a kiss in the direction I'm headed. *A kiss.* When was the last time a shop owner sent me off with a kiss? If I were in LA, I'd be thinking he was a creep and never go back, but not here. There's a vast difference between the cultures of East and West. I wonder if I'm supposed to deliver a kiss to someone at the store.

A left and a right later, I spot a sign displaying the word ECZANE. The pharmacy.

I'm relieved, but my first impression from the outside is that it is very different from home. Definitely different from the pharmacy chains we have on every corner in LA. This one is tucked away on a lane that is little more than an alley. It's only wide enough for pedestrians and motorbikes to get through. The storefront is small, the same size as the bakery and the butcher shop on either side of it. A bell rings as I enter. I'm thinking that I've been sent to a second-rate *eczane*, unless it has a massive underground vault filled with inventory.

The inside doesn't bolster my confidence. I count a half dozen people. Three aisles, two counters. One cash register. An attractive dark-haired man in a lab coat is explaining something to a customer leaning over the counter. With the shelves of drugs behind him, I decide he's got to be the pharmacist.

A teenager approaches me. "*Yardımcı olabilir miyim?*"

"English?"

"How can I help you, miss?" he asks cheerfully. He has a British accent.

He's wearing jeans and a navy blue T-shirt. He could easily have walked in ahead of me from the street. But no one inside raises an eyebrow, so I have to assume he works here. Still, I feel like I should be speaking to someone in charge about my prescription. All the Internet searches aside, I'm still doubtful that buying meds can be as easy as they make it sound.

"I have to speak to *him*. This is a..."

The guy in the white coat looks up at me. Immediately, I forget the rest of what I was going to say. Suddenly, I'm eighteen again.

The dark eyes are gorgeous. His eyelashes are so long that I wonder if Turkish men use extensions. His beard is thick. I think it probably makes him look older than he really is. I'd never thought much about it before, but I realize that I find facial hair masculine and very attractive. Then again, it could just be *this* man.

I can only see the back of the woman leaning over the counter. She continues to talk. But I don't blame her for wanting to extend her visit.

"You have a prescription?" the young man persists. "I'll take it to him."

The pharmacist nods at me and I get it. He's encouraging me to trust his employee.

"Okay. The prescription was written by my doctor in Los Angeles." I take the paper out of my purse. "I should have filled it before I came on this..."

Before I finish, the young man snatches the piece of paper out of my hand and takes it to his boss. No one cares about the circumstances of why I need to fill this prescription. I'm a customer, and they have a product to sell.

I'm *hoping* they have a product to sell.

I browse along an aisle, pretending to look for something while I wait. Menstrual hygiene products. Razors. Boxes of creams and ointments. Pain relief tablets and cough syrup. The products with western names are mixed with Turkish ones, and the price difference is huge. The young woman behind the cash register watches my every step, and I wonder if she's worried about me being a shoplifter.

I steal a look at the pharmacist. He's reading the prescription. I don't want to guess what he might be thinking. He'll know what my pills are for. I can't deal with the judgment of a stranger right now. Or worse, sympathy.

The main reason why I didn't tell anyone that I was going through therapy is the lingering stigma that is still attached to it, specifically in Elizabeth's eyes. I've heard her attitude about therapists for years.

They're all quacks.

The school social worker was useless.

The district psychologist didn't know what he was talking about.

When I was younger, I was bullied in school, and her response to the situation was, *Deal with it, or I'll deal with it for you. Why does everything have to be a crisis?*

Elizabeth never had any patience for drama. *I'll fix it for you.* In her mind, there's no such thing as process, only quick fixes. A person can't plan to work on something for two years, four years, ten years, or whatever. *If you're sick, take a pill. I want results now.*

That was why Jax might have felt pressured to sell Externus, despite the fact that he loved the work, the company, and the growth pattern. Elizabeth wanted results.

My mother's plan for how to get over my sadness about Autumn's death has two simple steps: first, marry Kyle; second, have another child.

This morning before I left the hotel, I arranged for him to have a separate room. I can't sleep in the same bed with him. I'm tired of acting like everything is great.

I work my way along the aisle until I come to a narrow door sandwiched between two shelves. It's covered with posters. Advertisements. Events. My eyes move from one to the next. Written Turkish uses the Latin alphabet with a few extra dots and marks on some of the letters. It's easy to pretend I can read it. I wish I could, but I can't.

"Your prescription is waiting for you at the register."

I'm pleasantly surprised to have the pharmacist deliver the message himself. He's standing next to me. This close, he's even more handsome than he looked behind the counter. And he has a deep voice that's warm and pleasant, with a hint of an accent. The woman he was serving is still at the counter, speaking to someone on her cell phone. And she's definitely giving me the evil eye.

"I don't have your prescription in loose pills. I gave you a box. A thirty-day supply. Will that be enough?"

"Yes. Yes. Thank you. That's great."

I fight my impulse to explain to him that I really don't intend to take the pills. Or why I'm filling the prescription at all. All the explanations my mother had wanted me to make to the hotel staff, I'd like to make to him.

There's no point. He's in no rush to walk away, and I study him. He's tall, and he smells good. *Osman* is sewn in red letters above the chest pocket of his coat.

"Are you Kemal Osman?"

He smiles with surprise. He's got perfect white teeth.

"How do you know my name?"

"A store clerk in the neighborhood sent me here. Maybe he's a friend or something?" I show him the card from the lamp shop.

"Ah, yes. My cousin."

I mention nothing about him sending a kiss.

"I'm very happy he sent you to me."

It might be my imagination. But the word *me* holds a punch. A sweet punch. I'm thinking he has to get back to work.

"Have you attended their performance?" He motions to the posters.

I wasn't paying attention, but he's referring to an advertisement for Istanbul's Whirling Dervishes. Men dressed in tall hats and white coats and skirts, and spinning in a circle.

"No, I haven't."

"Do you know about them?"

"Yes, actually. They belong to a Sufi order named after the poet Rumi. They seek a closer relationship with God through chanting, praying, and music. The whirling dance is a religious ceremony."

His eyes flash his approval. "How do you know all that?"

Wikipedia University. I don't tell him this, but I've been fascinated with Sufis for a while. Their history. Their rituals. I've learned that their way of life brings them nourishment of the soul. They whirl to lose their minds. Bring them to a higher plane of awareness. No doubt in the West they would suggest medication for this kind of behavior. "I've seen this same poster in a few different places around Sultanahmet."

"There is a great deal to see in Sultanahmet, but I wonder if you have visited other parts of Istanbul."

"I only flew in a couple of days ago."

"We have history every place you turn. It is in the air. We are a city of fifteen million people. There is so much to experience outside this part of the city."

Eighteen million, but I don't correct him. My information comes from the internet. He lives here. "I'm sure there is."

"Do you care to go see them?" He motions to the poster.

"I'd planned to see them sometime."

"The Galata Tekke is a popular Mevlevi Dervish hall in Istanbul.

That's where all the tourists go," he tells me. "There is a more authentic *semahane* at an old Sufi lodge in the Zeytinburnu section of the city. A university uses it as a campus now, but some practitioners come every other week for their meditation, and it is open to the public."

I stare at the poster and then steal a look at his face. His eyes are on me. Is he playing tourist guide or is he asking me out?

"We can have dinner afterwards, if you like."

He *is* asking me out. My lip twitches, and I bite it so I won't smile. This feels amazingly good, getting noticed by this guy. But the old doubts immediately rise to the surface.

Does he ask every American tourist who comes into the pharmacy for antidepressants out on a date?

He's reading my mind. "You would be perfectly safe. You already met my cousin. And you know where I work...Christina."

He knows my name.

Of course, he knows my name. He saw it on the prescription bottles.

"May I?" He holds out a hand for my cell phone.

I don't hesitate at all and hand it to him.

He adds his information to my contacts. Confidence oozes out of his pores.

"Ring me up. It would give me great pleasure to escort you."

By the time I'm back on the street, my face feels permanently flushed, and my heart is racing.

I don't know if I'll ever see him again or not. But something just happened. A good-looking guy was flirting with me. More than that. He asked me out. And I feel alive.

The lane is busier than before. I don't have to look at the map. I know how to get back to the hotel. But I'm not in any hurry.

An entrance to the Grand Bazaar at the end of the block looks enticing. I wander in that direction and notice the shoppers smiling at me. I smile back.

I pause near the arched stone entrance to the bazaar. A dozen tourists, all wearing electric blue T-shirts bearing the name of the same tour company, jostle me as they go by. Half of them stop and paw through leather purses hanging from a bunch of metal racks outside a shop. I imagine they're trying to get their requisite shopping done in the six or twelve or however many hours they have allocated for Istanbul.

My thoughts drift back to Elizabeth. I hope she's okay. I should tell Kyle about what happened with the robbery. He has a lot at stake in this sale too.

I dial Kyle's number. He doesn't answer the first time. It goes to his voice mail. He's in the middle of his workday. The images flashing through my brain all have a certain tall, black-haired Japanese woman in them.

The fact that those visions no longer bother me might have something to do with the attention I received from Kemal Osman. To feel attractive, to be the center of a person's attention, to receive a compliment—whatever the young pharmacist's motives were—filled a need in me. And I feel better about myself.

I dial Kyle again and he answers.

13

ELIZABETH

NOW

USELESS. Totally useless.

The embassy person she'd spoken with was polite enough, but a complete waste of time. What was worse, no one else would talk to her. No one in a supervisory role was "available." No one with higher security clearance would check on the information she gave them. Elizabeth might as well have been a nobody, because that's how she was treated.

She should have known. Regardless of her service record, regardless of her personal connections with the State Department here in Turkey, she had no life-and-death emergency. Elizabeth couldn't get the consulate personnel to consider the theft in the hotel room or her presence in the country as a situation that deserved any elevated level of attention.

Fine, she'd follow the procedure outlined for any Joe Shmoe. Make an appointment and come back to the consulate on the assigned date with the required forms.

Once the veracity of the documents is ascertained, a temporary identification card would be issued until a replacement...

Blah, blah, blah.

Humiliated, exhausted, frustrated, and fuming, Elizabeth took a cab back to the hotel. By the time she arrived in Sultanahmet, it was a little past twelve noon. Going to the police station would have to wait. Right now, she needed a shower, a change of clothes, and food.

The hotel manager immediately approached her when she entered the building. The police report wouldn't be ready for a couple of days. She was glad she hadn't wasted more time going there first.

Elizabeth was also told that she would be moved into a deluxe room overlooking the Hagia Sophia. Her entire stay would be *gratis*, courtesy of the management. Her meals should be charged to the room, as they would be compliments of the hotel.

"If you're looking for your daughter, Ms. Hall is in the hotel's Seasons Restaurant," the manager advised, eager to please.

Elizabeth went out, descended the stone steps from the lobby, and made her way along a flower-lined walk to the entrance of the restaurant. As she approached the glass-walled conservatory in the middle of the courtyard, she saw her reflection in the windows. She almost didn't recognize herself. The scruffy, poorly dressed woman staring back at her was old and tired. She'd aged ten years in one day, physically and emotionally. She leaned forward to wipe a smudge off her cheek. Her image distorted and melted away, replaced by the lunch crowd packing the restaurant beyond. Through the glass, she saw a young, dark-haired girl running between the tables, chased by her mother. The child burst through the door and bumped into Elizabeth. Startling blue-green eyes looked up at her, and she ran off.

The ground shifted, her vision blurred. What she saw was a hungry Kurdish child crying in an alley. The tightness in her throat felt like claws choking off her air, and a knot swelled in her chest.

The girl called her *Shaitan*. Satan.

Elizabeth fought back the lapse in her sanity and combed her fingers through her hair. She adjusted the sunglasses on top of her head. She was becoming soft in her old age.

The conservatory was octagonal shaped, with floor-to-ceiling glass and views of the lush inner courtyard. Wide doors opened to a terrace filled with more tables. She spotted Christina outside. She had her laptop open in front of her and a manila folder beside it.

She wasn't alone. A woman in a navy blue headscarf and a matching raincoat stood by her table. Her back was to Elizabeth.

She wondered if this was the same hijabi woman who'd been following them since they arrived. Same thin frame, same height. The same large handbag hanging from her shoulder as she'd seen this morning. It had to be her. On the street near the hotel this morning, Elizabeth had seen her speaking to her daughter. She wanted something.

Elizabeth started toward them.

A busboy carrying a loaded tray backed onto her path, and there was no way to avoid the collision. Plates shattered on the high-gloss marble floor. The noise of the crash silenced the dining area, and all eyes turned.

Elizabeth stiffened under the pressure of the glares. She was accustomed to standing on the side, to being the one who was critical of others. She'd labored hard in her life to earn that position. She refused to be the target of an embarrassing scene.

Other servers converged from every corner, making sure she was unharmed. A wave of apologies followed. In what was only seconds, order was restored, and Elizabeth started for Christina's table again.

The hijabi woman was no longer there. As she went onto the terrace, Elizabeth looked around her. Every table was filled. She focused on the women, on those wearing headscarves. She had vanished.

"That was an impressive entrance." Christina closed her laptop with a snap and planted her elbows on top.

"Par for the course." Elizabeth dropped into the chair across from her. "It's been a tough day."

"Get your passport?"

"I accomplished absolutely nothing. No police report. No passport. Nothing." She scanned the walkways in the gardens beyond the terrace. "Who were you talking to just now?"

"No one."

"I saw her standing by this table."

"Who did you see?"

Elizabeth knew Christina's moods and her demeanor. She recognized when her daughter was sad, depressed, or was in over her head and needed help. Right now, her flushed cheeks said that she was upset.

"You called Kyle and had an argument with him, didn't you?"

"Why do you think my life revolves around Kyle, Mother?"

"Because he's your boyfriend. He's the father of your child. Was," she corrected.

"Keep him out of it, will you?"

"Fine. Then tell me what's wrong."

Christina slid the manila folder next to her laptop across the table. "I found these among Jax's emails. I printed them out in the business center this morning."

Her first thought was that Jax had screwed her about selling the company. She was the finance person, he the engineer. When it came to the Externus start-up, he sat behind his desk and she pounded on doors to get every dollar of the financing they needed. Before he died, he had been dragging his feet, but she was ready to cash out. She wasn't getting any younger.

"Everything in this folder is about your past."

She didn't want to open the folder. He *was* screwing her over, but in a different way.

For her entire life, nothing had come easy for Elizabeth. The jobs, the money, having a child. After coming back to the US with Christina, she went to graduate school at night and got an advanced degree in finance. She needed a job, a way to support the two of them. Over a decade later, she met Jax York. They were working for the same company.

He was interesting and smart and harmless, and he was the kind of guy that needed someone to take charge of his life. Someone to help him with his business plans once he decided to branch off on his own. Elizabeth was good at those sorts of things. She enjoyed the challenge, and her financial degree was an asset in planning a future.

Not once in her life had she been tempted to marry. But with Jax and his ideas for Externus, it made sense financially. Also, he and Christina got along.

Jax York was sixty-two and she was sixty-eight when they got married. Neither of them cared about why he had been a lifetime bachelor or why she'd never married. Their past was their own, their secrets tucked safely behind separate doors.

All went according to plan. A lot of buzz surrounded Externus's startup. From the first day, they'd forecasted making it a four-to-five-year commitment. Build it and sell it. But then, this past year, Jax had suddenly become fixated on knowing more about Elizabeth's history. What she did before she had Christina. Why she left her job overseas and returned to the States. She answered some of his questions and ignored the rest. But she sensed that he hadn't given up. Looking at that folder now, she wondered what was inside.

"You can't ignore what's in here."

That was exactly what she was going to do. Elizabeth motioned to a server to come over and grilled him in Turkish on the luncheon specials.

"Do you want me to order for you too?"

"I can't eat after reading all this."

Always the one for drama, Elizabeth thought, placing her order.

The waiter was still collecting the menus when Christina started in on her.

"Jax was working with an investigator. He was digging into your past."

She drank her water, but it did nothing to loosen the tightness in her throat. The bastard.

"You weren't some freelance interpreter, backpacking your way through the world."

Elizabeth knew there would be no chance of changing the topic. Her daughter wouldn't let it go. Not when she was wound up like this.

"You worked with the State Department." She leaned toward her, lowering her voice. "You were CIA."

Elizabeth held up the glass for a busboy to fill as he went by.

Christina took the folder back and opened it, spreading the pages out on the table.

"You could go to jail for having State Department documents," Elizabeth warned.

"These are declassified. Anyone can access them."

She glanced at the pages. At the top of the facsimiles of memos and reports, *Top Secret* was stamped and X-ed out, with *Unclassified* appearing in block letters.

So much for confidentiality. Elizabeth knew any number of Jax's minions could have hacked in and gotten these, regardless of the security level. He called them programmers and gamers, but they were all thieves and hackers.

"You acted as liaison between our government and Saddam Hussein's people during the Iran-Iraq war."

Elizabeth ran her fingers over the white linen placemat. Average people were clueless about what their governments did. About what their military was capable of doing. The Agency recruited smart young people right out of college, trained them, and made them understand that the everyday life and death decisions of presidents and prime ministers and dictators had far more to do with power and profitability than with humanity. And that was true with *every* head of state. Elizabeth didn't think the recruitment practices or the CIA's purpose had changed over the past three decades.

"You're named in these documents. You *wrote* some of these memos."

"Of course, I did. That was my job."

Elizabeth did what her job demanded. What happened to *Thank you for your service*? No, that would be far too much to hope for.

"I don't understand why you're making such a big deal out of this." She kept her voice low. "So what, I never told you I worked with the government? What harm was done?"

"What harm was done?" Christina scoffed. "You were in Baghdad, and you facilitated the sale of chemical weapons to Iraq. You *knew* how and when Iraq would, and then did, employ gas warfare. It's all here. In these pages."

"Since when are you interested in politics? Or history?"

"I'm human."

"You're an American."

"Don't assume that everyone thinks like you and acts like you, just because of where we're raised." Christina's cheeks were a few shades darker. She thumbed through the pages, her fingers running across the sections she'd underlined or circled.

"You informed senior US officials regularly about the scale of the gas attacks on Iranian troops and on civilians. And on the Kurdish people in northern Iraq."

Elizabeth hadn't realized how deep Jax's hacks had dug into her past. She decided it was time to remain silent. She wasn't about to offer anything more until her daughter was finished. She needed to know the extent of the information she'd need to deflect or deny.

Halfway through the pile, Christina nearly ripped a page in half as she yanked it out and slammed it on top.

"*You* personally facilitated the sale of anthrax, VX nerve gas, West Nile fever germs, and botulinum toxins, as well as germs that caused effects similar to tuberculosis and pneumonia."

People at nearby tables sent them curious looks. "Keep your voice down."

"It's all spelled out. Right here. In black-and-fucking-white."

Elizabeth leaned forward and slapped her hand on the page Christina was reading. The entire table shook. "This is not the whole story. Take off your rose-colored glasses. What I did, I was directed to do. I served my country. *Our* country."

"Every guard at Auschwitz said the same thing."

"Easy for you to judge." Elizabeth paused until their server placed her salad on the table and left them alone. "You're naïve. Sheltered. Clueless about foreign policy and the hard decisions that need to be made in the interests of our country. What do you know about that time? What do you know about what was happening over there?"

"You tell me," she hissed. "Explain it to me."

"Alliances were shifting. After the Shah fell and we lost Iran, we needed Saddam. We needed his oil. He was an important friend."

"You bought him. And at what cost? He used those weapons against his own people."

"We didn't sell it to him."

"That is such a lie. You used Dutch and German weapons dealers. It's all here. *You* did it."

"Policy decisions are made in Washington. The job of the Agency is to gather data and analyze it. Make recommendations about potential outcomes. It's up to the military to engineer the strategies. Yes, we helped build up his weapons. But it was the Iraqis' call on what to do with them."

"So innocent people died. Men, women, children. And hundreds of thousands were driven out of their homes. You were responsible. This wave of refugees—"

"Don't be ridiculous. Nothing is that simple. No *one* person is responsible for any *one* event. I followed orders. I did my job. I was one cog in a vast, complex machine."

"Really? Your job? You're saying *everything* you did was for our government?" Christina spread the papers and pulled another sheet from the pile. "You saw a chance to cash in. And you took it. You profited from that evil. You had no conscience. No heart."

Elizabeth stared at the pages. She didn't think any evidence was left of the incident. She thought of Jax again and the private arguments they'd had about selling Externus. He pretended to give in, but all this shit was proof that he wanted to screw her in the end.

"You brokered a deal on your own for the sale of equipment from Italy that would speed up the production of chemical-filled artillery rounds and bombs. And you got caught. By *our* government."

"That's not true. I was only suspected. But it wasn't true."

They couldn't prove it. No one wanted to make her case public or even push it up the ladder. She wasn't alone. Others were doing the same thing. Everyone was a mercenary in those days. That's what wars do. They create a jungle where there is no law and order. Everyone makes a profit when they can.

As far as the U.S. government was concerned—as far as the Agency was concerned—there was too much dirty laundry. And the shit started flying when Saddam invaded Kuwait. Washington wanted it all to go away.

So she was out. She became *persona non grata*. Unacceptable. Unwelcome. They wiped her records. That was why she wasn't in the consulate's system today. That's why no one would help her. But somewhere in the dark closet of the State Department's records, she still existed. That's how Jax, and now Christina, got hold of these memos.

"How could you do it?" The anger came through in her daughter's voice, in the hard lines of her face.

Thank you for your service. The words reverberated in her head. How many times had she heard those words spoken to others? Addressed to some brainless, eighteen-year-old kid who never served overseas, who knew nothing of foreign policy or the military-industrial complex. People like Elizabeth and those she worked with were the puppeteers. They made kings. Took down monarchies. Destroyed governments.

She wanted her daughter to say those words to her.

"How can you live with yourself? How can you sit in front of me and pretend none of it matters? You're ruthless."

"You're calling *me ruthless*?" Elizabeth leaned toward her. "Have you gone hungry for a single day in your life? Did you ever have to worry about dropping out of school to work? Or about how to pay your rent? All you've ever known in your life is comfort. Well, I can live with myself. I sleep perfectly well. Because I did it all for you. Whatever I made, I spent it all on you."

"You can't blame me," Christina snapped.

"Oh, but I can." Elizabeth pushed her chair back and stood up. "I blame everything that is wrong in my fucking life on you."

14

CHRISTINA

NOW

IT'S 1:20 a.m. when I step out from the lobby to the street. There's a wicker bench with cushions, flanked by two pots of flowers by the door. I'm too restless to sit. Lights from the streetlamps flicker and dance on the yellow walls of the old hotel. I breathe in the night air. The sky is black, and no stars are visible above the city.

The hotel doorman is keeping a watchful eye up and down the quiet street, and on me.

He greets me in Turkish and then says, "Taxi for you, madam?"

"I've called. I'm all set." I show him the name of the car service on my phone.

This neighborhood and the hotel are intended to make the Western tourist feel safe and at home. All the staff speak some level of English. The doormen wear blue sport jackets and ties. The food is mildly seasoned, suited to the American palate. The comfort and service meet the five-star standard for any world-class hotel. But we're in Istanbul and—just as my pharmacist friend said this morning—there's so much more to the city than this neighborhood.

As I wait, I look up at the high walls of the hotel. I try to imagine this building during an earlier, much different period in history. What would a prisoner have to do to break free of an Ottoman jail? File off shackles? Scale a wall? Dig a tunnel? Create a diversion and walk past guards? I wonder if any succeeded in escaping.

I wish I could walk away from this hotel and my life, and become one with the city that stretches out over the hills as far as you can see. The culture and the four-thousand-year history are alive. When you walk through the neighborhoods, you can't help but feel its heart beat.

On the front step of an art gallery across the cobblestone lane, two cats growl and argue. One darts down the sidewalk, and the other chases after.

Kyle's flight gets in at three. He's supposed to come directly to the hotel, but I've decided to go pick him up instead. We have a lot to talk about. My call to him this morning was brief.

"Elizabeth was robbed. She lost her passport and license. Will there be any problem with signing off on a sales agreement?"

"We're putting the cart before the horse. There are preliminary offers, but we need to talk face-to-face with all the suitors. Let's make the deal and worry about signoffs after."

Maybe I'm more desperate than the others for this sale to be completed. The bonus check is my one-way ticket, the money gives me the ability to walk down this cobblestone lane into a new life.

Headlights shine in my face as a car approaches. A black Lexus SUV. It's the same company we used when my mother and I arrived three nights ago.

The vehicle pulls up front, and the driver steps out. The doorman speaks to him in Turkish. Satisfied with the response, he opens the door, and I climb into the back seat.

The good thing about online bookings is that I don't have to worry about the language. The driver knows he's to take me to the airport, wait, and bring us back to the hotel.

Once I'm in, the car glides away from the curb. Classical music plays softly. The temperature is perfect. The man behind the wheel is older and, from where I'm sitting, I can see a thin white scar along his jawbone. With the exception of greeting me with *Merhaba* when I first get in the car, he drives in silence.

Settling back in the cool leather, I stare at the darkened store fronts. We pass a couple of scruffy-looking dogs sniffing around a pile of boxes on the curb. They startle as we go by. Another cat sits on a wall above them, watching.

The streets are quiet and free of the daytime congestion. Two young men who look more like boys are pushing a dumpster down the road. Behind them, a trio of ragged children follows at a safe distance. Their faces are dirty. Their skittishness is not so different from the two stray dogs. Their vulnerability pierces my heart. They're barely older than babies.

I sail by them in my shiny black bubble—separate and sheltered.

I still mourn the loss of Autumn. I'll mourn her every day of my life, I imagine. And yet, this city holds...how many lost children? Hundreds, thousands who have no roof over their heads. No parents to go back to. No one watches over them. They don't know when or how they'll get their next scrap of food. Or if the next person who offers help is an angel or a devil.

I press my forehead against the window to cool my flushed face and think of the argument with my mother today.

If you enable the devil, does that make you a devil too?

I'm no theologian, but I'd guess that in every faith, the answer would be *yes*.

She arranged the sale and manufacture of outlawed weapons, knowing how they would be used. Knowing that real people would die or be displaced. Knowing that children who were lucky enough to live would end up like these homeless waifs, hungry and begging on the streets. And then she sidesteps any responsibility. Just part of her job, she claims. But she also did it for profit.

And how complicit am I?

The car pulls onto the highway, and Istanbul's lights become a speeding blur in my watery vision.

Elizabeth's words sit heavy on my conscience. I didn't grow up rich. We were middle-class comfortable. Elizabeth owned our house and she worked, and I reaped the benefits of it.

I never had to struggle to survive. As she reminded me, I never felt the desperation that goes with not having money. I never went hungry. I never searched through a trash dumpster.

Are my hands also red with the blood of all the people who have been affected by these wars?

Yes, they're stained. Indelibly. I've benefited from the choices Elizabeth made my whole life. I'm no victim. I'm complicit in so many ways. And I feel guilty as fuck. I wipe tears from my cheeks.

I had dinner with Elizabeth on the rooftop lounge tonight. But she made it clear that we were done with that earlier conversation. Let the past stay in the past, she says.

I didn't have much to say, but I thought of Jax and how he discovered all of this and never mentioned any of it to me.

To me, Jax was one of the truly good people I met in my life. Before working for Externus, I got to know him through Elizabeth and we hit it off. We shared the same politics, the same views, had similar interests. Later, after starting to work for him, I saw that his decisions balanced personal gain with social and environmental consciousness.

Digging further into his emails tonight, I've discovered he was also worried about Elizabeth's connection to the defendants named in a civil lawsuit recently filed in Baghdad. She was part owner of Externus. Questions about the company's liability are posed in vague, hypothetical terms in one of the emails he exchanged with the lawyer. References to "asset seizure" come up a number of times.

He was worried about his own complicity. But was he more concerned about securing his assets than what he'd discovered about his wife's past career?

I don't know all the answers. Nothing is clear-cut. Maybe I didn't know him as well as I thought I did.

Life doesn't consist simply of straight lines and primary colors. A person's behavior is usually all over the place. We're a mixed bag of good and bad, truth and lies.

That's true for Elizabeth. The same goes for Jax. And I can sit on my high horse and look down my nose at everyone, but it's also true for me. I'm still benefiting from the misery of others.

I think of Kyle and pull my forehead away from the window. How much do I tell him? Do I tell him anything?

As humans we're hardwired to sense when someone is watching us. Our body reacts with a feeling of unease. We get that prickling sensation on the back of our necks. Our brains are good at picking up on potential dangers. The presence of another predator. It's a survival instinct.

Right now, I know I'm being stared at. I look at the rearview mirror. The driver is watching me.

The dashboard displays numbers and gauges and gadgets, but the light doesn't illuminate his face very well. He's tall. The top of his head almost brushes the roof of the car. He's wearing a black jacket over a white shirt and black tie. His salt-and-pepper hair is short and wiry.

And the dark eyes in the mirror keep coming back to me.

I didn't tell Elizabeth I was going to the airport. Kyle doesn't know I'm coming to pick him up either. I suppose after this guy abducts me and a few days pass, they can trace my steps...

I have to stop letting my imagination go wild. This is not the time to let paranoia paralyze me.

There's nothing going on. My cell phone is in my hand. After what happened to my mother, I did think to ask the desk clerk about the Istanbul equivalent of 911 before leaving the hotel. *155*. I punch in the numbers now, but I don't hit the call button. There's no reason to. All he's doing is looking at a woman who was deep in thought a few minutes ago.

He's been quiet. Not unpleasant. He's a good driver. The soft music continues to play in the background. I wish I could engage in some small talk for my own sake. I don't know if he speaks any English.

He's still watching me.

"How many times a day do you make this run to the airport?"

"How do you know her?"

My heart leaps. My thumb hovers over the green button. Press it and the call goes through to the police. "Know her? Who?"

"Tiam. Tiam Rahman."

I shake my head, hoping he sees my look of confusion. "Is that a name that I should know?"

The car crosses two lanes and skids to an abrupt stop on the shoulder of the highway. The phone slips out of my fingers and tumbles to the floor. He turns and looks at me. His gaze is hard and frightening.

"How do you know Tiam Rahman?" he says again.

PART IV

I'm drenched in the flood which has yet to come.
I'm tied up in the prison that has yet to exist.
Not having played a game of chess, I'm already at checkmate.
Not having tasted a single cup of your wine, I'm already drunk.
Not having entered the battlefield, I'm already wounded and slain.
Like the shadow, I am and I am not.
—Rumi

15

ZARI

THEN

CELEBRATING birthdays wasn't traditional among the Turks or Kurds in Istanbul. Most of the refugees that she'd befriended here over the years didn't know what day they were born. Many had the first of January registered as their official birth date, for the sake of simplicity. Some even had the wrong year listed on their papers. If they had papers.

The registration process was a great relief to Zari. Using the January 1st date solved many of her problems. That was the date on Tiam's residency documents.

Still, on the third Saturday in September, she invited some of her friends, as well as Tiam's friends, to their apartment for dinner. She didn't tell any of them that her daughter's actual birthday had been two days earlier. It wouldn't have mattered to them anyway. But it mattered to her. The light of her eyes was now eighteen years old.

Zari had called Emine and asked if she could arrive early. Her friend was coming directly from work and bringing boxes of halva and baklava.

A deep camaraderie had begun when a nurse helped a homeless mother and her sick child in the halls of a hospital. Over the years, their friendship had evolved into a close and abiding sisterhood.

Zari helped when Emine's mother had a stroke and was

bedridden for a year, before passing away. She watched the grandchildren whenever the family needed an extra hand.

On her part, Emine helped her raise Tiam on her own. She helped her get a job and keep a job. She co-signed a lease so Zari could get an apartment, and then get her residence papers. The occasions where they supported one another were so numerous, and each one was woven into the fabric of their connected existence. Emine was a mother to her. A friend. A sister. Her *malak*, her angel.

When the doorbell rang, Zari dried her hands on a dish towel and pressed the buzzer on the intercom. She opened the door of her apartment and waited on the landing of the fourth story walk-up for her friend to climb the steps.

Emine was out of breath by the time she reached the door. She worked too much. At her age, six days a week in the hospital were too many hours to be on her feet. Streaks of gray hair had turned white in recent years. She wore them proudly. She said she'd earned them.

The women kissed each other on both cheeks and hugged. Shoes were left at the door. Zari took the boxes of sweets into the kitchen and put them on the counter.

Emine poked her head in the sitting room and the two bedrooms before coming into the kitchen.

"Where's your *çocuk*?"

"She takes art classes on Saturdays in Kadiköy. She'll be back by six and bring her friends with her."

"Such a smart girl, our Tiam. Nothing stops her. Nothing slows her down. *Allah iyilik versin.*"

God bless her. Zari prayed for the same thing every day.

"What can I do to help you?"

"Nothing! Everything is ready."

Zari pointed to the dolmas she'd rolled. They were already arranged on platters, alongside the triangular slices of kuku sabzi she prepared for dinner. She turned off the heat under the biryani and the soup simmering on the stove. The Kurdish salad was in the refrigerator. So was the yogurt drink. She'd made all of Tiam's favorite dishes for dinner.

She poured sweet tea in tulip-shaped glasses and placed a dish of walnuts and raisins on the tray.

Ushering her friend into the sitting room, Zari joined her on the thick carpet covering the floor. The two women leaned back against the Turkmen rug pillows Zari had saved up to buy last year.

This room, this snug apartment, was a blend of the person she was two decades ago and the person she'd become now. Colorful mosaic domes of Turkish lamps hung from the ceiling. Prayer rugs were folded and stacked in the corner, ready to be spread out when *adhan* was called out by the muezzin in the neighborhood mosque. On the wall, framed verses of poetry were depicted in calligraphy. Near one corner, the square table was her daughter's favorite place to paint and do her schoolwork. Beside it, a small bookshelf of dark wood was filled with Zari's own volumes of poetry. Tiam's schoolbooks were on the top shelf.

"Your house is clean. Your dinner is ready. As always, you've cooked enough to feed a hundred hungry people instead of..." Emine paused. "How many are coming?"

"I think ten. But I never know with Tiam. She might bring more friends home."

Zari glanced at the clock on the wall. She had to say what was on her mind before anyone else arrived.

"I went to the bank today and spoke to the manager. I asked him for a loan."

"A loan? What are you buying?"

"A car. I'd like to buy Tiam a car."

"But why?" Emine tsked, the colloquial Turkish way of saying *no*. "The congestion in Istanbul. The parking. The angry drivers. Why would you do such a thing to your good-natured daughter?"

Zari's intention wasn't for Tiam to drive the car every day. But with her frequent bouts of sickness, her breathing problems, Zari wanted her to have options. The university she'd been accepted to had multiple campuses. One of them was in the northeast part of the city. Far away from here. It would take too long if she were to depend on public transportation.

She explained all of this to Emine. Zari's friend had a car too.

Most of the time it was parked in front of her apartment building, but she still had it, in case she needed it.

"But when I was at the bank, the manager asked me why I'm taking out a loan when I already have so much money in my savings account."

"How much money have you saved?"

Zari leaned forward, studying the other woman's expression. "You should know. You put it there."

"Me? I've done no such thing."

This time, Zari was the one who tsked. "Everything around us has your stamp on it. The rug we're sitting on. The new coats Tiam receives every winter. I can go on and on. We both know what you've done. I am grateful beyond measure for your generosity over the years. But this time, I can't accept it. It's too much."

Emine shook her head. "Not me, my friend."

"There is no use denying it." Zari patted her on the knee. "I won't permit this. You can't put money into my account. You're still working to retire. You have grandchildren at your *sofreh* now."

"I tell you it wasn't me." Emine put the empty tea glass on the tray. "Someone else must be putting money in your account."

"If not you, then who?"

Emine started to get up. "I'll pour us more tea."

Zari put her hand out, stopping her friend. "You know something, don't you?"

"Think of it as a *zakat*, a contribution that *should* be made to you. Accept it. Spend it on your daughter. Buy the car she needs. Do whatever you want with it. You deserve it. It's yours."

Zari knew Emine too well. Sitting beside her was a woman who worked hard for everything in her life. There were no shortcuts. No easy roads. The words she'd just spoken didn't belong on her lips.

"You call me your sister. Then speak to me like one. Whose *zakat* is it? Why are they giving it to me?"

Emine rubbed her temples as if in pain. "Let it go."

"I can't. I won't. If you don't tell me, I'll go back to the bank and tell the manager that there has been a mistake. A bank error. The money isn't mine. They can do whatever they want with it."

"Please, Zari."

"I've learned from you. I work hard. I need no more charity from strangers."

She picked up the tray and got to her feet to get more tea.

"That money is not from a stranger. It was put there by your husband."

Zari stopped dead, grabbing the edge of the table. She couldn't breathe. Her heart beat was a pounding roar in her ears. The room swayed, and she sat down on the nearest chair.

"My husband?"

"Your husband. Yahya."

"Yahya?" She breathed his name as if she could bring him to life. "How? How do you know Yahya?"

He *was* alive, and the knowledge brought tears. For more than eighteen years, Zari had waited. She'd prayed. And she'd looked for him. She'd gone back to Ankara several times. She'd searched everywhere, there and here in Istanbul. On the streets. At the bus stops. In the Kurdish neighborhoods. She'd searched the lines of men preparing to pray at the mosque, hoping that one day her husband would be there.

"Where is he? Please, Emine." She dashed away tears from her face. "Where has he been? Why...why would you know, but not me? Where is he now?"

Question after question tumbled out. But she couldn't slow down long enough to hear the answers. Emine rose to her feet and gathered Zari to her chest.

"This can't be real. I didn't think I would ever see him again. He's alive. Is he well?"

"I'm not supposed to let you know. I was told never to mention his name. But he's been in Istanbul for a long time. And he's been watching over you and his daughter. Taking care of you and Tiam."

"Why wouldn't he come to us?"

Emine shook her head. Pulling out another chair from the table, she sat down. Their knees touched, and she took Zari's hands in hers. "He thinks that's not wise. It's not what he wants."

"He doesn't want me?" Her voice shook as the words tumbled out of her lips. "He doesn't want his wife?"

"Yahya is not the man you married. He has another life now."

"What do you mean, *another life*? Where has he been?" A hard thought pierced her chest. "Does he have a new wife?"

So many Kurdish families were torn apart after they fled their land. Lost to each other, they had to start again and make a new life.

"He went to prison, Zari. For ten years."

This was too much to comprehend. She struck her own chest with a fist. Why would he go to prison? Yahya?

"He joined a gang there. A criminal gang. And now, the people he works with, they are dangerous men. He is a dangerous man. The person he's become is different from the person you married. I'm telling you, these are bad people."

She couldn't believe any of this. Yahya was a good person. Smart and good. She still had his letters. "How do you know all of this?"

"Remember when Tiam was in the hospital for a month during her first year of high school?"

Zari would never forget those torturous weeks. She thought that her daughter would die. None of the doctors were offering any hope or encouragement. But Tiam had survived by sheer force of will.

"That was when your husband contacted me. He paid for everything. The hospital. The tests. The doctors. More doctors. He visited your boss and made sure your job would be waiting for you, even though no one could say when you would return to work. And he made me promise to keep his secret." Emine patted Zari's hand. "The money in the bank *is* him."

Zari pulled her hands away and wrapped them around her middle. Yahya. The pain in her heart wouldn't go away. "How did he find me?"

"You have papers now. You and Tiam have been in the government system for a long time. You use your real name, where you were born. Anyone can find you now."

A narrow bridge formed, stretching through a mist toward the man she loved. Toward the life she once had. Toward the happiness she'd once known. She needed Emine's help to cross it.

"Why did he go to prison?"

"I don't know."

"When did he come to Istanbul?"

"I don't know."

"Can I see him?"

"No."

"He doesn't want to see me?"

"He doesn't."

Emine's words were knives, ripping open her chest.

"I said it before. He's a different man from the one you married. He wants no connection with his past. He wants no one to know he had a wife."

"But he still feels obligated to provide for us?" she asked. If Yahya wanted to destroy the bridge between them, then why not walk away and forget them?

"He thinks he failed you as a husband. With things as they are, you're both better off being apart. And yet, he feels responsible for you. Financially. Tiam is his daughter. She's his flesh and blood. A piece of him. The love of a parent to a child never goes away. He'll be out there for her, watching, protecting, providing...forever."

Zari looked up at Tiam's books. At Tiam's shoes by the door. At Tiam's colorful array of headscarves hanging by the door. Her daughter's handprint was everywhere in Zari's life. But she was her daughter. Not his.

Sadness and relief swirled through her like twin spirits. She was glad Yahya didn't want to see her. For the first time, she realized she couldn't see him. Not today. And not eight years ago or whenever it was since he got out of prison. And not tomorrow either. How could she?

How could she face him and tell him she'd lost his daughter? Their daughter.

PART V

―――――――

Last night, when Irem's magic garden slept,
The wind of morning through the alleys stepped,
Stirring the hyacinth's purple tresses curled,
"Where is thy cup, the mirror of the world?
Ah, where is Love, you Throne of Djem?" I cried.
The breezes knew not; but "Alas," they sighed,
"That happiness should sleep so long!" and wept.
— Ḥafeẓ

16

CHRISTINA

NOW

ENDING the call and jamming the phone in my bag, I move away from the sliding glass door into the terminal, past massive gray pillars that are arranged in rows for the entire length of the building.

I'll be here, madam. Waiting. That's all the driver had to say for himself when he dropped me off at the curb. Are you fucking kidding me? Are you pretending that nothing happened? That you didn't scare me shitless?

My heart is racing, and my entire body is trembling. I'm relieved that I reached the airport in one piece. Too scared that he'd gun the engine and kidnap me, I shoved the door open and bolted.

Because of the late hour, there are fewer people in the long gallery of the terminal than when I arrived with my mother. A large coffee shop in the center of the huge space is open, and I consider stopping there, but I don't think I can hold a cup steady enough to drink it without spilling.

This airport is new. Istanbul has become a hub for so many airlines. The bridge between continents, cultures—a crossroads for all of us. People fly in, change planes, and fly out, but with the change comes a transition from one stage of life to another. In an airport, people give themselves permission to reflect on their past and ponder their future, so long as there are no distractions. But that doesn't describe me at the moment.

Everything had to happen today. I think of the documents on Jax's email and Elizabeth's rationalizations. Then there's Kyle and our long overdue conversation. The driver is the icing on the cake.

A monitor mounted on one of the pillars says Kyle's flight from Osaka by way of Tokyo has already landed. I check the time. He might still be coming through customs.

A trickle of travelers becomes a stream, and then a rushing river. Most are Japanese businessmen and tourists. I spot Kyle among them in the line funneling through.

His mussed hair and tired face show the effect of the hours he's been in the air. He stands head and shoulders over the others as he comes out. I've honestly never been so happy to see him.

He's surprised to see me waiting beyond the barrier. "What are you doing here? I told you I'd see you at the hotel."

When he reaches the end of the exit, I'm there waiting for him. I don't know if I intended to hug him, but I do and then pull away abruptly and shoot a glance toward the cars lining the curb, beyond the glass wall of the terminal. His tired smile quickly darkens into a questioning look.

"What's going on?"

The thought of what happened has me shaking again. My words tumble out on top of each other. "I came to pick you up. I hired a car service. But on the way here, the driver...well, it was scary."

"What exactly was scary? What happened?"

Pulling his luggage behind him, he leads me away from the crowd waiting for other passengers. He looks at the sliding doors.

"What the fuck did he do?"

This is Kyle. A lacrosse player and a frat boy in college. Since we've been together, I've heard plenty of wild stories from his old buddies. I know he's got enough 'alpha' in him to get into a fight. He's never had to on my behalf, but I know he would if the situation demanded it.

"On the way here, everything was fine. Then, out of the blue, the driver asks me if I know some Turkish name. It was so random."

Kyle frowns. "Okay. But that doesn't sound too scary. Was he being conversational? Maybe he mixed you up with another client."

"He pulled over to the side of the fucking highway to ask me this question."

I've got his full attention now. His eyes are blazing when he stares at the doors.

"Did he touch you? What did he do?"

"Nothing. He didn't do anything. But he kept asking the same question. It wasn't conversational. I didn't know what was going to happen."

He runs his fingers through his hair. "What did you say?"

I take a deep breath, holding it together. "I said I don't know anyone by that name. And I had to say it over and over."

Two grim policemen wearing vests and carrying machine guns walk by. They stop by an exit. Kyle is watching them. I can tell he's considering talking to them.

"What happened then?"

"He stares at me for what felt like forever. I was sure I was dead. Then, he just starts driving again and comes here. Like nothing happened."

"Is he out there now?"

"Yeah, he's waiting for us."

Kyle flexes his shoulders and nods toward the doors. "We'll take a cab back to the hotel. First, I'd like to say a few words to him."

We walk out of the terminal together. I'm not about to let him go out there alone. The black Lexus is waiting right in front, where he dropped me off.

But then the driver's door opens, and a young woman, wearing a black suit, white shirt, and black tie, steps out. I peer into the back seat, up and down the sidewalk.

"Who are you? Where's the driver that brought me here?"

"Good evening, ma'am." She has almost no accent at all. "An emergency call came for him. The dispatch office directed me to replace him."

"Where did you come from?"

"I work the airport transport route every night." She smiles at Kyle, obviously thinking he's the one to win over.

I don't believe her. "This is the same car. How did you get here? How did he leave? I was only gone for maybe ten minutes."

"The company directed us to exchange cars." She takes Kyle's suitcase. "The two of you are going to the hotel in Sultanahmet. I have the address."

"I need his name."

"Of course, ma'am. I'll have the office contact you with the information."

"Do *you* know him?"

"I am sorry, I cannot say. Company policy. They are very strict."

Kyle is shooting me a look that says, *Let it go for now.*

Inside the car, the music is on. She maneuvers through the congestion in front of the terminal like someone who does this all the time. Still unsettled, I'm scanning the vehicles around us.

"What kind of car is he driving?"

"My apologies, ma'am." She shakes her head. "The office will address your concerns tomorrow."

Kyle gives me another look and asks the woman if she has been working for this car service long.

That's enough to set her off. She doesn't stop talking for the entire drive back.

I know everything about her. She's a travel blogger. Grew up in some neighborhood in Istanbul. Studied for a year in New York. We hear about everywhere she's been. Everywhere she wants to go. Her boyfriend is from Morocco. She ticks off the names of a long list of celebrities she's driven when they were in Istanbul. She has lengthy opinions on the leaders of Turkey, Russia, Israel, the US. I know intimate details of her parents' health and occupations, her siblings' marital status. And there's a new litter of kittens in the alley next to her apartment.

I find it strange that she tells us all of this and still won't offer anything about the scary guy who drove me to the airport.

Regardless of all the chatter, I'm still jumpy. The first driver's threatening attitude is not part of the cheerful, welcoming vision I had of Istanbul. His questions and my answers keep replaying in my head. In the end, I'm not sure if he believed me. When he got back on the highway, I had zero confidence that I'd survive that ride.

As we arrive at the hotel, the reason for my nervousness has shifted to something else. The conversation I was planning to have with Kyle on the way back from the airport never happens. I'm thinking of the adjoining rooms I'd arranged for. I'd planned to prepare him for it before we got here, but it's too late for that now. And as the elevator arrives on our floor, I'm feeling like I'm trekking in shackles into a courtroom for crimes that should have been dismissed.

I use his keycard, and we go in. The connecting door to my room is open. He makes no comment whatsoever about why the closet is empty or why none of my things are on the desk or chairs. Between the two of us, I've always been the messy one.

"I need a shower bad."

He empties his pocket on the dresser, drops his suitcase on the bed, and takes out what he needs. I stare at his back as he disappears into the bathroom.

I leave his key on the dresser and go into my own room. It's only matter of time before he figures things out.

Sitting at the desk, I check my phone, but I have no new messages. I open the laptop and look through my new email. As far as the Externus acquisition goes, I've gone back and forth twice with the company lawyer today, and everything seems to be in line. I'm tempted to log into Jax's email and read more about the things he had uncovered about Elizabeth. But I already have a clear picture of who she is and what she's willing to do to get what she wants. There's no point adding more fuel to the fire.

I'm trying to keep myself busy, but at the same time I'm focused on what's going on in the next room.

Kyle is out of the shower. I hear him moving his things around. I close the laptop and walk to the window. Pulling back the curtains, I stare out at the rooftops of the city. The window is partly open. The air smells crisp. The sky is growing lighter in the east.

From a distant mosque, I hear a sound that's becoming as familiar to me as a church bell ringing the hour. The call for the morning prayer. I wonder if a certain young hijabi woman is awake and praying right this minute.

The city is rolling back the blankets of night, stretching, acknowledging Allah, and welcoming the new day. The air, the sky, the glow of lights, the hum of people, the tendrils of existence that make a place come alive...some of it has already become familiar to me. And some has yet to be discovered and explored. The realization is bittersweet. What I have right now is wearing on me. My life is exhausting. What is out there—beyond the domes and rooftops of this ancient place—is a new beginning. And I am ready to explore it.

"I can't think straight, see straight. I need to get some sleep."

Kyle's voice has me turn away from the window. He's standing in the doorway.

"Why do we have two rooms? Are we sleeping in this bed or that one?"

He's wearing gray knit boxer shorts and nothing else. His hair is wet. His legs are long and strong. The flat abs and the muscles on his arms and chest are proof he works out, regardless of all the time he spends on the road. There used to be a day when seeing him like this would take my breath away. When a mere look from him would have me climbing into bed with him. And neither of us would be getting any sleep.

It's different now. A glass wall exists between us, and what I see on the other side is no longer mine.

"You sleep there." I motion to his room. "And I sleep here."

"I don't understand."

"It's time, Kyle."

He lets out a frustrated breath. "Is this about Autumn again?" He doesn't wait for my answer. "Look, I said some things, and you said some things. But that's all behind us."

We'd had a few angry conversations about our daughter before and after she was born. "I did you wrong, Kyle. I wanted her more than I wanted you. I loved her more than I could ever love you."

"We've been through all this before. You treated me badly. Okay. I told you a dozen times that I forgive you." He runs a hand through his wet hair. "She's gone, Christina. And we don't have to do this now."

"When *should* we do it?" I ask. "Next week? Next month? When we're back in LA? And what's the point of waiting? You've moved on."

He bristles. "What do you mean, I've moved on?"

I didn't want to bring it up, but somehow my mouth has gotten ahead of my brain. "With Aimi."

His eyes narrow. "How do you know her?"

"Elizabeth saw the picture you posted on Instagram and showed her to me. I looked her up."

There are so many more photos of the two of them together on *her* social media page. I felt like a stalker going through them. It didn't stop me though.

"Aimi is a consultant. A headhunter. Our relationship is professional."

"I'm sure it is."

"This is ridiculous. What else do you want to know about her?"

I shrug. "Nothing. That's your room, this is my room, and Aimi is none of my business."

Kyle isn't giving up. He comes in and sits heavily on my bed, facing me. "I told you. She's a headhunter. She's always at the conferences. I met with her this time because she has an offer for me from one of the major gaming companies in Japan."

I'm not surprised that Kyle already has a job offer. He's good at what he does. He'll be an asset to them.

"But I told her I'm not making any decisions yet. Not until I talk to you."

"Me? How am I involved in this?"

"You seem to have forgotten this, but you and I are together. We're a team. I won't go anywhere without you."

This is not about our romantic relationship, and my brain clicks over from personal to business mode. I think of the financial aspects of this sale. We were each promised matching bonuses. Not a fortune, but enough to give us a healthy start. And then I think of Elizabeth. She's walking away with the lion's share of the money. But I know my mother. I've come to understand that I can expect nothing else from her when the business here is concluded. What is hers, she keeps. That's fine with me; I have no right to it. I wonder about Kyle though, and his motivation for us staying together. My mother keeps suggesting marriage and a baby. She doesn't want to lose him.

I'm becoming a real cynic, and I hate myself for it. My thoughts, my actions, the distrustful way I look at everyone around me—it's all Elizabeth's view of life. Talk about playing the blame game, I remind myself. I'm so broken.

"Well, I think you should accept the job. Go to Japan. Have an adventure. And I'll take care of our lease when I get back to LA. Unless you want to keep the apartment. In that case, I'll find another place."

"You're tired. I'm tired. We're not having this conversation now."

He can deny it all he wants, but I've said what has been on my mind. I don't know what else there is to say. A weight has been lifted off my shoulders. It's so much easier to run away than to stay and rebuild a relationship from shards and rubble. I grab my bag and start putting the laptop and my notes and phone into it.

"Where are you going?"

"Downstairs. I have some work to do."

"You can work here."

He's sitting half-naked on my bed. "Better Wi-Fi connection down there."

"When was the last time you slept? You look exhausted. Come to bed."

This is the problem with trying to break up with him in a civilized manner. He hasn't listened to anything I've said.

He tosses the decorative pillows on a chair and pulls down the cover. "Why don't you get in here with me. I know we'll both feel much better after we've had some sleep."

I can read the signals. If I get into that bed with him, we're having sex. We haven't had sex since I was eight months pregnant. My body is ready to do what he says, but my brain is saying *No way.*

"I have to go." I check my bag to make sure I have everything. I pick up my coat. I won't be coming back here any time soon, if I can help it. At least, not when he's sitting on my bed looking like he does right now. I head for the door.

"Who is he?"

The absurdity and the shock of his question make me stop and turn to him.

"Who is he, Christina? Who are you going out to see?" He pushes to his feet, coming toward me. "Tell me who he is. Don't jerk me around like this. I *know* there's somebody else."

My immediate inclination is to defend myself and remind him that for as long as we've been together, there's been no one else but him. Regardless of the model lifestyle of my mother, I've never been one for sleeping around.

"What makes you think there's a man? That there's someone else?"

"Because I've been watching you."

"What do you mean, you've been watching me?"

"You told me that this is your first time in Istanbul."

I think of the airport and how many flights I have taken this past year.

He motions to the bag hanging from my shoulder. "Do you want to take out your passport? Let's count the number of Turkish entry stamps you've got."

I hike the bag higher on my shoulder. I have no intention of showing him anything.

"You came to Turkey twice in the past year...*before* this trip. But every time, you lied to me about where you were going, and who you were traveling with. Why?"

I'd told him I was getting away with old girlfriends. I wonder how Kyle found out.

"It's not too much of a fucking stretch to figure out that there's someone else."

I head for the door. "There's no other man, Kyle. And you and I are done."

PART VI

Come, come, whoever you are.
Wanderer, idolater, worshipper of fire.
Come, even though you have broken your vows a thousand times.
Come, and come yet again.
Ours is not a caravan of despair.
—Rumi

17

ZARI

THEN

YESTERDAY'S SNOW lay gray and dingy along the sidewalk edges. A cold drizzle had been falling sporadically all day. In the large courtyard in front of the medical building, the bare branches of a tree glistened with a coating of ice.

Zari had grown to dislike doctors. She hated hospitals. For years now, every visit, every hospitalization caused her to die a little inside for fear that she'd never be taking Tiam home again.

Those same clinical centers called her daughter a medical miracle. Children diagnosed with cystic fibrosis rarely survived more than a few years. And yet, here was this angel, fighting insurmountable odds. Still spirited, still working, and still living her life at age twenty.

On the way in, Tiam stopped and hugged her. She was obviously sensing her nervousness.

"She won't listen to my lungs. She won't send me for an MRI or chest x-rays. She won't say things that will upset you. This is a university laboratory. They're different from regular hospitals. Today's meeting is about the future."

Zari clung to Tiam's words as she fought the usual paralyzing feeling of helplessness. She entered the building, staying close beside her daughter. They might call it something else, but the facility was all glass and stone and tile. And it was as stark and sterile as every other hospital.

In the glassed-in reception area on the second floor, a young woman dressed in everyday clothes was waiting for them.

Introductions were made. Zari stared at the *Genetics Technology Laboratory* badge hanging from a blue lanyard around the woman's neck. And beneath her name, *Testing Counselor.*

The old anxiousness roared back.

"Please call me Hatice," their host offered.

Hatice meant trustworthy. It was a good name, and Zari believed that such things mattered. The meaning of a name was often a glimpse of the road a person chose to follow or the challenge Allah laid in their path. Her voice was amiable, her eyes direct and kind.

She led them to a conference room near the stairwell. The two younger women had spoken on the phone prior to the appointment. Tiam was an adult. As a university student studying biology, she had taken control of battling her illness. She now decided which doctors she wanted to see or not see. What tests she should have and not have. What courses of treatment she wanted to pursue. And Zari supported her daughter. She was with her every step of the way, in whatever way she was needed.

Inside the conference room, the heavy seminar table of dark wood was large enough for more than a dozen people. The three congregated at one end. Zari and Tiam sat on one side, and Hatice on the other.

A thick folder marked with her daughter's name had been placed on top of the table. Sheets were extracted. The counselor chatted casually with Tiam.

Hatice finally addressed both of them. It was time to get down to business. "You are aware that before we perform the physical extraction of a blood sample, we need to gather as much information about your family history as possible."

An icy ball formed in the pit of Zari's stomach. She wished she'd asked more questions about why they were here. About what this visit entailed, and what her part in it would involve.

A cover sheet was removed from the stack of papers. Lines of empty check boxes filled the page. The woman's pen tapped lightly on the table as she prepared to start.

Zari read the heading on the questionnaire. "Why are you doing a genetic test when you already know my daughter has CF?"

"That is a very good question, Mrs. Rahman. Diagnosis isn't the only outcome of this testing. The results will assist your doctor in determining appropriate treatments. Science has advanced a great deal since Tiam was first diagnosed."

Zari worked in a pharmacy. She was a clerk, but over the years she'd read and learned a great deal. Especially about cystic fibrosis. She knew drugs were changing and science was advancing.

"In the same way," Hatice continued, "if Tiam someday decides to have a family, it's critical that we know the genome of her disease. Identifying the mutation is key."

An unexpected spark of hope raced through Zari. To think...her daughter could plan for five years from now, ten years from now, and could even consider having her own family.

"A family," she murmured.

"Yes. Typically, women with CF have healthy pregnancies, and their babies are born just fine. Of course, the potential father should be screened to determine if he carries a mutated gene, as well."

Zari needed a moment to catch her breath. Nervous or calm, stressed or hopeful, her emotions were spilling over in every direction. Every year of Tiam's life was a gift to them both. And now this...a road that she never imagined they'd be traveling.

"Do either of you have any other questions about that?"

Tiam smiled at her mother. "Do you have any questions?"

Zari shook her head. "No. I understand perfectly."

"Excellent. Now, these questions are directed at both of you. But," Hatice continued, addressing Zari, "we expect that you have more direct knowledge of your family history than your daughter, as well as the family history of Tiam's father."

"Yes, well, because of...events...it may be difficult to provide answers to all of your questions."

"Of course. Answer what you can. Whatever you remember will help us develop a more complete profile."

She started down the list. Name, date of birth, doctor's name. Tiam answered. Zari saw no harm in having her daughter repeat the dates that were on her government papers.

"Patient ethnicity." Hatice listed a number of categories.

"Caucasian/White," Zari answered in a quiet voice.

"We are Kurds," Tiam corrected.

"That wasn't one of the options," she told her daughter.

"Please check *Other* and write *Kurdish*."

Tiam was raised by her, but born to another. Without knowing it, her sweet angel was extremely proud of an ethnicity that wasn't hers. Of a history that she had no share in. But Zari had never revealed the truth to her daughter. She'd never said anything about their early years. About how her Tiam became Christina and Christina became Tiam. Tears welled up in her eyes, but she blinked them back as she continued to listen.

Hatice's questions shifted to pregnancy.

"I'm not pregnant."

"Has anyone else in your family been diagnosed with cystic fibrosis?"

Both sets of eyes turned on Zari. She rubbed her sweaty palms on her knees, trying to quiet her foot from tapping the floor under the table. "Not that I know of."

"Has anyone in the patient's father's family been diagnosed with cystic fibrosis?"

"Not that I know of."

"I see no results for a sweat test on Tiam as an infant. Was it done?"

Zari nodded, then shook her head. She didn't know. Her heart lurched to think a wrong answer could jeopardize what her daughter hoped to gain by this test. "She wasn't born in a hospital."

But she was. Zari held this child in her arms for the first time when she was only a couple of hours old.

"Let's get a little more detailed information about the family." Hatice paged down to a new form. "I'd like to get a list of all relatives on both sides, living and deceased, within a generation or two. And all their medical conditions and the cause of death, if possible. Shall we start?"

Zari stared at the form, but she couldn't see. Memories from the past were fighting their way through.

Twenty years ago, misery found new meaning when she arrived in Ankara with her newborn baby. There was no sign of her husband. The address she had—an apartment complex where he also worked—was a dead end. The manager of the building knew him, but said Yahya had disappeared. The man had no idea where he'd gone. Another Kurdish immigrant had already taken the job and moved his own family in.

The new people offered Zari and her baby a bed to sleep on in their crowded quarters for a few days. It was during that time that she found employment working for Elizabeth Hall.

Her new employer was pregnant, but she didn't show it during those early days. She lived in the complex and worked at the US Embassy. She offered Zari room and board and wages in exchange for doing all household chores and taking care of her child after she gave birth. Zari felt blessed, under the circumstances. Allah's will at work.

She never went with Elizabeth to the doctor's appointments. She didn't know what kind of medical issues the other woman had. Or her family. She had no idea who the father of the child was. She'd never seen Elizabeth with a man. She'd never even heard a name mentioned.

"Let's do the father's side first. His name?"

Hatice's question tore Zari's mind away from the past and forced her to pay attention to what was happening in this room.

"His name?" the counselor asked again.

The words wouldn't make their way past Zari's lips.

Tiam answered for her. "Yahya Rahman."

"Living or diseased?"

Zari couldn't do this. Her heart was too heavy. She couldn't lie. Yahya. Tiam. Neither of them knew what she'd kept hidden in her heart.

It had been two years since Emine told her that Yahya was alive. But Zari had continued on as if nothing had changed. She still looked for him everywhere she went. And there were glimpses. The driver of a car that parked for the long periods of time at the end of the street. The shadow pausing outside the window of the pharmacy where she worked. Each time, her emotions got the better of her. But she couldn't approach him, and she was thankful that he didn't either.

Tiam's cold fingers reached for Zari's under the table. "Missing. He's been missing for my entire life. We were refugees. My parents came to Turkey separately. They haven't seen each other in all this time."

Zari looked down and tears dropped from her chin onto their joined hands.

"His age?"

Forty-three. And he was out there on the streets of Istanbul. Watching over them, putting money in her account, buying a car for his daughter. Or rather, this angel that he thought was his daughter.

"How old would he be now?" Tiam asked quietly.

The lump in her throat kept getting bigger and bigger. She couldn't talk. She couldn't breathe.

"How about if I go get us some tea? My schedule is open for the entire afternoon."

Hatice's chair scraped the floor. Her footsteps were light. She left the folder on the table. The door closed behind her.

Tiam touched Zari's cheek. "I'm sorry, Maman. I shouldn't have brought you here. These questions bring back painful memories."

She used a tissue and wiped the tears off her mother's face.

"I know what you've done for me. How hard you've worked. How you've been both mother and father, sister and friend. You are my entire family. I know how faithfully you've supported me for my whole life. Through all these years of dealing with my sickness, you've been the bright light, the hope, the love that keeps me going."

Zari looked into her daughter's face. Her angel. Her gift from God. For the sake of her health, for the blessing of Allah, this child deserved to know the truth.

"I love you, Maman. We don't have to stay. Let's go. I can explain it to Hatice."

Zari shook her head and wrapped Tiam's hands in her own. "No, my love. We're staying."

"I won't put you through this. I saw how you fell apart, and she's barely even started with the questions."

Zari turned in her chair until she was facing Tiam. "I want you to have this genetic test. That's why we're here. Nothing makes me happier than to think of *your* future. But as far as these answers she's looking for..." She shook her head. "If I were to tell her that my mother had high blood pressure, or my father died of a stroke when he was in his thirties, it wouldn't mean anything. None of what I say will help them understand more about you."

"But Maman, the way the science of it works—"

"The way the science of it works is that there's a truth about me... about us...that you don't know."

Zari pressed a kiss on each of her daughter's cheeks. She had to make sure there would be no doubt of how she felt. A mother's love required no umbilical cord. The love she had for this child transcended genetics and anything else they could test in this building.

She couldn't love Tiam less, cherish her less. She could feel no greater pride for her.

"You are not Tiam." Zari held her gaze. "I didn't bring you into this world. You were born to another woman. Your name is Christina."

18

TIAM

THEN

NEVER IN MY entire life had I imagined that Zari Rahman might not be my mother. She took care of me. Loved me. Supported me. Encouraged me. She still does. She was the shoulder I cried on, the hand I reached for, the example I followed.

As a single mother, a refugee, a Kurdish woman, she has struggled to make a life in a country that for years discriminated against even the language that she spoke. In the face of the hostility of a world that has persistently stood against her, she wrapped me in her protective arms. And I found my true home in her embrace.

But, sitting in a conference room, Zari told me the truth and rocked my world. I've lived for twenty years as one person, but really I was another. The waves of shock and disbelief swept through me when she explained the horrifying circumstances when two toddlers had been swapped.

The first reaction that rushed through me was fear of losing Zari. My heart ached to think she would not be part of my life from that day on. She's everything to me, as I know I'm everything to her. But the worry dissipated like the morning fog on the Bosphorus. I'm twenty years old. No one can tell me where to go, what to do, whom to love. Zari is my mother.

Following that first day came resentment. But it is not directed at Zari. How can I understand a mother who leaves her child behind?

I can't help but think of the things that Elizabeth Hall deprived me off. Turks speak of America as the place of golden dreams. The land of infinite opportunity. The nation where the clever and the hardworking amass fortunes in an instant. America, the land of abundant riches.

Would I have spent less time in hospitals if I grew up there? I've been sick every day of my life. I was sick when Elizabeth took Zari's healthy child and left me behind. The United States is at the forefront of every medical innovation. Would I have new lungs by now to replace the failing ones inside of me?

I was denied a life there. A different life from the one I know. Still, if this were an alternate universe where I had the option of going with Elizabeth or staying with Zari, the choice would not be difficult.

I would stay with my true and loving mother. I would never choose another.

Weeks went by before my turbulent feelings subsided. Now, curiosity has become the driving force in my existence. I'm on the Internet all the time. I search the web, combing through it, looking for Elizabeth Hall. She's not difficult to find. And when I do locate her, I set up web tracking. Now, whenever her name shows up in any context, I know. She lives in California where the sun always shines, where the sky and the sea are blue.

I pore over her pictures of a gallery opening in Los Angeles one day. She's posing with a group of women. They're holding a check that is being donated to some charity. In another, she and three other people wearing tennis outfits hold a gold cup. Everyone is fit and healthy. They all dress well.

Her life is so foreign to me. I go to school and work, while Zari is at the pharmacy six days a week. We live paycheck to paycheck. Elizabeth is an executive for a big electronic company. On my screen, the plush world in which she lives is full of smiles and parties. I get no glimpse of the real woman who gave birth to me.

I study the images, searching for other ways to connect with her. The color of our eyes, the shape of our face, the angle of our cheekbones, the quirk in our smile where the right side lifts a little higher than the left. Do we have anything more in common? Am I at all connected to her?

I shouldn't care. But I do.

I don't want anything from her. I can't bring myself to contact her directly, but I still wish she could know that I'm here. That I have survived, despite rejection. Despite *her*.

It's during these endless hours of searching that something quite unexpected happens. Christina ends up accepting a friend request I send her.

She is me and I am her.

I follow every moment, every image, of the life that she shares with her friends. And she has no idea who I am.

19

CHRISTINA

NOW

A DAUGHTER'S relationship with her mother can be a lifeline, a buoy that keeps her afloat as she weathers the storms of life. Or it can sink her like a stone. For all these years, I've been trying to decide which kind of relationship I have with Elizabeth.

I've heard so many stories about my childhood. About how badly I treated my mother. The tales came from Elizabeth herself.

I tested her, pushed her, misbehaved. I acted out. From the very beginning, she says, I was a very difficult child.

When she tried to hug me, I became the classic stiff-armed baby, keeping her away. The next day, however, if she was busy or less inclined to offer affection, I attached myself like Velcro to her. I was clingy and afraid of being separated from her, inconsolable if I was left alone. My belief was that if she left me, she'd never come back.

As I got a bit older, I grew more defiant. If she made cupcakes, I wanted cookies. If she made pancakes, I wanted cereal. If we went out for steak dinner, I'd suddenly give up eating meat. When she bought me gifts for a birthday or Christmas, I wanted them returned.

No one is around to tell my side, if there is a *my side*. Elizabeth controls the narrative of those early years, and she says that I was difficult.

There's an incident I remember clearly. It happened when I was eleven years old. I overheard my mother talking to a friend.

"I'm sure I'd be devastated if something tragic happened to Christina. But I'd recover."

I was stunned. Her words decimated me. To this day, I don't know the rest of that conversation. *If something tragic happened...I'd recover.*

I was not essential in her life.

I was expendable.

She didn't want me.

One would think that the mother-daughter relationship would be the very definition of unconditional love. But Elizabeth and I seem to lack the gene. There is a disconnect that has always existed between us. As I grew into adulthood, the childhood stories and Elizabeth's constant reminders loaded me with feelings of self-blame and even shame. The difficult child has become a difficult adult. Every argument stabs and tries to draw blood.

The truth behind our toxic relationship eventually came out, though, when I became pregnant.

Before even telling Kyle about the pregnancy, I knew what his reaction would be. He didn't want a baby, but once I was over thirty, that was all I could think about. He'd be polite, respecting my decision to keep the baby, but I couldn't count on our relationship to survive.

While I was making plans on raising a baby without a father, I found myself consumed with learning what I could about my own father. My *real* father, not any of the men whom Elizabeth had relationships with while I was growing up.

Everything I read told me that my confidence, my feelings of self-worth, and my relationships with others were tied to knowing about him.

More times than I can count, I'd asked her about him. It was important for me to know who he was. Where he came from and where he went. I wondered why he rejected me, if he did, or if he was aware that I even existed.

When I was a child, Elizabeth told me I had no father...end of conversation. When I was twenty-something, she finally told me that she'd had some casual relationships with different men when she worked in Ankara. She became pregnant and decided to keep me. That discussion ended with no name. For a long time, I wondered if she even knew who my father was.

There was a lot wrong with me, and it all pointed back to that slippery slope of identity. I was an outsider, uncomfortable in my own skin. My insecurities carried over into my relationships with my mother, with my boyfriend, with the handful of people I considered friends. Regardless of all my flaws, I believed my child would be a blank slate. I could give her or him the confidence that I lacked myself. I could show the child the love that my mother held back and made conditional. I told myself I would be a better parent than Elizabeth was.

Like mother, like daughter. I was so consumed by what *I* was searching for that Kyle was left out of the decision-making process.

Genetic testing was something my gynecologist recommended when I was ten weeks pregnant.

"Some tests can check babies for medical conditions while they are in the womb. Others check their DNA for some genetic diseases."

I started the testing with my doctor, but I didn't stop there. One blood test led to another. Forty dollars to learn a little. A hundred dollars to swab your cheek and find out more. A search for medical conditions turned into an extensive hunt to know who I was and where I came from.

I'll never forget the warm day at the end of March this year. I was sitting at our kitchen table with my laptop open. A new email had arrived with the results of my family ancestry search. Everything else prior to that, folder after folder of medical records, hadn't brought me any closer to the answers I was searching for. That one page, blessed by the Mormons, the same test that millions of other people take, changed everything.

I stared at the paper. My entire family tree was jammed into one oval section on the map. The area included parts of Turkey, Iraq, Iran, Syria—where the four countries came together. Kurdistan.

There was no indication of any connection with Elizabeth's northern European roots. None.

The world I knew exploded in my face. Everything I thought. Everything I believed. It was all gone.

For all the years of not knowing who my father was, still there was a bond that tied me to Elizabeth. But that connection was now wiped out. My relationship with my mother, taut and frayed as it was, was severed with a suddenness that stunned me.

The mirror shattered and fell away, and I was looking into an empty void. I went searching for one parent and lost the other. I was now adrift and in danger of going under.

I clutched at that oval encompassing Kurdistan but repeated the test. It took long painful days and nights to confirm the results. And then, I realized my discovery was simply evidence of something I'd felt instinctively for my entire life.

I wasn't Elizabeth's child.

My research showed that all children who are separated from their mothers suffer trauma that will affect their bond with a new parent. This described us exactly: my difficulty living up to her expectations and her difficulty accepting me for who I am.

But if I wasn't hers, how did she get me?

I wasn't adopted. I had a birth certificate. A passport. A form that said I was born in a hospital in Ankara. The mother's name was recorded as Elizabeth Hall. The father's name was left blank.

If my discovery shed some light on our relationship, so much more of the truth remained hidden in the darkness. Asking Elizabeth wasn't an option. She was never forthcoming with information. The past didn't matter.

The truth, *my* truth, was a puzzle, and I had to find the missing pieces.

Kyle was in Japan on business. I went to Jax.

"I need a couple of weeks off."

He didn't argue, didn't ask me what I was going to do or where I was going. "Take as much time as you want. But come up with a good story so Elizabeth stays off your back."

We had all been working hard, starting the process of getting the company ready to sell. I fabricated a lie to my mother about some reunion in Greece of college friends, and I left.

Ankara is a huge, sprawling city of red tile roofs and high-rise buildings, teetering on the edge of Turkey's great central plateau. As the plane flew over the city, I spotted a huge gray fortress sitting on a peak in the center of it all, looming protectively over the urban jumble below. It was a sign. That first view of Ankara Kalesi, a symbol of power and continuity, became a source of strength for me.

And once I was in the city, other signs spoke to me. The crispness of the air, a particular slant of light across the pavement, the sounds and smells.

Something rose inside of me. A feeling surged and flowed through my veins and arteries more powerfully than anything I'd ever experienced growing up in Southern California. And in an instant I realized what it was. For the first time in my life, I felt I was where I belonged. I was coming home.

The feeling was short-lived. The hospital where I was born had long since been replaced by a soaring building of blue and white, glass and chrome.

Who I'd once been, the very place of my birth, had disappeared. It was the perfect metaphor for my life. Reality had been replaced by façade. Truth was replaced by pretense. In a subterranean office, an archival crypt where they kept the old records, they'd buried me.

I had my passport and my birth certificate. I could prove my identity. Soon after, I started looking into my medical files.

They were all here. A birth record under my name. Hospital follow-ups. Months of visits and repeated periods of hospitalization. I was a very sick child. The first year of my life I spent more days inside the walls of the hospital than outside. Records of tests and more tests were jammed into the folders.

In the midst of the reports, I found a long summary in English of a diagnosis for my condition. Cystic fibrosis.

The words leaped out at me. Cystic fibrosis. The prognosis was terminal. Respiratory and digestive failure imminent. *Patient survival unlikely...*

Cystic fibrosis. Debilitating and deadly. And I had it.

Except I don't have it. I've *never* had it. The tests my gynecologist ran made no mention of it.

But Elizabeth's baby had it.

Those were the first tears that I'd shed since arriving in Ankara. Not for myself. I cried for the child who never lived. The baby who died of cystic fibrosis. I even shed tears for my mother, thinking how tragic it must have been to be told this news. I still didn't know who I was. Or how Elizabeth ended up with me. But there was an innocent baby who never lived, who never had the life that I'd been given.

A day later, maybe it was two days later, I was still in a fog. I mourned like I'd never mourned before. There was a small park across from the hotel. The breeze was chilly, but I hardly noticed it. The lights of the city had come on, and I settled on a stone bench. I was feeling the jagged edges of grief scraping my mind raw.

I'd come here to find myself. But instead, I lost another part of me. I lost a person I was somehow connected to, but never knew.

I should have called Elizabeth then. She had lost a child and found me. Raised me. But my mind flickered back to those words I overheard so many years ago. *I'd be devastated. But I'd recover.* Of course, Elizabeth would recover. She'd recovered when it mattered. When she lost her own baby.

Once again, I was an outsider. An outcast. And even more than before, I didn't know who I was. I only knew who I was not.

Sitting in the park, with the spring night swirling around me, I felt a numbness creeping in. Apathy spreading through my bones like the winter cold. But there was a baby growing inside of me. For her or his sake, I had to shake the dark mood. To escape, I turned on my phone and went on social media. I looked to see if I had any friends in Ankara.

None.

Any friends in Turkey?

One. Apparently, we'd been friends for eleven years. Her page had no posts, and I didn't know anything about her. I messaged her.

How do I know you?

Her answer came back immediately. *I am you. And you are me.*

I hopped on the next flight to Istanbul.

THE FIRST TIME we saw each other was after I left Ankara. I met with Tiam at a little café in Eyüp, a neighborhood in Istanbul. The sun was warm coming through the large windows, and our tea sat untouched. I longed to hear about her. She wanted to hear about me. We each wanted to know what the other knew about our childhood.

For thirty years I slept in the real Christina's bed. I wore her shoes. I lived her life. I called her mother my mother. All during the flight from Ankara, I feared that when we met, there would be drama and open resentment.

I realized immediately that I was wrong. There was not even a hint of tension between us. Coming together felt more like a reunion. We weren't two strangers. It was as if we were sisters. As if we'd known each other for our entire lives.

After hearing Tiam's story, I had to fight the inclination to call Elizabeth in California and shred her, scorch her with a hundred horrible but fitting words. I wanted desperately to tell her that the sick child she'd abandoned in Turkey so many years ago was sitting right in front of me. I wanted to curse her for taking me from my real mother without her consent.

Tiam wouldn't let me.

She amazed me from those first moments. Bright and beautiful and self-aware. She didn't want anything from me or from her birth mother. Her only wish was that perhaps someday an opportunity would present itself when she could face Elizabeth.

Of course, I wasn't going to leave Istanbul without meeting my true mother. Tiam and I took a tram to their apartment in a Kurdish enclave on the other side of the sparkling waters of the Golden Horn. She called Zari but said nothing about me, except that she was bringing home a new friend for dinner.

20

ZARI

THEN

In Kurdistan, a person can knock at anyone's door, and they will be greeted with warm hospitality. It was part of Zari's faith as well as her culture to welcome guests. The belief that Allah was All-Generous was woven into the fabric of who she was. She'd raised her daughter to be the same. And more days than not, Tiam would call to say that friends would be accompanying her back to their apartment for dinner, or to stay the night.

Tiam was generous and pure of heart. People recognized her quality and were drawn to it. And Zari loved her all the more for it.

To prepare a meal for two or twenty made no difference to Zari. Their grocer was down the street. Their butcher kept late hours. She'd gained so much experience feeding large numbers of people over the years that Emine teased that she should open a restaurant.

Tiam's call this afternoon was brief. "I'm bringing a new friend to dinner, Maman."

She didn't mention a name, nor did she say anything about who this new friend was. Generally, she would offer something like, *We take classes together,* or *She's the cousin of so and so,* or *We met when I was waiting for my appointment at the doctor.* At the very least, she would mention a name.

As she started the rice, Zari sighed. She was terrible with remembering the friends' names. She constantly mixed them up. Azra would be called Zehra, and Zehra became Nisa. Oh well, at least they were properly fed.

Tonight, for some reason, Zari's heart was beating faster. She felt hot and flushed. There was a jitteriness in her stomach that she couldn't explain. Tiam had been doing well with her recent change of treatment. It had been four months since she had last been hospitalized. The feeling Zari had now was different from the anxiety that plagued her whenever Tiam's health took a downturn.

Trying to ignore it, she made enough food to feed a dozen. Some of Tiam's friends were vegetarian now, so Zari always had some meatless dishes, just in case. At the last minute, she ran to the bakery and bought some fresh bread and baklava.

As she put the purchases on the counter, she realized the restlessness wasn't going away. She couldn't understand what was happening to her. Maybe it was menopause. She was fifty-two. Her doctor told her she'd be showing the signs soon. Going into the bathroom, she stared at her flushed face in the mirror.

She was getting older. The years had etched their marks around her lips and on her forehead. But her eyes were the same, and they grew misty now as memories of years past came back to her.

Back in Qalat Dizah, many nights Yahya would call before coming home for dinner. She would never forget the flip in her heart as she waited for him by the door and saw him coming down the lane. She flattened her palm against her stomach.

There had been no warning when he appeared in the crowd the day Tiam graduated from pharmacy school. The class assembled in the quad, all of them dressed in their black caps, gowns, and white sashes. Zari had been filled with such pride, and she cried as she held on to Emine and watched the child she raised stride across the stage to receive her diploma. She didn't know what made her turn her head, but as Tiam descended the steps, Zari saw him. For a moment, their eyes met. Yahya. How it must hurt him to look on them. Always from a distance. Always from the edges of their lives.

And then he walked away.

Gazing into the mirror now, Zari brushed away the falling tears.

She loved him. No matter who he was, or what he'd become, or what life he led. There had never been another man except for him. He would always be her husband. Her love. She'd given him her heart and had never taken it back.

Why was it that even as she aged, the tide of her emotions ebbed and flowed as if he was her moon, her sun, her universe?

She couldn't have her daughter arrive at the house and see her like this. Taking a deep breath, Zari splashed cold water on her face and dried her eyes.

Going back into the kitchen, she texted Tiam.

Where are you, angel

Almost home

Tiam had her own key. Zari walked to the window overlooking the street. Her heart continued to feel unsettled, her body restless. Spring was late this year. It was too cold to open the window. Scanning the passersby from her fourth-floor vantage point, she saw her daughter and the woman she was bringing home. She could only see the tops of their heads. Her friend wore no hijab, and she was carrying a large bouquet of flowers in her arms.

Yahya brought her flowers every Friday after Jummah.

Zari raced to the kitchen and drank a tall glass of cold water to calm herself. Going back to the door of the apartment, she opened it and heard their footsteps on the stairs. The two were coming up, whispering in English.

As they drew closer, Zari's heart pounded harder and faster. The friend's lilting tone and her soft laugh dug into her memories.

She heard her own voice in the timbre and pitch of the words. The happy laughter of a toddler sitting on her lap. The soft skin of an infant's round face pressed against her shoulder and neck, small fingers clutching her hair.

My maman.

Could it be? Her throat burned from the force of the tears struggling to break free. She was afraid she might collapse before they ever came through the door. Dreams belonged in her mind. She was imagining things.

Zari backed into the sitting room and held onto the nearest chair.

"We leave our shoes outside," Tiam told her, speaking in English. They were on the landing.

"Here, give me your coat."

"*Teşekkür.*" Thank you.

"You can speak English with her. She's very good."

"*Teşekkür*," she said again. There was an emotional catch in her voice.

Tiam came in first and saw Zari. Her smile was wide, her eyes bright. "Maman, I want you to meet...Why are you crying, Maman?"

Zari's gaze was fixed on the young woman who stood behind her daughter.

"Hello, Mrs. Rahman. Thank you for having me in your home for dinner."

Zari looked past the bouquet of flowers being held out to her. She stared at the cleft in her chin, the high cheekbones, the curly hair, the lovely hazel eyes that immediately reminded her of Yahya.

"Maman, please meet my friend Christina."

It was possible. It was happening. She was here.

Zari shook her head fervently. Her prayers had been answered. "No. No. Come here, my daughter. You've come back to me."

PART VII

...In and out, above, about, below,
'Tis nothing but a magic shadow-show,
Played in a box whose candle is the Sun,
Round which we phantom figures come and go.
— Omar Khayyam

21

CHRISTINA

As I sit in the hotel's business center, I wonder if Kyle is sleeping. He has a gift for compartmentalizing his life that I envy. Relationship, work, and daily routines don't interfere with each other. And when he needs sleep, he gets sleep.

He's not completely wrong. It's true that I already came to Istanbul twice this year—in April and again in June. But my trips weren't for a rendezvous with some boyfriend. Each time, I came to see my family. My *real* family.

After that first trip to Ankara and Istanbul, I went to talk to Jax. He was more than my boss. He was married to Elizabeth, but he was also my close friend and mentor. I grew up without a father figure in my life, and he was the closest thing to it for me. I needed someone to confide in. He was the only one I could truly trust.

It's still hard to fathom that he's really gone. I can picture him now, sitting in his cluttered office like Jabba the Hutt, his glasses perched precariously on the end of his nose, surrounded by a forest of computers and monitors and gaming apparatus. Over the past couple of months, I finally found the answer to why I'd felt like a square peg in a round hole for my entire life. For years, I'd lived as one person, but actually I was another. Jax knew I hadn't been my usual self lately, but he'd chalked it up to the pregnancy. With his pale blue eyes fixed intently on me, he listened quietly as I told him everything.

After my April trip, after being reunited with my birth mother, I was overwhelmed by such a chaotic tangle of love and guilt and wonder. It was unforgettable, that moment in Istanbul. We stood—Zari and Tiam and I—holding onto each other in an embrace that could not be broken for a very long time. That embrace has not been broken since.

After learning the truth about my history, it took me days to subdue the rage coursing through me for everything these two women had been forced to endure. But if Tiam was tolerant of what Elizabeth had done to them, Zari didn't want to talk of Elizabeth and was only interested in me. My real mother gathered me over and over again in her arms. She was so filled with love and joy. Love was—and is—a powerful force in her, and as I stood there with her arms around me, I felt its tender shoots spreading through me, all the way to my heart.

When I left Istanbul, I consented to Tiam's wishes. She wanted to be the one to reveal the truth to Elizabeth when the time was right.

Jax could have arranged the meetings for the sale of Externus anywhere, but he chose Istanbul. I wasn't supposed to be here, but I wondered if he was trying to help Tiam meet Elizabeth.

He's gone, but this trip is sure to provide that moment of reckoning. Elizabeth is with me. I'm still waiting for Tiam to initiate contact with her. I've seen her at the airport, at the hotel, at the tram station. Each time, I think *this* is the time when she'll approach and speak to Elizabeth. But every time, she disappears.

I called Tiam last night when I arrived at the airport. The voice mail I left her was a little rattled. Now, with the sun edging over the buildings to the east, I wait for her response. I don't have the name of the driver yet, but I want to know if she has any idea who it might have been, and why he was asking about her.

I think of Kyle upstairs. I didn't leave him on a positive note.

I don't fault him for thinking I'm having an affair, even though there's never been anyone for him to be suspicious of. I don't have any male friends now that Jax is gone. Still, I could have been more forthcoming about these trips. My lack of honesty with him stems from the way Elizabeth treats him and talks about him. For more times than I like to remember, she's bluntly told me how she wishes she could be in my shoes, and she isn't only talking about my age or my career. She's talking about my relationship with Kyle.

Tiam's text finally arrives. We'll meet in an hour by the stone benches that line the walkways on the east side of the Suleymaniye Mosque. I pack up and leave through the lobby. The day promises to be cool and clear, but it's too far to walk. The morning commute has begun in the city, however, and I don't want to take a cab. The last thing I want is a driver like last night.

One of the hotel doormen suggests an alternative.

"You can board the tram by Hagia Sophia, Miss Hall. Ride it to Eminönü. From there, the walk is uphill but manageable. Ten minutes, at most. The Suleymaniye Mosque is a very large place. You cannot miss seeing it when you leave the tram."

I definitely won't miss it. I don't tell him, but I've been there before. The second time I came to Istanbul, Tiam took a couple of days off from work, and we saw a great deal of the city. The beautiful Ottoman-era mosque was one of the first places we visited.

The tram runs every ten to fifteen minutes, but I don't have to wait long before it arrives. Standing amid a crush of commuters and tourists, I hold onto a chrome pole and think of ways to convince Tiam not to put off her meeting with Elizabeth for much longer. I don't want her to miss this chance. But at the same time, I feel for her. I can understand her hesitation. She wishes that her disease hasn't made her so terribly fragile and weak. Her argument with me when we spoke on the phone before I got here was that she wants to face her birth mother as a strong woman. She wants to stand in front of her and say, *You were wrong to give up on me. Look at me. I'm thriving in spite of you.*

This past spring, Zari knew instantly that I was her daughter. For the past three days, I've been pointing out Tiam to Elizabeth at every opportunity. I've shown her pictures, hoping a similar recognition would dawn on her. There are plenty of similarities between them.

Knowing what I know, I see the resemblances every time I look at them. Shouldn't a mother recognize her own daughter?

As we approach my stop, I join the crowd around the tram exit and step off when the doors open. I climb the hill, following the winding streets, and make it in less than ten minutes. I know where I'm going, and I'm anxious to get there.

Meeting here versus some coffee shop near my hotel was my suggestion. I love this place. The first time Tiam and I came to the mosque, I had waited near the fountain by the ornate tomb of Suleyman the Magnificent while she went inside for the Friday Jummah prayer. The magnolias were in bloom, and their sweet fragrance filled the air. I was filled with a sense of peace that I hadn't felt for a long time.

After the prayer service was over, Tiam collected me and we climbed a narrow stone stairway to a wide gallery overlooking the bright, airy expanse of prayer space. Above us, the golden dome of the Suleymaniye soared heavenward. We sat on the thick red carpet, surrounded by brilliance and simple splendor, and talked for hours.

As I hurry along now, warm from the climb, I turn my face to the light breeze. Broad granite walkways enclose the green lawns around the mosque. I pass by buildings that house schools, a hospital, a library, and a soup kitchen. They're all part of the mosque complex. From its earliest days, Suleymaniye was not only a place of worship. It also served as a charitable institution, a center that fed thousands of the city's poor every day—Muslims, Christians, and Jews alike. The history of the place helps explain the aura of warmth and welcome that surrounds it.

It's still early in the morning, but the grassy area is already crowded with tourists and pilgrims. By the wall facing the shimmering waters of the nearby Golden Horn and the Bosphorus, I spot Tiam. The mask I've noticed she's been wearing the past few days hangs limp around her neck. She's struggling to walk and has to pause every few steps to catch her breath.

She sees me too, and the way her face lights up touches me. Raw emotions I've been keeping a tight lid on break free. Tears are rolling down my face by the time we are in each other's arms.

"I've missed you."

Her voice is thick with feeling. "The baby. My God, Christina. I'm so sorry."

I called her from the hospital after Autumn was born. We spent hours on FaceTime and laughed at how my daughter would open her eyes and stare at the screen whenever Tiam whispered her name. I sent more than a dozen pictures for Zari to see, and called her that night when Tiam was home. Our mother became emotional and cried happily while I spoke to her. I promised to call back again when we were released from the hospital.

My next call, only a few days later, shared the devastating news. After Zari heard about her granddaughter's death, Tiam told me she knelt sobbing on the floor, her face raised to the sky and her fist striking her chest. The last time I had called Tiam from the US, she said Zari is still grieving our loss.

Tiam's face and mine are pressed together, and I feel our tears mingling. Neither of us is in any hurry to let go of the other.

"I wanted to do this in the terminal and every time I've seen you." My voice cracks. "I want you in my arms and in my life."

"I actually planned on walking up to you at the airport and hugging you and letting Elizabeth figure things out on her own. That was why I showed up when you arrived." She pulls away and takes my hand, leading me to a stone bench. "But this week has been very hard."

Tiam looks paler, thinner than when I saw her in June. She's also wheezing. I can hear the congestion with every breath she takes.

"What's wrong? You're having more trouble."

"Change of seasons. Allergies. Anything can set me off."

As we sit, a ferry at the pier far below us sounds its horn. I glance over the wall at the blue-gray domes that form a cascade down the hill, toward the waters that have provided Istanbul with its lifeblood for two millennia. Across the Golden Horn, buildings cover the hills to the east, and they sparkle now in the morning light.

I worry about her. It pains me to think of how she suffers with this terrible disease. She told me that she is on a list for a lung transplant, but the list is long. Perhaps too long. Still, she has great spirit, my Tiam. She is a true fighter.

"Tell me about the driver last night," she says. "You sounded upset on the message you left."

I describe him as well as I can. Today, the incident doesn't seem as scary as last night.

"There may be a million men in Istanbul who fit that description." She shakes her head. "But I know so many people through my job and through the hospital where I get treatment. Also, there are the two volunteer groups I'm involved with now, trying to help Syrian refugee children in Istanbul."

I am you. And you are me. That's true, but Tiam is also the far better me. I know of the educational projects she's involved with. I've donated online to the nonprofits. But money isn't enough.

"The only thing I can think of is that some of the men involved with the program, and the relatives of those children, become very possessive of the teachers. They think because we're women we need protection."

The explanation makes sense. I wasn't harmed. He did drop me off at the airport.

"What did you say when he asked how you knew me?"

"I told him you and I were social media friends and that we were hoping to connect when I came to Istanbul." I couldn't say any of this to Kyle last night.

"He must have seen us together, or he wouldn't have asked the question."

"I almost spoke to you at the restaurant yesterday, but then there was Elizabeth's commotion."

Tiam looks around her, and I suspect she's searching to see if someone is watching us now.

The morning sun reflects brightly off the high granite walls of the mosque, and it draws my eye.

"Suleyman ordered that his imperial mosque should be built on the highest hill in the city," Tiam says. "He wanted to show that he was greater than the Roman emperor who built Hagia Sophia."

"I think he succeeded."

We're both aware of the people walking past us. To any casual onlooker, we're just two friends sitting together. But there are no eyes on us that I can tell.

The downside of what happened last night—leaving the hotel in a strange car in a city that is still new to me—is the residual fear.

"Oh, I have something for you." Tiam searches in her bag and produces a piece of paper. "Remember our conversation in June? We talked about Elizabeth's friends in Ankara around the time I was born."

I finally know who I am. I know that my mother and father are Zari and Yahya Rahman. But Tiam—the real Christina—knows only half of her history. I've told her that Elizabeth will not be any help in identifying the father, but we decided that perhaps there is another way of finding out the truth.

"Did Zari think of anyone?"

"Yes, she remembers a woman named Patricia Nicholls. She was a good friend of Elizabeth around the time I was born. They were in each other's lives. Always together. She lived in the same apartment complex and worked at the American Embassy."

Patricia Nicholls. That name hasn't come up in any of the information I got through Jax's emails. But I haven't read everything in those folders, either. If she was close to Elizabeth, I can't help but wonder whether she was involved in the same criminal activities. I haven't shared with Tiam anything that I've learned. I decided it's best to keep all of that to myself for now. I'm afraid if she knows to what extent Elizabeth was involved with the attacks on the Kurdish people, she won't want to meet her birth mother.

"The woman is now retired and living as an expat in Istanbul. She even has a vacation house in Bodrum on the Aegean coast."

I glance out at the city's rooftops down the hill. "It's curious that we're here in Istanbul and Elizabeth has made no mention of her. You'd think she'd want to pay her old friend a visit."

"Perhaps they haven't been in contact in the years that you've lived in California."

I look at the name, phone number, and address on the paper. "I've never heard of her."

"Maybe she knows the man Elizabeth was with when she became pregnant with me."

I understand Tiam's need for answers. I've been there. I flew halfway across the world to find out who I was.

This is one thing I can do for her. She can't call Patricia Nicholls, but I can. Or at least, I can open the door.

"I'll let you know if something turns up on this." I add the information to my contacts. "But just as important, when are you going to talk to Elizabeth? Please don't let this chance get away from you."

"I'll do it. Soon."

"She's only here another week."

Tiam takes an inhaler out of her bag and administers a dose. Her cheeks are flushed.

"Why don't you join us for dinner tonight?" I suggest. "Come as my guest, as my friend. We don't have to explain anything. I'll make sure Elizabeth is there. I should have thought of this before. You don't have to say anything to her if you don't want to. No big scene, but at least you'll get to talk to her. What do you think?"

"I have to go to work this morning, and this afternoon I have a treatment at the clinic. I can see how I feel afterwards."

I'm relieved that she's considering it. This game of cat and mouse is painful to watch. I want Elizabeth to know, to realize her real daughter is alive. I believe Tiam needs to let go of the weight she's been dragging around too, and say what's on her mind.

"Can I come with you for your treatment?"

"To the clinic?" She looks surprised.

"I'd like to. Unless Zari is already going to be there."

"I don't let her. Not for the treatments. She gets too nervous. Seeing her stressed upsets me." Tiam stands up. "By the way, just as you asked, I haven't told her you're in Istanbul."

"Thank you." My plan is to go see her after the Externus sale is finalized. After Elizabeth is gone. Next week, Tiam will take me back to the house to surprise her.

Tiam texts me the address for the clinic. "I'm warning you. One errant tear, one sad look, one mention of the words *I'm sorry,* and out you go. You're only allowed to come with me for my treatment if you smile."

"I'll smile." I place a kiss on each of her cheeks and hug her.

She starts along the walk with a wave. I watch her pass by a grouping of magnolias. I hadn't noticed them when I came in, but they're now crowned with golden yellow leaves. In a month, those branches will be covered with the fuzz-covered buds of next year's flowers.

Tiam disappears through an archway by the mosque, and I brush away my tears. Today, she's paler, weaker, struggling more than she did even yesterday. But I'm here. Whatever it takes, whatever she needs, regardless of the cost, I'm here to make sure she gets it. And I won't let her give up the fight.

I don't want to lose her.

22

ELIZABETH

ELIZABETH GLANCED around the early lunch crowd. More than half of the tables on the patio of the hotel's courtyard restaurant were occupied, mostly by women. Thirty years ago, large expat communities made up of Brits and French people and Italians and Iranians made Turkey their home. It was cheap, comfortable, and civilized. From the languages she could hear being spoken around her, she guessed the same mix of people were still around.

She motioned to the waiter to bring more tea. Kyle was supposed to arrive in the middle of the night. Still, it irked her that it was already eleven thirty, and she had yet to see them down here. Christina should have let her know about the schedule of the meetings, but she hadn't shared anything yet. She was too distracted by digging into ancient history.

Elizabeth wanted the sale of Externus to go smoothly. The three of them were supposed to meet this afternoon with one of the interested companies here in the hotel. What room, what time, and what she needed to bring or say were all a mystery, however.

She was savvy with money and financing. Put a balance sheet or an accounting ledger in front of her, and she could make the dollar signs light up. But Externus was a gaming company, and she knew no more about the intricacies of gaming than she did about brain surgery. She took care of the finances of Externus, and Jax was the expert on the computing side. He knew everything about the products and the industry, so he took lead on most things. He ran the meetings and made the decisions. She'd pushed him to sell, and once he agreed, it was up to him to see it through. She was simply supposed to be the financial presenter and the decoration on his arm. But Jax had died.

She hated the feeling of not knowing everything about her business. Knowledge was power, and she hated not being in control. Too late. Once Christina joined Externus, Elizabeth hung on to the vague hope that she could rely on her daughter as an advocate on her side. But Jax and Christina became a tag team. Quickly, she recognized it was the two of them, conspiring with one another, and usually against her. The investigating Jax had done into her background was just the latest of his treacherous double-dealing. It was low, even for him.

She wondered if her daughter had shown the files to Kyle.

Elizabeth wanted to put the past behind her. All of it. Her career with the CIA. Her marriage to Jax. This moronic gaming company. She wanted to put Turkey behind her too. She didn't care for these nasty feelings of guilt that had been gnawing at her since they arrived. She wanted to take her money and run, fast and far. She already knew her next two stops after leaving Istanbul. A couple of weeks at the Post Ranch Inn in Big Sur to rejuvenate her, and then a trip to White Desert in Antarctica.

Still, for all his naïve idealism, Jax had proved to be a great partner. At least, his company was. Elizabeth had worked hard all her life. When this was over, she'd be finally able to relax, to travel in style with no need to stop anytime soon.

The chatter of feminine voices on the patio hushed, and Elizabeth knew the cause without even looking up. Kyle was making his way through the glass double doors onto the patio, and two dozen sets of women's eyes were fixed on him.

She couldn't blame them. Her own pulse fluttered as he approached her table.

"Good morning, Elizabeth. Or is it afternoon?"

"Not yet."

He leaned over to kiss her on the cheek. She turned her face slightly, and his lips brushed against hers instead. She got a whiff of his cologne—spicy and masculine—and fought the urge to lean in and inhale more of it.

"How was your flight?"

"Long." He motioned for a waiter.

And he didn't have enough sleep. Deep lines fanned out from the corners of his eyes. A clenched jaw muscle flickered.

"caffè Americano...and leave the menu," Kyle ordered. "You have tea. Do you want anything to eat?"

Elizabeth declined and watched him glance back toward the door. He was waiting for Christina, she decided.

"When and where are we meeting today?"

"We have nothing until Friday."

Today was Wednesday. "Friday? What about the Russians?"

"We were supposed to meet with their reps this afternoon, and then with all three companies on Friday. But the Russians postponed."

"Is anything wrong?"

"No, it's better this way. If Jax were alive, it'd be a different story. He'd meet with each of the principals individually, try to sweeten the deal. But with him gone, there's no point and they recognize it."

His coffee was delivered, and he told the server to come back for his order.

As Kyle took a sip, Elizabeth glanced appreciatively at him. He had that handsome Nordic look that just got better with age.

"We have the Divan Meeting Room reserved all day on Friday," he continued. "We'll have a meet and greet at ten. At eleven, Christina and I will do our presentations, and after lunch, we'll do a Q&A. You should be ready if there are any questions about the numbers, but I don't foresee it. The buyers were sent the relevant data on products and projected revenue, and I've been in contact with the decision makers. All three companies plan to make an offer. We'll finish accepting the closed bids at four. You'll announce your decision Monday morning. And that's it."

"Thank you. I feel better knowing the schedule." She was annoyed when he shot a glance toward the door to the lobby again. "Friday is Christina's birthday."

"I don't think it's in our best interest to postpone the meeting."

"No, of course not. But we can do something for her tomorrow night."

"Whatever you want."

Whatever I want. Elizabeth watched Kyle turn his focus on the menu. His eyelashes were long and flecked with gold. He was truly a gorgeous specimen of the human male, even in his present tired condition. The constant looks of the women at nearby tables hadn't escaped her attention. She relished the thought that they might be wondering if she and Kyle were together.

The year before she married Jax—five years before Christina threw herself at Kyle and they moved in together—Elizabeth ran into him in the wine bar at the airport in San Francisco. She'd met him twice before. He was in sales, a rising star in the same company where she and Jax worked.

"Where are you going?" she'd asked him over her glass.

"Back to LA. How about you?"

"Calistoga Ranch, Napa Valley. A girlfriend has a time-share and invited me to go, but at the last minute she cancelled."

"That's too bad."

Every time she'd seen him, Kyle had been flirting with someone. Why not, she decided. "I have the place to myself for the weekend. You want to join me?"

That was all it took. And those three days were the best sex she'd had in decades.

She brought her cup of tea to her lips now to hide the heat of the recollection. Elizabeth didn't know why she was thinking of that today, after so long. So much had changed since then, and they both had successfully pretended that it never happened.

"You hadn't forgotten that Friday is Christina's birthday."

"Of course not."

"Where is she now? Still in bed recovering from a wild night with her prodigal boyfriend?"

His eyes narrowed, and Elizabeth recognized her comment was

inappropriate. Considering their history, it was definitely better not referring to that topic with her future son-in-law.

"She's down here somewhere, working."

"When did she come down? I didn't see her."

"Since early this morning, I think."

"How early?" she asked. "I came down at eight for breakfast. No one was in the business center. I haven't seen her, and we have a few things we need to chat about."

"She was down here working for you, for Externus. We're trying to sell your company."

"Always defending her."

"Someone has to," he said shortly.

"Why are you such a bear this morning?" she asked, putting her hand on his arm. "What's wrong with you? I'm on your side."

He shook off her touch. "I don't need you to be on my side, Elizabeth. I'm here to do a job for you. Let's keep it at that, okay?"

She felt her temper flare. She wasn't ready to let this conversation go. But her eyes were suddenly drawn to a man in a dark suit and tie standing on the garden-lined walkway leading from the lobby. He was tall, with broad shoulders and salt-and-pepper hair. Something about him ignited an ember of worry in the pit of her stomach. He removed his dark glasses, and recognition prickled along her spine. Elizabeth knew exactly who he was.

"There's Christina," Kyle said suddenly, pushing up to his feet.

Elizabeth followed his gaze and saw her daughter marching across the courtyard, heading directly for the man.

23

CHRISTINA

"You're the driver who took me to the airport last night."

We're only a step away from each other, and there's no doubt in my mind he's the one. His voice, his hair, even the scar running along his jaw.

He turns to me and puts his sunglasses back on. Out here in public in the daylight, I find nothing frightening about him. He could easily be mistaken for a member of the hotel management or staff. Maybe he is, except that he's wearing no name tag.

"I believe you are mistaken. If you will excuse me."

"Wait a minute," I tell him, blocking his escape route toward the lobby.

The man is middle-aged, sturdy looking, and wearing a blank look intended to convey that he doesn't recognize me. I don't buy that for a second. I saw his eyes as soon as he spotted me coming toward him. He remembers me all right.

"I have a good memory for faces. You picked me up in a black Lexus SUV on the street in front of the hotel. You took me to the airport, and a different driver brought me back here. I know it was you. We can call the car service if we need verification."

He says nothing for a moment and then his attitude changes. "Of course, ma'am. I am sorry that I did not remember immediately. I drive so many people. And please accept my apologies for the incident. It was sudden and unacceptable to question you in that manner."

His apology sounds sincere, and it sort of sets me back. Maybe what happened wasn't as dramatic as I remember it. I think of the conversation I had with Tiam this morning about the men from her volunteer work.

"I hope my answers to your questions put your mind at ease, at least. Ms. Rahman and I are friends. Is that enough for you?"

"It is. I thank you and wish you a good day, ma'am."

"But why did you want to know about—?"

"You will please excuse me, ma'am. I must go."

He brushes by me and goes up the steps into the lobby. His departure is so abrupt that it takes me a couple of seconds before I realize the reason. Kyle is striding toward me. I look past him and realize he's come from Elizabeth's table. I start toward him.

"Are you okay? Your mother said she didn't see you all morning."

"Of course I'm okay." I gesture toward her. "She's waiting for us."

He walks beside me. "Did you get my text about the meetings today?"

"I did. Everything is moved to Friday."

We reach the table, and Elizabeth starts in on me before I sit down. "Who was the man you were speaking to just now?"

Her tone is way sharper than it needs to be. I didn't sleep at all last night, and the effect of it is starting to wear my patience thin. "It doesn't matter. You wouldn't know him."

"Christina, who was he?"

"It doesn't matter."

"For God's sake, why can't you answer the question?"

Kyle sends me a look. He has no patience for fights, especially when it's between Elizabeth and me. I wonder if he's told her our news. I guess he probably hasn't, or she'd be more wound up about my poor decision-making skills than a stranger I was talking to.

"He's the driver who took me to the airport last night."

"Why didn't you say so?" Kyle shoots a glance at the door to the lobby and starts to get up. "I'd like to have a word with him."

I put a hand on his arm and stop him. "No, don't. He apologized. It was all a misunderstanding. It's done."

He stares at me for second and then settles. "Okay. If that's what you want."

Elizabeth is just getting started. "You went to the airport last night? You said Kyle was using a car service. Why didn't you tell me you were going? What a careless thing to do in the middle of night."

A waiter shows up at the table, asking if I'd like to see a menu. Thankfully, that curtails the barrage for the moment.

"No, thank you."

I need a short nap before I go to meet Tiam, and getting something to eat from room service would be better than staying here.

"I finished my presentation for the buyers and sent it you," I tell Kyle before Elizabeth can say anything more. "Can you look through it?"

"Yeah. I'll do it this afternoon."

I turn to her next. "Patricia Nicholls."

She nearly chokes on the sip of tea she's just taken. I wait as she clears her throat. Her face is guarded by the time she looks up at me.

"She was a friend of yours when you were living in Ankara. Right around the time I was born." I'm not giving her the opportunity for any denials. And I'm not going to play the game of her not remembering the woman's name. "She's retired and lives in Istanbul. Now that we have a couple of days with nothing to do, why don't you give her a call? We can go visit her. Or maybe we can invite her to come to the hotel for lunch."

"What for?"

"For old time's sake."

"I haven't spoken to her for years. I really don't feel any driving need to renew the acquaintance."

"Okay. Then if you don't mind, I will."

"I *do* mind. She was *my* friend." Elizabeth's voice is getting icier. "You don't even know her."

Kyle shoots his signature look my way again. The frown that says, *Let it go.* But he has no idea what is motivating me.

"But I'd like to get to know her," I say in a reasonable tone. "We're all in Istanbul, and Patricia is a connection with the first couple of years of my life. I'd love to hear what those days were like."

"How did you find out about Patricia Nicholls?" Kyle asks.

"Her name comes up in some of Jax's private emails."

I look directly at Elizabeth. She doesn't know if Patricia was or wasn't mentioned in the file I showed her yesterday, but I'm hoping the threat is enough to trigger a reaction. Even though Tiam asked me, I can't exactly call the woman out of the blue and ask her if she knows who got her friend pregnant thirty-three years ago. I can't even imagine her speaking to me. But by doing it this way, at least I know I'm chipping away at the wall Elizabeth is hiding behind.

"What emails?" Kyle wants to know.

"I'll call her," Elizabeth breaks in immediately. "We'll see what her schedule is like. Do you have a number for her?"

"Did you buy a phone?"

"I got one this morning. It has a Turkish number."

She digs her phone out of her bag and slides it across the table to me. I put Patricia's information into her contacts. She's the first entry. I hand it back to her and stand up.

"No lunch?" Kyle asks.

"No, thanks. I'm really tired. I'm going up for a nap." I gather my stuff. But before leaving, I drop my other news on Elizabeth. "I made a reservation tonight for four people at eight o'clock at the Hamdi Restaurant, by the ferryboat pier. Does that work for you?"

"Who's the fourth?" Kyle and Elizabeth ask at the same time.

"It's a surprise," I tell them, turning away.

PART VIII

Fair is the leisure of life's garden ground:
Pleasant is friendship's voice and mirth's soft sound.
Sweet are the perfumed flowers; yes, yes, what bliss
Soothes like hope's fresh scent of loveliness?
...From the pure lily I heard this clear song:
'Happy their peaceful life who work no wrong;
Sweet idle flowers, whom heaven's sweet airs do kiss;
No conquering king hath joy more fair than this.'
— Ḥafeẓ

24

TIAM

CHRISTINA IS PACING on the sidewalk in front of the clinic when I arrive. As I wait to cross the street, her worry is clear as a winter sky. The furrowed brow. The lips compressed into a thin line. She pauses and rubs her hands against her thighs. I've seen all of this before in my mother. I'm well aware of how my health affects those who care for me, who love me.

Although I've been following her on social media for twelve years, the past six months are what really count. Christina has become one of us. She is family.

When she sees me crossing over to her, she smiles. We greet each other with a warm hug, and she doesn't let go immediately.

"Everything I'm going through today is routine," I tell her. "So there's nothing to be worried about."

"Awesome." She looks up at the four-story white granite building. "What do you want me to do? When we get up there, I mean."

"Keep me company. Talk to me."

As we go up in the elevator, I fill her in on what will happen.

"First, the nurses will do the normal check-in requirements—blood pressure, temperature, and things like that. Then the doctor comes in and checks me out. After that, they hook me up to an inflatable percussion vest. That beast of a machine loosens up the mucus in my breathing passages. Then they listen to my lungs again."

They're expecting me, so right away they put me in the room with equipment I need. Nurses and tech aides sail in and out, doing their thing. I've been here so often that I know everyone. The staff all speak Turkish, and I translate as much as I can for Christina. She listens carefully to everything.

I love the fact that she wants to be here. She doesn't have to do it. Even though she found me—or rather, we found each other—our lives could have continued on separate paths. But she is interested in what's happening to me. Since our meeting this past spring, she's taken hold of the ties that connect us, and she hasn't let go. We talk to each other every week, and we trade messages even more frequently.

After her car accident, she called me from the hospital. The hours we spent on FaceTime, knowing she wished I were there in the room with her and Autumn, was precious to me. After the baby died, we spent hours on the phone again, both of us grieving. I've had many friends in my life, but the connection I have with Christina is different —it goes much deeper.

And now she's here, sitting next to me.

A nurse comes in with the list of my medications printed out on a form. She wants me to double-check it.

"You take *all* of these?" Christina asks, glancing at the list. "This is your daily regimen?"

"Pretty much. On average I take fifty pills a day. Medications, supplements, enzymes, laxatives. Then I have the nebulizer every morning and night. On top of that, I have these lung-clearing exercises and sinus rinses. It goes on and on."

It's one thing to hear about my condition over the phone, it's another for her to be here with me during a session. Zari is one of the strongest women on the planet, and yet even her spirit bends under the weight of her worry when she comes to the clinic. That's why I don't tell her about the appointments and the tests unless I need to be admitted. The less she knows the better. I hate to see her suffer.

"When did you first know that you were sick?" Christina asks.

"I don't remember a time when I felt like other kids. I've never been healthy."

I tell her about when I was a little girl. I'd stand to the side in the schoolyard or the playground and watch the other children race around. I admit I was pretty envious, but that was my life. And I missed a lot of school days.

Being honest about a debilitating disease doesn't exactly make for cheerful conversation. I know this, so when she glances at all the gadgets around the room, I change it up.

"By the time I was five years old, I'd heard the doctors say *kistik fibroz* so many times that those were the first words I learned to spell. Everyone was so impressed."

"Well," she says with the crooked half smile that makes me think of Zari. "My first attempt at spelling wasn't so well received."

"Tell me, what was it?"

"Fuck you."

I burst out laughing. "You didn't."

"I did."

I burst out laughing. "How old were you?"

"I was five."

"How did that happen?"

"A couple of boys in the neighborhood were arguing on the street. One of them said it and then spelled it out for emphasis. I thought it was pretty cool."

"And so you shared it at home?"

"I told Elizabeth *Fuck you* as soon as she walked into the house that afternoon. And she wasn't by herself. She had a friend with her."

"No!"

"I said it clearly and proudly. *Mommy, fuck you. F.U.C.K. Y.O.U.* I remember being so tickled with myself."

My laughter starts a new coughing fit, and she watches nervously.

"I should get someone."

I hold on to her hand and make her wait until I catch my breath. In a moment or two, it passes.

"What did she do?" I finally ask.

"Oh, it was a total meltdown. She spanked me. Grounded me. I had to go to bed with no supper. It didn't matter that I'd come to learn the phrase innocently. There was a lot of yelling and drama, and my poor babysitter got fired." She shakes her head. "Elizabeth has always been big on discipline, and she's very slow to forgive an offense. And that was one of the first of many crises in our household."

I've learned a great deal about Elizabeth in the years since I found out she's my mother. Her public persona seemed to indicate that she was leading a perfect life. A beautiful life. That was the face she showed the world. Hearing about Christina's childhood gives me another lens to see her through. I find it fascinating. Question after question burns on my tongue every time we speak. But I don't ask them for two reasons. I don't want to feel envy about the life I was deprived of. And second, I don't want Christina to feel any sense of guilt.

"What about now? Does she still get angry with you?"

"All the time. I think during my pregnancy and after losing Autumn, she consciously toned it down. She's perpetually disappointed in me."

"That's impossible," I protest. "You're kind. You're educated. You're independent. You have a great job. You're smart."

"Thank you. But I have *not* turned out the way she wanted. Whatever her expectations were, I've never been able to meet them."

And as a very sick baby, neither did I.

I've had chances to walk up to Elizabeth and start a conversation this week. I've practiced my speech numerous times. Christina has said she'll be there to support me, and I know she'll help me get through it. But every time, I've used the excuse of not being strong or healthy enough to justify backing out. The truth is that I am intimidated. I know I'm not good enough for her. To go to her and say *I'm alive* isn't enough.

"Tell me, did Zari ever talk to you about all of this? About CF? I mean, when you were younger? You had to be scared."

It's far more pleasant to talk about Zari than to think about Elizabeth.

"All the time." We had many important discussions about being sick. "I think I was ten or eleven years old when I asked her if I was going to die from it."

"Jeez. What did she say?"

"She told me that people could die from CF. But she said that children also drown in bathtubs and get hit by cars. The important thing to remember was that I was a fighter and I was alive now and that she'd be beside me every step of the way."

"I'm sure the only thing I would have heard was that I could die from it."

"Exactly. We often hear only the worst," I tell her. "But at the same time, I started to understand the reason for all the salty food we ate and for my constant stomach aches. I think I stopped complaining about the medicines and the doctors and the hospital stays after that."

The nurse comes in and tells me that the doctor is running late, but he'll be in to check my lungs in ten minutes. Then they'll connect the vest.

When she goes, Christina leans against the treatment table where I'm sitting. "If you could take a day off from all of this, what would you do?"

I think about all the activities that I've missed out on. There are a million things. I know what Christina is doing, though. She's thinking of doing something nice for me. The last thing I want is for her to feel obligated.

"I'd do nothing," I tell her. "I'd lie in bed and do nothing but read and read and read."

She laughs. "What do you like to read?"

"I love reading romance novels. I have to read so many technical articles about pharmacy that reading about love and new beginnings is a welcome change. So on this day off, as you call it, I'd read about a woman like me falling in love. It would be a story that makes me believe happily ever after exists for people who are sick like me."

Christina looks toward the light pouring in through the large window. I know she's trying to keep her emotions in check. I kick myself inwardly. "I didn't mean for it to come out sounding so morbid."

"It didn't."

"You're being nice to me."

"I am." She smiles.

"Has there ever been anyone?"

"Of course! Thousands! Zari always beats them away with a broom." We both laugh.

"Seriously. Even in the best of worlds, relationships can be difficult."

"They're complicated for me. I have many male friends who are colleagues, or that I know through my girlfriends. We often go out as a group for dinner or movies or to university events or lectures. But my relationships with men are pretty much platonic."

I don't tell her that most of my friends are now married and have children. Of my unmarried friends, six more are having weddings this year.

"Platonic because of religion?"

"To some extent, I suppose. Of course, Turkish men can be quite... um, ardent. But the ones I associate with are respectful. We tend to spend time in small groups. And then some fall in love and marry. Not me, though."

"You're beautiful and kind and smart. What's wrong with men these days?"

"You're repeating my words back to me. I think we are great fans of each other."

"Tell me there's been *someone*."

"Well, there *was* a classmate at the university that I had feelings for. And a young doctor at the hospital. And the brother of a good friend who lives in Australia and visits twice a year."

Christina is the first person I feel comfortable talking with about men and relationships. I'm thirty-two years old, and I can't really discuss it with my friends in Istanbul. They'd know who I'm talking about. And, as much as I love Zari, talking about men with her is out of the question.

"There are four or five others I could name that I secretly hoped would ask me out, but none of it has happened."

"Why?"

"Because of this." I wave at the machinery around us.

"Wait. Your choice or theirs?"

I smile and shake my head at the darkening expression in her face. She looks so much like Zari right now. "Does it make a difference?"

"*I* think it does."

"It wouldn't be fair to drag a partner down this path with me. But, to be honest, men rarely get close enough to have a conversation about it."

"Assholes."

I laugh and my chest hurts. Christina waits until I clear the mucus, but this time she doesn't panic.

"Can you spell that?" I manage to gasp.

"Gladly...and I'll do it to their faces."

I motion for water from the cooler in the corner. She gets it for me.

"I think the only good men exist in romance novels."

"I don't believe that. There have to be some good guys left out there. I'm not giving up hope for you."

Our relationship might be new, but it's a special one. We're two very different people because of our upbringing, culture, religion, even schooling, but I feel that our lives are connected on so many levels.

"Speaking of men, your boyfriend Kyle flew in last night."

"Yeah, he did. But he's not my boyfriend anymore. I broke up with him last night."

The furrow in her brow has reappeared, but Christina seems more resigned than sad about it. She knew it was coming. Back in June, she told me she had her doubts that their relationship would survive once the baby was born.

"After we're done helping Elizabeth sell the company, we'll go our separate ways."

I'm not exactly sure what to say. "I'm sorry."

"No worries." She's trying to sound cheerful, but I can feel a deeper disappointment that she's pushed inside of her.

"So when your business is finished here, will you live in LA?"

"No." She waits while a nurse rolls a piece of equipment into the room and then goes back out. "At least, not on a permanent basis."

I already know that she's planning to stay around for a while after Elizabeth leaves. She told me she wants to spend some time with Zari.

"What would you think of me moving to Istanbul?" she asks.

"I think it would be wonderful, but it's a big step."

I immediately think of Maman and how many times in recent months I've thought about what would happen to her if I were to die. As if I needed a reminder of my condition, the breath catches in my chest, and for a few moments I struggle.

Christina's eyes go wide with alarm, and before I can stop her she's out the door. Seconds later, she comes back in with a nurse. I raise my hand to indicate to them I'm okay. She comes and stands next to me, touching my face, wanting to make sure for herself.

I love the idea of her moving here. I can't say it out loud, but I've already lived well past my life expectancy, and having her in Istanbul will make all the difference for Zari.

"I suppose you'll want me to share Zari with you." I cock an eyebrow at her.

"I'll insist on it."

"You're *not* sending me back with Elizabeth."

"Fine. But I want my name back."

"Not happening. I'm keeping the name Tiam."

A young doctor walks in as we're talking. Immediately, he looks at me, at Christina, and then back at me. He thinks we're arguing.

"*Merhaba.*"

I've seen him here once before. In Turkish, I introduce him to her. She nods and fades back toward the window.

He's all business and listens to my lungs as he asks his questions.

"*Öksür.*"

I cough as he instructs.

"*Tekrar.*"

I do it again.

"This one *is* quite handsome. Is he one of the assholes?" Christina asks softly. I can hear the laugh in her voice.

"One of which assholes?" the doctor asks in English, never looking up as he continues what he's doing.

I smile as she slinks over red-faced to inspect some equipment in the corner of the room.

"I was complaining about tech aides in the radiology lab," I lie, speaking in English. "You're definitely not in that category."

"Handsome or asshole?"

"Both."

"Okay. I'm sorry I asked," he says, winking at me.

He goes back to listening to my lungs. The clipboard on the bed next to me has some of my test data from this week. The oxygen saturation measurement result is underlined in red, and the other tests are also bad.

"I don't—"

"*Türkçe konuş,*" I say immediately, asking the doctor to speak in Turkish.

He gives me the news. My life has always been about the fight to stay alive, but I'm losing the battle, little by little. He says they'll try the vest today, but he wants me to come back tomorrow for more tests.

He goes out, and a nurse comes in. Christina joins me next to the bed.

"He has definite potential for becoming one of my assholes," I say to her.

She laughs and watches the nurse put the inflatable percussion vest on me.

Seeing her standing so attentively, feeling her optimism, knowing she's here and planning to stay obliterates my fears. For the first time ever, I'm not worried about tomorrow. I know Zari will be taken care of.

25

CHRISTINA

BEFORE TODAY, I had no personal experience with the mental and emotional toll that comes with watching someone you care for suffer.

Standing in that clinic treatment room, I wasn't the caregiver. I wasn't in charge of making decisions. I didn't have to do anything but keep Tiam company. Still, I worried. I found myself pacing my breathing involuntarily to the machine that she was hooked up to. When they asked her to cough to clear her chest, I discreetly coughed. Each time the doctor came back to check on her progress, my palms were sweating. I was anxious to hear his findings. The entire time, however, I held back my tears, bottled up my emotions, and pretended I was handling it.

The expressions on the faces of those who moved in and out of the room clued me in. I needed no translator to understand what they were thinking. No one was happy with how Tiam was doing.

Being in Istanbul and seeing Tiam's condition only confirm my plans. The moment Elizabeth made the offer of a bonus upon the completed sale of Externus, I knew what I wanted to do with my share. I haven't told anyone about it yet. The money is going toward Tiam's treatment. But after what I've seen today, I realize that financial assistance is not the only thing she needs. Her disease seems to be far more advanced than I thought.

Questions regarding Tiam's prognosis clutter my mind. My knowledge of CF and its treatment comes from online searches. Definitely not the most reliable source. I have no idea if what she's receiving as treatment is adequate. I want to know if she's on a waiting list for a lung transfer. And if she is, how long is the waiting time in Turkey. Another thought occurs to me. If I can somehow get her to the US, would the wait be any shorter there? Would the operation be more successful?

Right now, watching her undergo these treatments, I have no opportunity to ask these questions. I don't even know if she'll confide in me. She's trying to protect Zari. I'm afraid she'll try to do the same thing to me by holding back the truth.

By the time the session is over, four hours after we went in, a tension headache is pounding away above my temples, but I paint on a smile to hide it.

"I can't have dinner with you and Elizabeth tonight. I'm sorry. I need to go home and sleep," Tiam tells me as we walk out of the clinic. "Can we postpone it?"

She's pale and obviously spent. Her eyes have dark shadows beneath them.

"Sure. Tomorrow night?"

"I can try."

I'm relieved about putting off the dinner too. Whenever this reunion takes place, I'm supposed to be both bystander and mediator. But I'm worried about Tiam. Today I've had a glimpse of what Zari has gone through for the past thirty years. She's watched a child she loves struggle month after month, battling to stay alive. She's known from the time Elizabeth left that Tiam's illness is critical.

The time I had with my daughter was far too short, but I recall how her every twinge ripped at my insides as I worried. The hospital staff told me she was going to be fine. Still, I was consumed with watching her, pacing the room with her tiny body in my arms. And after they moved her to the ICU, they kept telling me she had a good chance of pulling through. I wanted to believe them...until I couldn't. And then she was gone.

Zari has lived with the specter of imminent death hanging over Tiam for decades. It drains the life out of me just thinking of it.

I tell Tiam that I'll take her home, but she refuses, saying she'll be fine. We argue about it, but she's adamant. So we get separate cabs. Before we part, she promises to text me in the morning and tell me how she's doing.

As I arrive at the hotel, I think to check my messages. I have a few. Kyle wants to see me about the presentation. Four texts come from Elizabeth's new Turkish number, summoning me.

"Ms. Hall. Your mother wishes to see you," a registration clerk announces as I walk through the lobby. "She's in the courtyard."

My plan of sending a group text to Elizabeth and Kyle about the need to reschedule dinner is pointless. I'm certain she'd send hotel security to collect me if I don't see her.

Before I go out, I get some water in the lobby and search in my purse for something to take for this headache. The box of medicine I filled yesterday is at the bottom.

For a moment, my mind turns to what my life could be like in Istanbul. I'd call Kemal Osman and ask him to bring his cousin, or maybe some other friend, to accompany me and Tiam to see the Whirling Dervishes. Kemal and Tiam are both pharmacists; maybe they've met before. They might have a great deal in common.

My schemes for matchmaking are interrupted as another text comes from Elizabeth. She's telling me that she's moved from the courtyard to the rooftop terrace.

I find a couple of acetaminophen tablets in a side pocket of my bag and down them with a sip of water. I'm starting to recognize the faces of many members of the hotel staff, and they know me too. They smile and greet me by name as I pass by. Two Turkish-speaking men dressed in dark suits are standing near a window. My attention is immediately drawn to the taller of the two, but he's not the driver from last night. Since exchanging a few words with him at lunchtime, I'm no longer frightened by our encounter. How he knows Tiam and why he was asking about her continue to stir my curiosity, however.

I go to the terrace, and Elizabeth waves to me from a sofa as soon as I appear. The September sun is dropping into a golden western sky.

The air is still comfortably warm, but Elizabeth has had them light a heater nearby.

"Where were you? I've been trying to find you all afternoon. People at the front desk said you left the hotel."

"I went for a walk."

She pats the seat on the sofa next to her. As I sit down, a white-jacketed waiter approaches, replacing Elizabeth's empty glass with another cocktail. I shake my head at the offer of seeing the drink menu.

"I could have come with you."

"No, I needed some time on my own."

"I'm glad that Kyle arrived safe and sound. Aren't you?"

"Absolutely." I have my answer about whether he'd said anything to Elizabeth about us. "So what's the emergency? Why did you send me so many texts?"

"This dinner tonight. You know how much I hate surprises. Tell me who's coming or I won't be there."

My head hurts too much for me to argue. I motion to the waiter. "I've changed my mind. May I have a cup of tea?"

"Yes, ma'am."

Elizabeth continues as soon as he goes. "It's Patricia Nicholls, isn't it?"

"Have you called her?"

"I tried but she didn't answer."

"Did you leave a message?"

"Of course. I said that I'm in Istanbul and told her where we're staying. That's all."

She drinks down half of her standard old-fashioned. From her slurred speech, I suspect she's had a few already.

"I still don't understand why you care at all about seeing this woman. All this nostalgia crap you carry around about your child-hood is exhausting. Patricia was old thirty years ago. She's probably a doddering old biddy by now. There's nothing that she can tell you that I haven't already told you...numerous times."

Whether we make contact now or not, I already plan to get to know Patricia Nicholls when I can move here. Perhaps after a lunch date or two, she'll be willing to share a few glimpses into Elizabeth's old life, particularly with regard to the men. Maybe what I'm hoping for is too great a stretch, but I think it's worth the effort. I'll do anything for Tiam.

My phone buzzes with an incoming text. It's Kyle, telling me that two changes to the contracts need to go to the lawyer and come back corrected by Friday. He's in the business center, and he wants me to go over them with him.

I text him back, saying I'll be there in five minutes.

"You can relax," I tell her, standing up. "Dinner tonight is pushed back to tomorrow night. Same restaurant. Same hour."

"I can't," she argues. "You can't. Kyle has already made a reservation for the three of us. We're celebrating your birthday a day early tomorrow night."

How appropriate, I think. It's really Tiam's birthday this week. Zari told me that I was actually born in March in a mountain village in the eastern part of Turkey.

"I'll work it all out with Kyle."

"I'm warning you. I don't want Patricia to join us for dinner," Elizabeth says curtly. "If she decides to contact me, and she wants to come and chitchat over tea, maybe. Not dinner. Do you understand me?"

I find it amusing that she's already decided who my guest is.

"Promise me." She's not giving up.

"I've got it. Patricia won't be joining us for dinner."

The server delivers my tea, but I leave it on the table and walk away. I'm already wondering what kind of scene Elizabeth will make if Tiam shows up at this birthday dinner as my guest. As I go down to the business center, I start to have second thoughts about the two of them meeting for the first time in a restaurant. Elizabeth has seen pictures of Tiam and caught glimpses of her. What if she decides to be rude or belligerent? It isn't beyond her to behave badly.

The idea of a casual dinner doesn't seem so great anymore. Right now, my head is hurting too much to think of an alternative. Maybe tomorrow, after I speak to Tiam, we can think of something else.

Kyle is the only one in the business center. When he sees me coming, his expression darkens. He's still upset about the way I ended things.

"What do you have? What do we need to do?" I ask as I pull out a chair and sit at the adjoining workstation.

He slides his notes in front of me, and I go over them. The changes he wants in the contract have to do with taking out the noncompete clause, so the current Externus programmers' jobs will be protected. I agree with what he's suggesting. I open up my laptop and write an email to the company lawyer, identifying the changes.

"Does Elizabeth know?" he asks after I send the email. "About us?"

"I didn't say anything. I don't think it's any of her business."

"I agree. Let's keep it that way." He stacks the papers next to his laptop. "Everything is a lot more complicated than I imagined it would be. We just want to keep things going forward, smooth and easy."

"What do you mean *complicated*?"

"You and Elizabeth are hiding something from me."

"What are you talking about?"

He sends me a look that says I should give him some credit. "All you had to do was mention something about emails today, and she agreed to call some old friend of hers from thirty years ago. You black-mailed her."

"My mother and I have a lot of baggage. But my private life is mine," I remind him. "Especially now."

"I want this sale to go off without a hitch, Christina."

"So do I." I meet his gaze, happy that our conversation is about business. "Whatever is going on between Elizabeth and me, it has nothing to do with Externus."

"Really? Nothing?" He turns in his chair until he's facing me. "Then why Istanbul? Have you wondered why Jax planned to meet with buyers here?"

"I don't know. Because it's closer to Moscow? Because it's neutral ground for all three potential buyers?" I think of what I revealed to Jax after my first trip. It was after our talk that he picked Istanbul as the location for the sale. "Good airport? Nice hotels."

"He could have done this so easily in Osaka last week. All the companies that are coming this week were there. He could have even pushed the price up by luring other midsize companies into a bidding war. Everyone in the business was there in Japan."

"Did you suggest it to him?"

"Yeah, I did. But he was dead set against it. He said we'd hold the auction here. Period."

My mind drifts back to my conversation with Jax again. His marriage with Elizabeth was a business transaction from the start. He wanted to start a company. She knew how to raise funds and make him look good with investors. Beyond the business side of things, they were a terrible match. Each of them lived their own lives, had their own friends, and did their own thing.

"I don't want to do all this work and have it shit the bed at the last minute." He's not giving up.

Kyle is a perfectionist. Whatever my problems are with our personal relationship, I've never had any doubt about his ability to do his job.

"With the exception of this change we just sent off to the lawyer," I ask, "what can go wrong?"

"Elizabeth is your mother. So *you* should know." He plants his elbows on his knees, keeping his voice low. "After what you said to her, I was afraid she'd turn out to be a loose cannon, so I did some poking around into her background."

"You went through Jax's emails?" I ask, knowing Kyle is capable of digging into those same files.

"No. I did a search on the dark web, just to make sure."

Deep within the internet, where regular search engines don't go, the dark web is a world with no borders and no boundaries. If the internet most people know is the Wild West, then the dark web is located in the Nine Circles of Hell. As a programmer in this line of business, I understand the importance of this largely hidden back alley off the information highway. Laws and regulations don't apply here. Nations can't censor you. Knowing how to navigate its paths is a powerful skill, and Kyle and I both have it. I already guessed that the information Jax collected about Elizabeth's past and her involvement with illegal arms sales must have come from there.

"It's clear she was CIA," he tells me.

"I know." I shrug noncommittally. "Jax was digging up old dirt. That's where I found the stuff. In his back-and-forth emails with a hacker."

"She was involved in some dirty business," he continues. "Looks like she made some money from it. Money that might have gone into Externus."

"I don't know what she did with her money from her old job. She always worked when I was growing up. She needed a paycheck." I tell him the rest of what I know. "Jax collected pages of declassified material before he died. But how does all of that affect what we need to do?"

"Then you know about the kill list?"

"What kill list?" Kyle knows something that I don't. Now I'm worried.

The dark web did not get its name or reputation without good cause. It's where criminal elements across the planet buy and sell a plethora of illegal commodities. Identities. Weapons. Sex slaves. Drugs. It's a clearinghouse where contract killers find murder-for-hire offers and other lucrative employment opportunities from governments and businesses that want lethal results and no repercussions. It's a meeting place where hideous crimes originate.

"The kill list that has Elizabeth's name on it."

"Who wants her dead?"

"Two years ago, a Kurdish group came up with names of people they hold responsible for war crimes. Some of them were sued."

"I know about the civil suits, but my mother wasn't named in them."

"Yeah, well, she was on another list. A hit list."

This is getting worse and worse. "So someone is going to come after her?"

"I don't know." He rakes his fingers through his hair. "The list is long, and it's more than two years old. But I think it's a Salman Rushdie kind of thing."

Before I was old enough to understand anything about politics, I heard that the British Indian writer was on some list for disrespecting Islam and the Prophet in his work. As far as I know, nothing ever happened to him.

"I think Jax knew about it," Kyle says. "And coming to Istanbul was intentional."

"Jax wouldn't do that." As soon as I say it, I'm not really sure. I try to force down my doubts that he might have intentionally put her life in danger by bringing her to Istanbul. "Besides, couldn't someone hurt her in LA or New York or anywhere?"

"I suppose. But I don't really know."

"But you're saying she's in more danger here in Istanbul?"

"I don't know. Maybe. Maybe not. She's been here how many days now?"

"Four."

"Has she left the hotel?"

"We went to a *hamam* together, and she went to the consulate by herself. She's been out in public. We went to the Spice Market."

"And nothing happened to her." He frowns. "Maybe the best thing for all of us would be to keep her in the hotel, watch her, finish the sale, and get her on a plane home."

"She still has to go to the police station and the consulate for her passport."

"I told her I'm going with her tomorrow. But maybe your dinner plans for tonight are a bad idea."

"I already postponed them."

"Your mother asked me to make a dinner reservation for your birthday tomorrow night. I'll change it to the restaurant here in the hotel."

"That sounds good."

He hesitates a moment and looks directly at me. "I suggest that we not mention any of this to her."

There's no doubt in my mind that Elizabeth will be on the next flight out of Istanbul if she hears anything about a kill list, regardless of how old it is. She values her life way more than any money from this sale.

26

ELIZABETH

THE PEOPLE GOING down the city street swept Elizabeth along. The mask she was wearing pinched her face. The shoving, heaving stream surrounded her, crowded her, lifted her. It was difficult to breathe, and she couldn't move right or left. She was one with this surging mass of humanity.

With every step, pain shot upward from the soles of her feet. She'd lost her shoes somewhere. Her clothes hung on her body like a sack. The crowd jostled her, and the mask slipped. She managed to jerk a hand free of the crush and push it back in place.

A sudden pop and a hissing sound, and she inhaled a sickening sweet smell, like rotting apples and chlorine. She knew what it was, and panic gripped her.

On either side of the street, apartment buildings exploded and collapsed as she passed by them. They crumbled with deafening booms, sending up plumes of smoke. Dust and debris filled the sky and descended like a shroud on the crowds behind her.

The rushing human current became frantic and turned into a stampede. Shouts and cries competed with the sound of buildings crashing and falling like dominoes.

Elizabeth ran with the rest, but she knew she couldn't let them in on her secret. *She* was the force causing the destruction around them. *She* was death.

Another blast, and she tripped over something in the road. She went down hard.

A body. A child's body. She reared back on her knees. It was a thin, dirty bundle of rag and bone. She stared at the pale face. Elizabeth recognized her. She'd seen her in the Kurdish neighborhood and had imagined her running in the restaurant. She was everywhere.

The crowd separated and veered around Elizabeth. Bodies became a blur, but they were a fortress, protecting her. They guarded the hand that had come to destroy them. They thought she was one of them, a victim, an innocent. They didn't see beneath the mask.

Smoke and dust formed a swirling maelstrom around her, muffling the sounds from above. It was just her now and this child.

Against her will, she touched the emaciated cheek. The flesh was cold and lifeless. The Kurdish girl was dead.

The child's eyes slowly opened. Thin fingers reached up and pulled away the mask from Elizabeth's face. Bloodless lips moved, and two words were whispered.

Shaitan. Devil.

ELIZABETH SAT bolt upright in the bed, gasping. Grabbing her chest, she tried to breathe, but she couldn't get enough air into her lungs.

Everything around her was dark, swirling, alive. Smoke filled the room, burning her eyes. The cloying odor of rotten fruit and chlorine was overwhelming. The hissing sound was coming from somewhere in the darkness.

She had to be still sleeping. She was trapped in her nightmare. Wake up, Elizabeth.

"*Wake up.*"

Her scream echoed in the room. Tearing off the duvet, she leaped out of bed, landing on her hands and knees on the carpeted floor. She couldn't think, but her instincts told her one thing. She had to get out.

"Get out."

She scrambled on all fours toward the smudged shape of the door.

Her fingers climbed the wood and found the knob. It slid out of her grasp, and she fell flat on her face. She pulled herself up again and yanked at the knob, but the door wouldn't open. She pounded on it and screamed for help.

She stopped as she realized the hissing was right beneath her. The smoke was coming in from under the door. Understanding ripped through her.

Nerve gas.

They had taken her to Kurdistan. The poison was swirling around her. Smoke filled the air. But Saddam was dead. She'd played her part in those attacks, but that war was over.

Halabja had been the worst. She'd reported the eye-witness accounts in her memos to Langley. She'd seen and studied the photographs. There were so many.

The streets had been littered with the Kurdish dead—men, women, children. So many young ones died, a grayish-green slime oozing from their mouths, their frames contorted, fingers grotesquely twisted in pain.

The lucky ones died within minutes. As the shells exploded and the gases spread and settled, death was everywhere. First, the birds began falling, then animals, then humans. Once it reached the lungs and entered the blood stream, breathing stopped so abruptly that people simply dropped as if frozen. It was all there, recorded for posterity in the photographs.

All across Halabja, apocalyptic horror spread with lightning speed. A woman in her kitchen, cutting beets, was found dead, still holding the knife in her hand. A father stretched across a doorway, his face forever petrified in a scream. In his arms lay a lifeless infant. Five thousand or more breathed in the chemicals and were dead within minutes.

In her office in Ankara, she and the others pored over pictures taken by a journalist who arrived just after the assault. The Agency would point the finger at Iran, but she knew who was responsible. Elizabeth knew. She was the one wearing the mask.

She stared at the tube spewing smoke and gas into the room from beneath the door. They were coming after her. It was her time to die.

Panic obliterated all thought now. Crying for help, she threw herself at the door. Clawing at it, she twisted the knob, and it slammed open against the latch bar. She tore at it and stumbled out, gasping for air.

The hallway was empty, silent as the grave, and she ran.

27

CHRISTINA

A SHARP KNOCK at the door drags me up from the depths of sleep. I hear my name. It comes again, and I sit up with a start. My heart is racing, and I try to clear away the clinging dreamworld clouding my brain. The knocking becomes louder.

"Christina!"

Throwing back the covers, I jump out of bed. I open the door to Kyle's room. He's standing on the other side.

"Let me in, Christina." It's Elizabeth's voice, muffled by the banging.

He sends me a curious look. "What's going on?"

"I have no idea."

He walks in, and I close the adjoining door before hurrying to let her in. Everyone up and down the hall must be awake from this ruckus.

The three of us had a late supper in the restaurant. Elizabeth was tipsy before we sat down, and she was totally wasted before we were done. I helped her up to her room. That was at ten thirty. I check the clock. It's almost four in the morning.

I open the door, and Elizabeth rushes in, pushing me back and yanking the door shut behind her. She's wearing no shoes, no robe. She's in her nightgown, and her eyes are wild.

"Oh my God, I'm so glad you're up! They're after me."

"Who's after you?"

I try to go out and look out in the hall, but she puts her hand on the latch, stopping me.

"I had a nightmare. Then I woke up. And there's gas everywhere. Someone was pumping it into my room. I didn't know where it's coming from." She grabs her chest. "I think I'm going to have a heart attack."

"Let me call for help."

She grabs my arm, stopping me. Behind me, Kyle switches on a light.

"No. I'm fine. Terrified...but fine." The moment she spots him, I'm forgotten. "Thank God you're here!"

Elizabeth walks right into his arm and starts crying. My mother is crying. He's whispering some nonsense in her ear. And she holds onto him, her face pressed against his naked chest, her bare arms wrapped around him.

Watching her is more than a little awkward. I've been relegated to the background. But that doesn't stop me from worrying about her.

"Did you see anyone?" I ask her. "Did someone break in?"

"No. The door was latched."

"Was there gas? Did you really smell it?" Kyle asks.

"I think so, but I'm not sure."

"Did you see anyone in the hallway?"

"No one was outside."

"Wouldn't the other guests smell it if it was coming from the hall?" I ask.

"How do I know? I woke up and it was there."

Kyle is looking at me over her head with raised eyebrows. He doesn't believe it either. This is a five-star hotel with security personnel that are on high alert, as it's been just days since a room burglary. And the likelihood of a gas attack only in her room? A *gas* attack? Impossible. I wonder how many more drinks Elizabeth had after I helped her back to her room. And then there's the sleeping pill that I know she takes every night when she travels. I decide it probably wouldn't be wise to bring up any of those things.

He tries to extricate himself, but she's not letting him. Kyle is dressed only in his boxers. She's in a thin nightgown. Every time I see her like this, I get impressed all over again how good she looks for her age.

Remembering that I'm only wearing a T-shirt and underwear, I grab the hotel robe off the end of my bed and stuff my arms into the sleeves.

"There was a tube," she tells Kyle. "Someone fed it under my door."

"What, a pipe bomb sort of thing?"

"No. No. A plastic tube. The gas came through it."

"How do you feel now? Are you okay?" he asks, obviously trying to calm her down.

"I can breathe. But I'm scared. I'm definitely *not* okay!"

Kyle's eyes meet mine over her head again. His expression is apologetic, and I shrug. In all the years I've watched men go in and out of Elizabeth's life, I know she's never excluded anyone based on his age, looks, wealth, or nationality. Before Jax, Elizabeth was an equal opportunity serial dater. Maybe if we were still together, I'd be pissed off at her for clinging to Kyle, but I no longer have any right to be.

"Are you sure something *did* happen?" I say, loud enough to get her attention. "You said you had a nightmare."

She finally pulls away from Kyle and glares at me, saying nothing.

"Did you call the front desk?" I get the second robe out of the closet and hand it to her.

"No, I came here."

I want to crawl back into my bed and pretend none of this happened, but Elizabeth isn't going anywhere.

"How about if you and I go back to your room and check things out?"

She turns to Kyle. "Would *you* come with me?"

We are facing a minor dilemma. Kyle's clothes are in the next room, and right now there's no way we want to explain our breakup to Elizabeth. He sends me a pleading look.

"No, I'll go with you," I pick up my room key, my phone, and the second key I have for Elizabeth's room.

"Wouldn't it be safer if you came?" she asks him again.

"You're in good hands," he assures her. "Christina is quite capable. I think the two of you can handle just about anything. But we can always call security if you want."

"I don't think we'll need it," I tell him, steering Elizabeth ahead of me into the hall. He mouths *thank you* before heading for his own room.

The hallway outside my room is deserted. I'm amazed, considering the din. The swish of the elevator around the corner is the only noise. She takes my arm, and I motion to our bare feet and matching robes.

"Twins," I say, trying to distract her.

"Do you really think I dreamed all of it?"

"You had a few drinks last night."

"No more than usual," she says defensively. "And I can hold my liquor."

The elevator door opens as soon as I press the button. We get off on her floor, and I sniff the air in the hallway, looking for any sign that what Elizabeth said might be true.

Near her door, there is a piece of clear plastic tubing about two inches long. I show it to her. "Is this what you saw?"

"I told you I didn't dream it." She takes it out of my hand and studies it.

"Mom, this could be from anything." I motion to the closed doors up and down the hall. "Remember when we were going in to dinner, all the excitement when that Turkish pop star cruised through the lobby? She and her entourage—including her roadies—are staying here. This could have come from a smoke machine. Musicians use them at concerts and clubs and parties. Somebody dropped this."

A room door closes somewhere on this floor, and Elizabeth jumps. She immediately hands me the tube and motions that she wants to go in. I unlock the door.

There are no strange smells inside, either, only the lingering scent of Elizabeth's perfume. She switches on the light and waits by the door. "Check everything."

I walk through, opening closet doors and going into the bathroom. Nothing is out of place. Her daytime and nighttime skin regimens are lined up on a shelf. Back in the bedroom, the covers on the bed are pushed back, and her bathrobe is draped over the back of a chair. Her purse is sitting on the desk. I already know that she received the replacement for her credit card yesterday. Liras and loose change are piled next to the purse. There's also a bottle of Jack Daniels and an empty tumbler beside it.

To try and make light of the situation, I make a big show of checking everywhere, even the dresser drawers. "Everything looks good. No murderous clowns hiding under the bed or in the shower."

She doesn't look amused. "Open the windows."

Her tone is as irritated as it is condescending. I'm sure she would have been in a much better mood if Kyle had come back here with her, but I don't want to start an argument this early in the morning. I do as she says. As I open the windows, the sight of Hagia Sophia makes me pause. I breathe in the smells of dawn and stare at the golden spotlights illuminating the ancient walls and minarets.

I hear Elizabeth moving around the room behind me. As she ducks into the closet, checking the room safe, I think about this imagined gas attack, the declassified files I've seen, and what Kyle told me in the business center yesterday. Even knowing what I know, it's still difficult for me to believe Elizabeth's name is on some hit list. I wonder if she already knows about it. But how could she? She's technologically literate, but hardly an expert.

The more I've been thinking about it, the less doubt I have that Jax planned this trip to Istanbul for a reason, and that it had nothing to do with business. He wanted to bring Elizabeth back to where she'd be faced with her past and the guilt she'd tried to bury. He was bringing her back to the scene of her crime, more or less. The Kurds consider areas in eastern Turkey to be part of Kurdistan.

Her nightmare tonight about gas being pumped into her room has to be a subconscious reminder of the wrongs she's perpetrated in her life. The ghosts of the innocent dead, murdered with chemical weapons and nerve gas, are haunting her.

"Are you all set?" I ask, turning away from the window. "Can I go back to bed?"

She's sitting on a chair now, her feet up on an ottoman, watching me.

"What's going on between you and Kyle? Why two rooms? Why separate beds?"

Of course, she would have noticed it. Elizabeth sees everything. None of Kyle's clothes were lying around in my room. Only one side of the bed was slept in.

"I'm not discussing my private life with you." I try to keep my tone clear of any hostility.

"Christina, I'm your mother."

You are not.

"You can talk to me," she continues. She's obviously gotten over her scare. "I've been around the block a few more times than you."

"Good night." I start for the door.

"I'm telling you. This is not the time to be stupid." Her tone is sharp, and it pisses me off. "Kyle is *not* a guy that you walk away from. It doesn't matter what he says. Do what you have to do. Hold on to him."

Against my better judgment, I pause at the door and look back at her. "Spoken by the woman who has walked away from every relationship in her life."

"Jax died."

"The one exception. He saved you the trouble of divorcing him after the sale of Externus."

"Don't fool yourself. He wanted the same thing. He couldn't wait until I wasn't looking over his shoulder." She points a finger at me. "But don't confuse him with what you've got. Jax was nothing. He was nowhere near the man Kyle is. If those tabloids weren't stuck with picking celebrities, he could be crowned Sexiest Man Alive."

It makes me want to throw up when she says stuff like that. She's done it before, more times than I care to remember. The image of

Elizabeth tonight, wrapping herself around Kyle's half-naked body, makes a bitter taste rise into my throat.

"The three of us are still going to be here for a few more days," she continues. "I'll talk to him. I'll fix it for you."

"There's nothing that needs fixing."

"I think there is. I know him. I know how to talk to him. And I know how you are. I can convince him to give you another chance."

My anger is bubbling beneath the surface, hot and molten, and I'm about to explode. But in advance of the impending blast, a sickening clarity forms.

"I'm done with Kyle," I tell her, "My relationship with him is over. But clearly you're not."

"What do you mean, over?"

"I mean we're done."

She's looking at me, and the wheels are spinning behind her blue eyes.

I might as well say it. "I just realized something. You're ready to jump right in, aren't you? Well, go ahead. Be my guest. Make your move."

"You think I won't, if I want to?"

"Go ahead."

"Maybe I already..."

She stops whatever she's about to say, but she's already said too much. Silence hangs in the air.

"Don't be ridiculous." She pulls the belt of her robe tighter. She can't look at me directly. "Kyle is yours. And all I care about is you. Your future. Your—"

"Stop."

I open the door and step out. I've always suspected it. The way she'd look at him or let her touch linger on his shoulder or his waist. I guessed at what Elizabeth just confirmed. Still, I wonder when it happened.

Their age difference wouldn't matter to either of them. Kyle was always a player before we got together, and I've seen quite a few of the women who had paraded through his life. He had his choice of all types and all ages. I suppose that only added to why I never felt secure in our relationship. And maybe, deep down, that was my excuse for becoming pregnant, knowing we'd have to end it after. What we had could never be permanent.

As I wait for the elevator, I feel lighter. My head is clearer. Little by little, the truth about my world is revealing itself.

The adjoining door to Kyle's room is open when I get back. He's in bed, but I can't tell if he's sleeping. I close and latch the door before climbing into my own bed.

Lying there in the dark, I think of Tiam. First thing in the morning, I have to call her. We'll figure something out. Between the two of us, we'll make her meeting with Elizabeth happen.

28

ELIZABETH

ELIZABETH HAD EXPECTED they'd have to wait at the police station, but this was beyond the pale...even by Turkish standards. They'd told her at the hotel that the written report of the burglary would be ready when she got there at nine o'clock. But it was noon by the time a clerk handed her a piece of paper. At least it was signed and stamped. It was good enough for her to take to the consulate.

Elizabeth was grateful for Kyle's calm manner and his polite interaction with the paper shufflers. She knew it was because of him that she hadn't been given even more of a runaround. They were right on the cusp of the midday dinner hour, and they could have easily told her to come back the next day. That's the way bureaucracy worked.

"Do you want to stop for lunch?" she asked Kyle as they left the police station.

"You have an appointment at the consulate that you don't want to miss," he reminded her.

She checked the time. He was right. They only had an hour to get there.

Their taxi crawled through the heavy traffic. Every light along the way went against them. People jammed the sidewalks and rushed into the crosswalks.

She looked at the faces. Ever since she'd arrived in Istanbul, she hadn't been herself. The burglary had thrown her. Facing the cab driver's interrogation made it worse. The child's face she'd seen in the alleyway in the Kurdish neighborhood refused to go away. Her words continued to chip away at her conscience. Elizabeth was losing control.

And then last night, she'd awakened, thinking that her room was filled with poison gas. She needed to pull herself together. Running out of her room screaming in her nightgown was outrageous. No one was trying to murder her in her sleep. It was just a relief that she didn't call the front desk and make a complete fool of herself.

It was this city, this country. Memories from thirty years ago were nagging at her. She thought she had been done with them, buried them deep, never allowing them to scratch the surface. And the man she'd seen yesterday—Christina's driver to the airport—couldn't have been who she thought he was. He was simply another product of her overloaded brain.

As they approached an intersection, she saw a woman carrying a screaming baby across the street, and an image flashed through her mind of another child and another time...

Elizabeth tried to restrain a toddler in her seat on a flight leaving the Istanbul airport. Red in the face, the little girl screamed and contorted her body to fight her.

"Maman. Maman."

"I'm right here, Christina. I'm only putting the belt on while we take off."

The little girl shook her dark curls, kicking the seat in front of her. "Maman."

"Flying can be so difficult when they're that age." An Englishwoman sitting across the aisle leaned over to put her two cents in. "She's a pretty little one. Your daughter?"

"Yes, my daughter," Elizabeth responded.

"Annem değil." The child shook her head, still screaming. "Anneeeee!"

"She speaks Turkish already?"

"Her nanny."

The flight attendant arrived with a carton of milk and opened it for them. "Maybe this will help, ma'am."

The child kicked hard at the milk and the hand holding it. "Maman."

The carton splashed out onto the floor, and the attendant jumped back.

"That is bad, Christina. You're a very bad girl."

Large tears rolled down the round cheeks, and the hazel eyes looked up into Elizabeth's face. "Tiam."

"Who is Tiam?" the Englishwoman asked.

"The nanny's daughter. Christina misses her little friend."

Elizabeth came back to the present and turned abruptly to Kyle, sweat trickling down her spine. "I don't want to stay in Istanbul after Friday."

His eyes shifted from whatever he was reading on his phone. "The decision about a buyer has to be finalized before you go."

"Why can't we do that right after they submit their bids? Why wait until Monday?"

"The potential buyer gets a period of forty-eight hours to retract their offer. That's why you can't give them a decision until we know they can't back out of it."

"I don't have to stay for it. You can represent me."

"Neither Christina nor I have the power of attorney. And if you walk away prematurely, it could make the buyers nervous." He patted her hand. "Today is Thursday. Be patient. We're almost there."

Elizabeth grabbed his hand before he could withdraw it. It was large and cool and strong, exactly what she needed. "Tell me you two are staying together."

His eyes were tired when they met hers. "I don't want to have this discussion with you."

"Why not?" she asked. "I know Christina isn't the easiest person to live with. And God knows, you could do better than her. But I want you to be—"

"Stop."

"There's nothing worse than a jealous woman. She must have said something nasty to you when you got in. Whatever it was—"

"I said stop." He pulled his hand free. "I know what you're doing, Elizabeth."

"What am I doing?"

"You put her down, and then I get angry and defend her. You want me to think she needs me in her life just to stand up to you. As if that will keep us together."

Elizabeth didn't know why the tactic shouldn't work. He seemed driven to protect her.

"Christina doesn't need me. Give her a little credit."

"Okay, maybe she doesn't need you." She leaned toward him and lowered her voice. "But we're family, for all intents and purposes."

"No, we're not."

"It's in your best interest that we are, though. You told me yourself a conservative estimate of what I'll be walking away with is fifty mil after the sale."

Four years ago, she'd arranged for loans and investors to come up with nine million dollars for Externus. After the sale on Monday, there would be taxes that had to be paid, the half-million each she'd promised to Christina and Kyle, and the loans she had to pay back. After all of it, she was still walking away with a bundle. But she wondered how long she could travel and live a life of luxury before she got tired of it. Eventually, she'd want to settle down.

"I need you in my life," she said, latching onto Kyle's hand again. "I want you to think of any investment you want to make. Tell me anything that you want to do, and I'll fund it. You supply the dream, and I'll make it happen."

He pried his fingers out of her grip once again and looked into her eyes.

"Thank you, but I'm not interested. Once we're done with Externus, I'm moving to Japan. The sale means the end of line for you and me."

29

CHRISTINA

I SIT up in bed at the sound of the housekeeper's knock, and I'm shocked to find out that it's already quarter past ten. I go to the door and open it a little.

"I need an hour. Okay?"

"Yes, ma'am." The young woman nods politely and pushes her cart down the hallway.

I can't remember the last time I slept this late, but Elizabeth's 4:00 a.m. crisis might have had something to do with throwing off my schedule. Before jumping in the shower, I check my phone for any calls or messages. There are two texts from Kyle.

on the way to police station with your mother now. to consulate next. then back to hotel

The message was sent at eight thirty this morning. The second one has the time for our dinner reservation at the hotel restaurant. He's made it for three people.

Before changing it to four, I decide I should send Tiam a text.

Hey soul sister. Love you. Dinner tonight?

When I come out of the shower, the light on the hotel phone is flashing, indicating a message. Tying my hair up in a towel, I cross the room and pick up the handset.

"Hi, Elizabeth. Surprised to hear from you. I'm home this morning. Call me."

The voice belongs to an older woman whom I suspect is Patricia Nicholls. I'm surprised at getting the message. But when I think about it, I realize that she must have asked for "Ms. Hall," and the hotel operator directed the call to my room rather than my mother's.

The decision whether to return the call or wait for Elizabeth takes about two seconds. I call Patricia's number. A quiet, noncommittal voice answers the phone in Turkish, and I immediately introduce myself.

"Hello, Ms. Nicholls? This is Christina Hall. I'm so excited that you returned my mother's call."

There's a pause on the line before she responds. "Elizabeth's daughter? Christina?"

"Yes. I'm in Istanbul with her."

"Really? How nice. What are you two doing here?"

"Touristy stuff. Sightseeing." I try to keep my tone light and decide to say nothing of the company business.

"Is Elizabeth there with you? Put her on the phone."

"She's getting a massage at the spa right now. But she told me if you called, I should see if you'd like to get together while we're in Istanbul. The three of us could have lunch, maybe."

I've become such a good liar.

"Today?"

"We're only here through the weekend."

"I see." She pauses before continuing. "Tell me how Elizabeth is doing. I haven't seen or heard from her in years. I didn't even know she had my contact information."

"It's easy to find anyone online these days."

"Of course, I didn't think of that."

"She lost her husband, you know," I say in the soft voice of a grieving daughter. "Two months ago. It was very unexpected."

"Oh, I'm sorry. I didn't know she was married."

I offer pieces of the truth about Jax and how he died, and our conversation takes on a more casual tone. She has a lot of questions about Elizabeth and what she's been doing. I'm truthful in answering them, for the most part. And then I tell her about my own tragedy regarding Autumn.

Oddly enough, that news is the absolute icebreaker. She'd love to meet with us today.

"Can you come to my place?"

"I'm sure we can manage it."

She gives me the address, and I compare it to what I already have in my contacts. It's the same. I say goodbye, telling her Elizabeth will be thrilled to see her.

Patricia lives in Beyoğlu, a different neighborhood from where we are. To get there, I'll need to take a cab or hire a driver.

As far as showing up alone at her house, that's all neatly arranged in my mind too. I'll tell her the truth when I arrive, that Elizabeth had to go to the police station and the consulate to replace her lost passport.

This meeting is only an introduction, a first chance for the two of us to get to know each other.

I dress, throw on my makeup, and grab my bag. At the front desk I ask about a car service that can take me to the address, wait for me, and then bring me back. The receptionist suggests the same company I used to go to the airport to pick Kyle up. I decline and ask for another.

"Limousine Services is another one that we use." She rattles off the information. It's a bit more expensive than the standard driver services. Am I willing to pay the higher price to engage them?

Of course I'll pay the higher price to engage them.

Twenty minutes later, a white Mercedes town car pulls up to the door. The doorman checks the credentials of the driver. I do too. She's a woman in her forties. Quiet, polite, none of the talkativeness of our driver two nights ago. I give her the address and sit in the back seat.

The leather seats give off the smell of luxury. The smoked glass windows cut me off from the real life that pulses through the streets outside.

I think about Patricia Nicholls and our conversation. A switch was flipped when I mentioned Autumn. The loss of a baby is tragic, and that obviously connected with her. She didn't say something heartless like *You're young, There'll be another,* or *God works in mysterious ways.*

I fight down the sudden ache rising in my chest. Since the first day at the hotel, when I imagined Autumn crying in the crib, I've kept myself busy so I'd have little time to think about my daughter. But she's always there on the edges of my thoughts, reminding me and helping me to do what I must. Even today, when I was speaking to Patricia Nicholls, Autumn was there.

She's gone from this life, but still she gave me permission to use her name to help Tiam...another lost child.

After Tiam had given me Patricia's name, it took only a quick online search to learn Elizabeth's former colleague is eighty-two. But our brief conversation assured me that she's extremely sharp. I consider calling Zari and asking her what she can tell me about Patricia, but I decide against it. Zari still doesn't know I'm in Istanbul.

The car crosses a broad bridge over the Golden Horn. Tracks for the trams run down the center of the roadway. On the outside of wide sidewalks, the railings are lined with fishermen.

I've been here before with Tiam. I've seen these hardworking people. Day and night, in every season, they stand here trying to catch enough for their next meal. These fish are needed to feed their families. I wonder how many of them are immigrants. I focus on the women fishing alongside the men. I think of my mother.

Zari was an immigrant, and there is so much that I am curious about. I can't wait to spend more time with her and learn more about her history, my history.

The Galata Tower rises in the distance. Tiam told me it was once the tallest building in Istanbul. When it was built, it anchored one end of a massive sea chain that the Turkish rulers used to close off the entrance to the Golden Horn. Even then, governments were all about control, raising the walls, keeping out the very people whose lands they'd destroyed.

As we come off the bridge, my driver immediately cuts off the main road, and we make our way through busy neighborhoods. These twisting roads and alleys are jammed with refugees from Syria, Lebanon, Palestine, Iraq, and Iran. They're on the streets—Kurds and

Arabs and Iranians, as well as Uyghur Turks—selling whatever goods they can carry on their backs or push on their handcarts. The alleyways, crowded and dirty, remind me of sepia-tone photographs of immigrants in New York City. Those people, desperate people searching for a better life, had arrived at Ellis Island with a lifetime of belongings jammed into one suitcase.

As we drive through the streets with tenements rising on both sides, I see the dogs and the cats and the ragged children with hungry looks on their faces. They stare at this white symbol of luxury passing by them.

I feel ill. I'm embarrassed about what I represent. I'm ashamed of the life I was raised in, thanks to Elizabeth. I recall what she said to me when I confronted her with the crimes she'd committed.

Have you gone hungry for a single day in your life?

Many of these people are the victims of endless wars and upheaval. In wave after wave, they've been driven from their homes by governments motivated by greed and the insatiable thirst for power and influence. They are the lost and the dispossessed, trying to scratch out a place to live.

When the city thins out a little, I check my phone for any messages from Tiam. Still nothing has come back. I send her another text.

Call me Sherlock. Going to see Patricia.

I worry that there's something wrong. She's usually very quick with her replies, especially when we're in the same time zone. I consider calling her, but the map on my phone says we are getting close to Patricia's address.

I glance out the window, not surprised at all by the change. No garbage on the streets. No laundry hanging out to dry in the alleyways. The very picture of gentrification. Of course this would be where an expat would live. Here, between well-kept apartment buildings, I see old houses surrounded by gardens and high walls with gates. We slowly work our way past a large park with manicured green grass and flowers between brick walkways. The only dogs allowed in this neighborhood are on leashes. The traffic is still heavy, but there are fewer people on the streets.

We turn up a narrow side street that will take us to Patricia's home.

I glance at my phone to see if there's anything from Tiam. Still nothing. Worry has planted a knot in the pit of my stomach. I recall how washed-out she looked after finishing the treatment yesterday.

A car comes out of nowhere, cutting us off. My driver slams on the brakes and hits her horn.

It all happens so fast. Two smashes explode around me in rapid succession—my window, and then the driver's. Pebbles of glass shower me. She's screaming in the front seat as doors are yanked open.

I try to fight off the hands reaching in to grab me. But before I know it, I'm being dragged bodily from the car.

PART IX

O how long shall we, like children, in the earthly sphere
Fill our lap with dust and stones and sherds?
Let us give up the earth and fly heavenwards,
Let us flee from childhood to the banquet of men.
Behold how the earthly frame has entrapped you!
Rend the sack and raise your head clear.
—Rumi

30

TIAM

AN HOUR after my mother leaves for work, I go down the stairs to the street. Normally, I take a bus and the tram. Today, however, I call for a cab. When I get in, I ask the driver to take me to the hospital.

My breathing has been getting worse day by day, but I've been trying to pretend nothing is out of the ordinary. Ordinary for me, at any rate. It's not unusual for the slightest thing to set me off at any time. The change of seasons. Allergies. A temporary worsening of the city's air quality. Sometimes there's no reason at all. Still, I've been ignoring my situation all week. I can't do that any longer. The sticky mucus is building up, and yesterday's treatment wasn't effective in clearing my lungs. The doctors at the clinic confirmed it. I was asked to come back today, although I made sure Christina didn't know anything about it.

After all these years, I've come to understand my body and my disease. I know why I struggle to breathe and how to handle the pain in my stomach. I know the signs. And I know the consequences if I don't react right away. The clinic can't help me. My condition is much more serious.

I'm so tired. So worn out.

The emergency room people surround me as soon as I walk in, for I'm a familiar face. This is the same hospital that Zari brought me to thirty years ago. It's one of the best pulmonary care facilities in the entire city. They already have my medical records. They know that the bronchodilators and the medications are part of my daily routine, and I don't come to them unless it's critical.

An IV gets inserted into my arm, and they start the intravenous antibiotics and the steroid shots. Next come the breathing tests, before they put me in the vest. Then I wait for the lung specialist to come.

Even though I know the procedures and understand their value, I'm exhausted and frustrated. There's nothing I can plan for. My life isn't my own. My body is tired. Sometimes I just want to give up. How easy it would be to curl into a ball and die. I wish the choice was mine, and that I were brave enough to do it right now and be done with it.

A text from Christina lights up my phone.

Hey soul sister. Love you. Dinner tonight?

Her message immediately dispels the doomsday cloud surrounding me. I look at the sun shining outside the windows of the hospital and blink back my tears. I can't bring myself to answer her message and tell her where I am. Maybe things aren't as bad as they seem. I make a pact with myself that if the doctors can somehow work their magic and I walk out of here today, I'm showing up for that dinner.

The hope of flaunting my health and my accomplishments at Elizabeth is fading. The truth has to come out—for my sake and for Christina. Even for Zari. But our meeting doesn't have to be a showdown. It only needs to be the final stitching of a wound that has been bleeding far too long.

The doctor comes in, with another on his heels. They take turns listening to my lungs. They speak to me calmly and ask the standard questions. But I see how they both avoid looking into my eyes. It doesn't matter. I don't require a committee report to tell me how badly I'm doing. Right now, I'm like one of those fish on the Galata Bridge sidewalk, flopping around, unable to breathe. I don't need someone to confirm it.

When I ask them about the next step, they become evasive,

looking at their clipboards and the monitors and anywhere but at me. Then, with a vague comment about needing to go and consult and look at test results, they slip out the door. The vest continues to thump and pummel my chest. It takes great effort not to tear it right off my body.

Another text comes from Christina. *Call me Sherlock. Going to see Patricia.*

I wish I were strong enough to pick up the phone and thank her for everything she's doing for me. I consider texting her, just a few words. But as I'm trying to decide, my mother sails through the doorway, and I immediately put the phone down.

"Why didn't you call me?"

Her eyes are on the equipment and the IV attached to my arm. She is pale and already tearing up.

"I looked in your room before I left this morning. I thought you were sleeping."

I don't dare tell her that I stayed still intentionally when she checked on me. I didn't want her to be worried.

I switch off the power to the vest for a moment. "How did you find out I'm here?"

"Emine called me."

I should have known. We might not be related by blood, but Emine is the best auntie anyone could wish for. And when it comes to my health, she has everyone in this hospital on high alert.

There's not much clearing in my chest. Every breath is a painful struggle. The mucus is too thick. Zari switches on the vest again. She stands close to me, and I think of all the times when she'd be clapping me on my back, encouraging me to cough. Or picking me up and running outside to get me to the hospital.

One time, she closed the door of the taxi on her fingers in her rush, but she didn't say anything about it. That night, standing at my bedside after I was admitted, Emine noticed her friend's swollen hand, though she had tried to hide it. Three broken fingers. Not a word or a whimper.

"I spoke to the nurse outside. She says they're going to admit you."

I shut off the machine again. "The doctors are coming back. They're still consulting."

"They're too afraid to give you the news themselves."

I knew this was going to happen, but still I blink back my tears.

Zari kisses my forehead. She caresses my face. She knows me so well. "You can do this, my love. They'll help you breathe. They always do. You'll be out before you know it."

But it could be too late. Today is Thursday. Christina has done everything I asked her to do. She's hidden the truth from Elizabeth and given me plenty of chances to make myself known. But I was looking for a momentous scene filled with flaring emotions. A movie-ending kind of meeting. Maybe I've read too many books, watched too many films. But I didn't take my chance when I had it. I didn't walk up to Elizabeth and say, *Here I am. Your daughter. Alive.*

There's more than mucus clogging my chest. The words I need to say to her are suffocating me.

It took Elizabeth thirty years to return to Istanbul. What are the chances of her returning in my lifetime? My future is not measured in years.

A nurse comes in and tells me they'll be moving me. But I'm not going into a regular hospital room; they're taking me to ICU. The little hope I have left drains out of me. Tears fall in droplets onto the vest. My breathing becomes ragged, I'm starved for air. My mother turns the machine back on.

"Don't give up, little one. Please don't. Not now." Zari is right there, kissing me. She is the mother of all mothers, the lioness beside me protecting her cub.

I cling to her arm. She doesn't know what Christina and I had planned for this week. She doesn't even know that her real daughter is in Istanbul.

I'll never forget their first meeting this past April, and when the time came for Christina to go back to America. Maman was afraid that she'd lost her child forever. Afraid she'd never see her again.

For what felt like a lifetime, she'd lived with only the slimmest hope that someday her lost daughter would come back to her. Back into her life. Into our life. And now that she'd seen Christina, held her, cried with her, Zari feared that she'd be lost to us again. And then in June, when she visited us again, it was the same when the time came for parting. Zari grieved both times Christina left.

A mother's love. I've felt it my whole life. I could never be jealous of the affection between those two. I've never thought for an instant that Zari loved her more than she loved me. Her heart has more than enough room for the two of us.

I turn off the machine and take out the mouthpiece again. "Christina is in Istanbul."

Zari brightens immediately. "Where is she staying? Will she come and see us? Have you seen her?"

"I saw her yesterday."

The glow in my mother's face immediately dims. "How did she seem to you? The baby."

"She's still very sad." I shouldn't have said the words.

Zari taps her chest, signifying her grief. She is still mourning the loss of her grandchild.

My breaths are getting heavier, and nothing is clearing. I'm not coughing and expelling the mucus as I should. I scratch at my throat, wishing I could tear it open. Each word I speak steals air. I have to be precise.

"Call Christina. I need her here."

I dial the number and hand her my cell phone. The mouthpiece is back on. The phone rings and rings and goes to voicemail. She must be with Patricia Nicholls right now.

"Where is she staying?" Zari asks. "I can leave a message for her at her hotel."

With each tick of the clock, my body is collapsing around me. My heart is beating too fast, my thoughts are becoming a jumble. I feel like I'm racing toward a cliff edge. But before I go over, there's so much I need to do.

I free my mouth from the device. "Elizabeth is with her."

I don't know what kind of reaction I was expecting, but my mother's hand immediately wraps around my wrist. I realize that she's holding on to me...and not just in a physical sense. I see it in her eyes.

She's keeping me close. This connection is meant to be a lifeline. It's the hope and love that she feels I need right now.

She's right.

"Get her for me?" I show her a text from Christina that has the hotel where they're staying and Elizabeth's new room number. "Please. Bring the woman here who gave birth to me...the woman who abandoned me."

31

CHRISTINA

THE WINDOW SHATTERS, spraying me with shards of glass, and the car door is yanked open. My driver is screaming, and strangers are invading the confined space.

As a man grabs for me, I try to fight him off. His hands clamp onto my wrists like steel bands, and I throw myself backward, trying to wrench free of his grip. I kick at him as fiercely as I can, catching him in the hip. It's not enough, and he drags me out into the lane.

Two cars sandwich ours between them, one in front and another in back. The narrow side street that connects the larger roads is lined with high walls and back gates and garage doors. No pedestrians. There is no one to call for. No one who can help. That doesn't stop me, and I scream at the top of my lungs.

Another man comes to help him, and I'm lifted like a writhing, twisting sack of potatoes. All my fighting and squirming comes to nothing as they shove me face down in the back seat of the car in front. One of them wrenches my hands behind me and zip ties are wrapped tight around my wrists and ankles. They gag me with a rag and jam a burlap bag over my head.

No gunshots were fired, but I'm worried about my driver. I heard her screaming too, and I don't know if they're putting her in the other car or leaving her there.

It's hard to breathe, and my heart is beating so hard that I think it will rip a hole in my chest any second. They stuff me down on the floor of the back seat and cover me with something that feels as heavy as a rug.

In the midst of my panic, what Kyle told me yesterday comes to me. The kill list with Elizabeth's name on it. This is why I'm being kidnapped.

Moments later, car doors slam, and we're speeding through the streets. I have no idea where they're taking me. The only sound I hear is the electronic techno music they've cranked up loud enough to drown out any muffled cries for help. The beat matches my pounding heart, which is about to explode with fear. I don't know what is going to happen to me, but my brain is going haywire with imaginings that are nasty and final.

A memory of my accident from two months ago cuts into my thoughts. I recall two things happening while I was in the middle of it —the feeling of extreme vulnerability, and the sensation that everything was inevitable. I couldn't stop time or the cars that were about to hit me, no matter what I did. It's the same feeling now. It must be what a rabbit experiences the moment before the coyote's jaws clamp down. There's nothing I can do to stop this. My fate is no longer in my hands.

I try to listen to the few words that I can hear over the music.

"*Gidelim. Sol.*"

"*Kızdı.*"

I recognize the last word. It means 'angry'. Someone is angry.

"*Sonraki sokak.*"

Sokak means 'street'.

We drive and drive until it feels like I've been in this car for an eternity. I don't know if I'm still in Istanbul. I could already be outside the city. I could be halfway to hell.

Suddenly, the car jerks to a stop and doors open. The thing that covers me is thrown back, and I'm dragged out and hauled like dead weight into a building. They yank me along a passageway that smells damp and moldy. We go into what feels like a larger room. A heavy door squeaks open. One of them pulls the bag off my head, shoves me in, and slams the door shut.

I lie there on the floor, listening to them talking as they move away. Then another distant door closes. A chair scrapes in the room outside my door. Then all the noise dies.

My heart struggles to find a rhythm. My eyes are slowly getting accustomed to the light. My entire body is trembling. I wonder if I'm in shock. Another memory flashes through my mind. Autumn's peaceful face. She looks to be sleeping. But I know she's dead.

Am I dead too? I blink back the tears clouding my vision and focus on my surroundings. I'm alive...for the time being.

The room is small. Ancient rusted pipes come out of one wall, run the length of the dark ceiling, and disappear into the opposite wall. A dim bulb hangs at the end of a thin wire in a corner. It's the only source of light in the room. There are no windows. No furniture. The walls are bare, and layers of paint are flaking off the wall.

The zip ties on my wrists are so tight that my fingers have gone numb. One of my legs is cramping. The smell of mold is just part of a whole bouquet of rotten odors. I landed on a filthy rug that smells of urine and vomit and God knows what else. It's stained with dark spots. I don't want to think what might have caused them.

I squirm around until I'm able to push myself into a sitting position. A cold, wet droplet hits me on my forehead and runs into my eye.

I blink a few times in panic and inch backward until I'm against the cold wall. I count my breaths and try to calm the wild beating of my heart.

I think back to the emails in Jax's files and try to recall the contents. I should have paid more attention to Kyle's warning of what was on the dark web. I should have been smarter, more vigilant.

Dying has never frightened me. Even during my accident, I only worried about the baby. But maybe it's the idea of a violent death that terrifies me now. I don't believe I'll ever walk out of this room again. And there's no doubt in my mind that my abduction is directly tied to the hit list containing Elizabeth's name.

They have me, and I have a feeling I'm the worm wriggling on the barbed hook. They expect that she'll take the bait. And then, they'll reel their trophy in.

Another drop of water falls from the pipe onto the rug.

A snippet of a different memory comes back, the same one that has played and replayed in my brain for years. *I'm sure I'd be devastated if something tragic happened to Christina. But I'd recover.*

Those words of Elizabeth's are more relevant now than ever.

But I'd recover.

Huddled against that wall, I wonder what she'll do when they contact her. And I'm certain they will. Would she try to negotiate for my release? Would she put her own life in danger? Would she die for me?

Elizabeth is the same person who left behind a sick child and took another mother's healthy one in its place. The thought doesn't fill me with optimism.

There's a pattern in the way she's always lived her life. Her existence is safe and privileged. She treats life like some produce she's brought home a week ago from the grocery store. This peach has a spot. This apple is bruised. This banana is already turning brown. I'll take them back and get replacements. She gave birth to a baby who turned out to be sick, but she knew exactly how she wanted to handle it. And she recovered. She'll recover after me too.

Once the kidnappers reach out to her, my guess is that she'll turn the problem over to Kyle.

And what will he do? Kyle who already has plans of moving on to a new job and a new life in Japan. My mind is clear enough to recognize that I've already burned the bridge in our relationship and decimated whatever soft spot he might have once had for me. There is no going back on that one. He has no reason to stick out his neck. He'll contact the Istanbul Police and the US Consulate, and they'll all have a nice, sparsely attended memorial service for me back in California. I'm pretty sure they'll never recover my remains from the Bosphorus or wherever it is they dispose of bodies here.

Zari and Tiam are the only ones who will truly miss me. The only ones who will mourn my loss. Their faces linger in my mind. My family.

How pathetic and maddening that Elizabeth should get away with robbing us of the lives we were intended to live thirty years ago, and now she'll do it again.

Another drop of water falls, spattering and then blending irrevocably into the dark stains on the soiled rug.

32

ELIZABETH

ELIZABETH ARRIVED with Kyle at the consulate, certain their business here would go more smoothly than it had at the police station. She had an appointment, and they got there on time.

She started for the gate, and Kyle told her he was going in search of coffee. She could see a line of shops and restaurants across the street, within easy walking distance. He would meet her back here when she was done.

After passing through security, she was directed to follow a blue line on the floor through long windowless corridors that ended at a crowded waiting room. There, behind wire-reinforced glass, a sour-faced clerk took the forms and fees and pictures and told her to sit. As before, they gave her no special treatment. The attitudes never rose even to the level of cordial. It didn't matter that she'd worked for more than two decades for the government.

Every seat was filled, so Elizabeth stood with her back to a huge seal of the State Department plastered to a wall. As she watched the people jammed in the enclosed space with her, she felt completely detached from their lives.

Many struggled with the language once they reached a window. Others had difficulty understanding the forms they had been given to complete. Bits and pieces of conversations reached her.

"Do you have a pen I might borrow?" a woman with a German accent asked her.

Elizabeth hiked her purse higher on her arm and shook her head.

An old man leaning on a cane held out the form he'd been handed. "*Mesheh komakam koneed?*" he asked in Farsi. Can you help me?

She turned her back, pretending she didn't understand him.

Something about this situation rekindled thoughts of her childhood. Moving from one army housing unit to another, Elizabeth turned her back on the other kids. She didn't need them. There was no point having friends that she'd be leaving behind. The detachment process was too exhausting. She could stand on her own two feet.

Today, the people that she was being forced to wait with were dreadfully needy. Desperation hung like a yellow haze in the air. But Elizabeth was neither needy nor desperate.

When she was called back to a window, a limited-access passport was handed to her. She was told that she could use it when the time came to leave Istanbul.

Leaving through the gates past the armed security personnel, she was happy to find Kyle waiting for her. She wanted to go back to the hotel, wash the stench of the consulate off her, and have a drink.

She showed him the new ID. "Is this enough to verify my identity for the signing?"

"It should be."

He motioned for one of the waiting taxis and gave the name of their hotel as they climbed into the back seat.

It was amazing how much power a little slip of paper could bestow. Elizabeth already felt safer, more confident, more in control of her life. She could go where she wanted, escape unwanted company, and put the past behind her.

"What time is our dinner reservation?" she asked.

"Six."

"Plenty of time."

She dialed her daughter's number. The cell rang and rang.

"Plenty of time for what?"

"To get a manicure and pedicure at the hotel salon."

The call went through to her voicemail. Elizabeth didn't leave a message.

"I was going to ask Christina to join me." She looked over at Kyle. "I didn't buy a birthday gift for her. I thought the bonus would be enough."

She dropped the cell phone into her bag.

"She's *working* for that bonus," Kyle said. "A birthday gift should be separate."

"Look who's talking. What did *you* get her, other than a business trip to Istanbul?"

He didn't answer.

"I'm teasing." Elizabeth nudged his shoulder with hers. "Come on. Tell me."

"What I give Christina doesn't concern you."

She glanced at Kyle's face and his long lashes. He was all concentration as he typed away on his phone, pretending that Elizabeth wasn't even there. She tried to guess at what he'd bought Christina. Maybe they weren't done. One could only hope. If Elizabeth couldn't have him for herself again, she still wanted him in Christina's life.

From all appearances, though, her daughter had ruined it. She wondered if Christina had driven him away or if they both had a hand in messing it up.

"What's the deal while you two are in Istanbul? " she pressed. "You have adjoining rooms. Sex or no sex?"

She was trying to get a rise out of him, but an incoming call ruined the opportunity. Kyle spoke Japanese to whoever was on the other end. She didn't understand anything that was being said.

Elizabeth knew he was fluent in Mandarin, and increasingly competent in Japanese and Korean. That was part of what made him so valuable to Externus.

There didn't seem to be an end in sight to his conversation. She looked out the window at the office and apartment buildings and the storefront shops and restaurants. Food carts were on every corner, and people were bustling about on the sidewalks like a colony of ants. She was bored and impatient to get back to the hotel. She needed a drink more than she needed to get her nails done.

Kyle ended one call and immediately placed another. This time, he spoke English.

"Yes. The order was placed by Kyle Phillips."

She turned toward him, watching his profile. A five-o'clock shadow darkened his chin and jaw. He looked hip and rebellious.

Elizabeth recalled when a dreamy-eyed Christina broke the news to her. *Kyle thinks we should move in together. I know he's had plenty of relationships, but he's never lived with someone. And he wants me.*

At the time, the thing running through Elizabeth's mind was that it was unfair to other women for a man like Kyle to be tied to one person. But since then, she'd come to appreciate the pleasure of having him around.

"I'd like to change the delivery date from tomorrow to tonight," he said. "Yes, the same room number."

Her interest was piqued, and Elizabeth hung on every word.

"Lilac. Jasmine. White calla lilies."

He was reviewing what was going into the bouquet.

"You're certain the jasmine is fragrant, right? Yes. Make sure it is. Thank you. Yes, deliver it as soon as you can. That's great."

The sting of jealousy was sharp and unexpected, and Elizabeth felt it pierce the tough outer skin of her ego. No man had ever paid this much attention to any gift she'd received. Not even Jax. And that bastard was her husband.

"I know someone who likes jasmine."

Kyle looked up from his phone. For the first time since they'd gotten into the cab, his expression was gentler. "She needs some cheering up."

"She needs sex to cheer her up. A bouquet is a great start to getting her back into your bed. Well done, my boy."

She made a mistake of touching his arm, and he jerked it back as if he'd been burned.

"What's wrong with you?" he asked loud enough to draw the eyes of their driver in the rearview mirror. "There are times that I wonder if she's really related to you. I mean, what parent says things like that. How can you treat your daughter the way you do?"

Elizabeth turned away. His words stung. She treated Christina better than she deserved. She'd given her everything.

The cab rumbled across a bridge, but she didn't see the shimmering water below. Instead, in her mind's eye, she saw the red-faced child being placed in her arms.

From that very first moment, she was terrified of holding Christina too tightly or handling her the wrong way. The baby was weak. She cried all the time. She wouldn't take her milk. Ten days after coming home from the hospital, she had to take her back. Christina was hospitalized for a week that time. Three days later, they were back in the emergency room. Elizabeth's life became an ongoing nightmare of doctors, a crying baby, and sleepless nights.

And then there was Zari's daughter, Tiam. Six months old, round-faced, happy, and energetic. Curious and affectionate, she melted into Elizabeth's arms whenever she picked her up. Tiam was aware of everyone and everything around her. She was the very model of those healthy, beautiful babies on TV.

Life wasn't fair. The universe had played an ugly game on her. Elizabeth put up with it for as long as she could, and then she decided to change the rules. She had the money and the power to deal herself a new hand.

Kyle was correct. She wasn't her real mother. But she'd earned the right to be critical of Christina, to correct her, and to make sure she appreciated the life Elizabeth had given her. It didn't matter that Christina didn't know the truth, so long as she understood all the privileges she'd been given and was grateful to the person who continued to provide them.

Had Elizabeth said things she shouldn't have from time to time? Had she been too strict or too critical of her? Maybe, but that was what a young woman needed to succeed in this world. A woman had to be tough and smart and, at times, callous.

Elizabeth felt a headache coming on. She didn't want to think about the past.

She sat back and closed her eyes until the cab pulled in front of the hotel. She waited for the doorman before getting out. Kyle was already standing by the door. She hurried in ahead of him.

"How about we meet down here at five thirty?" he called after her. "We can have a drink before going to dinner."

Elizabeth waved a hand at him. Whatever. She'd be well fortified when she came down to face those two. And she'd come down when she was damn well ready.

When she reached her room, she kicked off her shoes, peeled off her jacket, and went to the desk. Yesterday she'd ordered a bottle of Jack Daniel's to be sent up. Pouring herself a healthy inch into the bottom of a tumbler, she breathed in the biting fragrance before letting it roll around on her tongue. The liquor warmed her throat as it went down.

"Better."

She splashed a little water on top and then espied the message light flashing on her hotel phone. Taking another sip, she pressed the button on the speakerphone.

"Hi, Elizabeth. Where are you? I've been here all morning."

She immediately recognized the old voice. She'd heard it yesterday on Patricia Nicholls's answering machine.

A second message followed.

"I'm afraid I can't sit around all day, waiting for you and your daughter to show up. Call me tomorrow. Maybe we can try again over the weekend."

"My daughter?"

Curious, Elizabeth looked up Patricia's number on her cell and called her. The phone rang until the message machine kicked in.

"Patricia, it's Elizabeth. What do you mean, waiting for us to show up? We're playing phone tag. And by the way, I meant what I said in my last message. She doesn't know. *No one knows.* So keep it zipped. Hear me?"

She ended the call and then tried Christina's cell phone. There was still no answer. She tried her hotel room next. Again, nothing.

She called the front desk. "Have you seen my daughter today?"

"Yes, ma'am. This morning. Ms. Hall hired a car service for the day and left the hotel."

"Did she say where she was going?"

"No, ma'am."

Elizabeth hung up. Useless. Sipping her drink, she considered whether Christina was bold enough to go see Patricia on her own.

The bad news was that the answer was yes.

Her pregnancy had done something to her. It had changed her. Maybe it had to do with hormones, but Christina was a different person from the one she used to be.

The good news was that something had changed her mind, and she hadn't gone through with paying that woman a visit.

33

ZARI

Zari never wanted to come back to this hotel. When she left it the last time, thirty years ago, she was rushing a sick child to the hospital. Today, she was hurrying to find Elizabeth and convince her to see that child, now grown, who lay in the ICU, struggling to stay alive.

She's mine. Mine. You can't take my daughter away from me. I won't let you.

The words she'd wanted to say all those years ago played back in her mind. She was mourning the loss of her Tiam. At the same time, she'd been ready to fight. Her daughter had been stolen away. Zari's vulnerability as an illegal immigrant had been used by Elizabeth to take a child that didn't belong to her.

Zari had no voice, no rights, no one to support her claim. But she'd been willing to fight—to physically fight—to do anything. She was a beast unleashed. But by the time she got here, Elizabeth was gone. She'd kidnapped Tiam. The anger Zari felt all those years ago was back again. The desperation she felt burned her. The sensation that a piece of her heart was torn away, cut out with brute force made her want to cry out in pain even now.

She paused on the steps, taking deep breaths, forcing herself to remember why she was here. What she had to do.

She'd come here because of Elizabeth's biological daughter, the beautiful soul she'd cherished every day since.

Zari remined herself that she was truly blessed, for now Tiam and Christina were both her children. One of them she raised. The other she lost and then found again.

Raw and painful emotions flared again in her chest as she recalled her conversation with Emine, before she'd left the hospital this afternoon.

"The level of oxygen in her blood is extremely low. Her legs and her stomach are swollen. What she's going through right now isn't another flare-up. The doctors think her organs are in danger of shutting down. That's why they're moving her into ICU."

"But she's been there before."

"This time is different."

Every time Tiam was admitted, the doctors warned her it could be the last time. Over the years, the old established treatments stopped working. New experimental ones weren't readily available in Istanbul. They told her a lung transplant might help. But the waiting list was long. And even if one became available, there was no guarantee that Tiam's body would accept the new organ.

Zari would not allow herself to think in terms of days or weeks or months. The medical profession relied on statistics. Based on their graphs and reports, her daughter had already lived well beyond the life expectancy of CF patients. But the men of science knew nothing of Allah's will. Or her faith. Or Tiam's fortitude.

Zari kept the torch of hope lit. She'd never allowed it to be extinguished. But this time, it was flickering like never before. She believed Emine's words.

Elizabeth would not remain in Istanbul for long, and there was no telling when she would be back. But it was Tiam's wish to meet her birth mother, just once, before she disappeared from their lives. And Zari would go to the end of the world to grant her wish, no matter how it tore at her heart.

Reaching the landing of the stairwell, she straightened her hijab. She smoothed the front of her coat. The thought of having to face the woman who'd wronged Zari and both of her daughters filled her with anguish. But once again, she reminded herself why she was here.

As Zari stepped out onto the hallway, she was surprised to come face-to-face with a security guard. Life had come full circle.

"*Otelde mi kalıyorsun?*" he demanded. Are you staying at the hotel?

Years of living in this city had given her confidence. She was now in this country legally. She had papers, a good job, and a community of friends. She wasn't a twenty-one-year-old mother, wild-eyed and fearful of being deported.

At the same time she wasn't blind to the ongoing hostility toward her people. She could read it in this security guard's face. Someone who looked and dressed like her wouldn't stay in this hotel.

"*Kalmıyorum.*" Zari quickly told the guard that she wasn't staying here. She showed him her pharmacy badge and let him see the inhalers and medications at the bottom of her bag. They were Tiam's emergency supplies; she always carried them with her. But today, they were supposed to look like a delivery. "*Eczanede çalışıyorum.*"

"*Misafir kim?*"

"Elizabeth Hall." She told him the room number she'd been given by her daughter.

On the way here, Zari had tried Christina's cell phone again. But she could only reach her voicemail. Now she worried about her too. Where was she?

The guard scrutinized her badge again and finally motioned for her to go ahead.

There was no guarantee that Elizabeth was in her room. Asking the front desk about a guest's whereabouts would be met with suspicion; she'd be ejected from the hotel, or worse. And she strongly suspected Elizabeth would have her arrested if she approached her in public.

She stopped at the door. Her heart was drumming wildly in her chest. She wiped her sweating palms on her thighs and then raised her fist to knock.

Thirty years melted away. Christina, gasping for air, was draped over her shoulder. Zari was once again the frightened and angry young mother. Back in Ankara, when she'd realized her baby had been stolen, coming to this hotel in Istanbul was the only thing she could do.

On that horrible day, she had seen a confirmation sheet in Elizabeth's apartment for a reservation to this same hotel. Zari had to get her Tiam back. The bus trip had been a nightmare, but she'd arrived here, as ready as she could be to confront her foe.

Blindly, she'd climbed the back stairs from the service entrance, only to realize she didn't know which room was Elizabeth's. Luckily, she found a cleaning maid, who showed her mercy and checked her log of guests.

"No, she's not here. Ms. Hall and her baby have already checked out."

Now, three decades later, worry again clutched at Zari's throat. She murmured a prayer and focused on her reason for being here. She knocked.

"What is it?"

Elizabeth's voice was the same, but she could hear the brusqueness in the response. Zari knocked again.

She heard footsteps approach the door, and then there was silence. She tried not to squirm. She guessed the other woman was staring at her through the security hole. She'd changed a great deal over the years. Zari was rounder in the face, the deep lines fanning from the corners of her eyes bore proof of the hardships she'd endured. The style of her hijab had also changed. She now used a silky scarf and tied it with a bit of style, the way Turkish women wore theirs.

"Who are you? What do you want?"

"Your daughter sent me."

A latch clicked, the door opened, and Elizabeth stood waiting with an expectant frown on her face.

Zari thought of the first time they'd met, and the memory of the two of them, standing inside an open doorway in Ankara, came back to her.

"What did you say your name is?"

"Zari Rahman."

"And whose beautiful baby is this?" Elizabeth held out her hands.

Without giving it so much as a thought, Zari placed her two-week-old infant in the woman's arms. "She is my baby."

"Look at those eyes. Her skin is to die for. And she is an armful." She bounced Tiam and ignored Zari when she reached out to take back the baby. "What brings you to Ankara?"

"My husband, Yahya Rahman, was working here. But they tell me he has disappeared."

Elizabeth turned away, still holding Tiam, and led her into her apartment. "A difficult situation, I'm sure. Maybe I can help."

There was something very possessive about the way Elizabeth held the infant, and Zari's instincts told her to take her child back and run. But she couldn't. She was desperate. She had no home, no husband, no money, no job.

What choice did she have? Convincing herself of the American woman's good intentions, Zari answered her questions, accepted her offer of employment, and moved into the apartment with Tiam that same day.

Elizabeth's sharp tone now cut through the curtain of the past, bringing her abruptly into the present. "Where is Christina?"

Zari studied her. Elizabeth had aged, but the years had been very kind to her. The hardness in her piercing gaze, however, was exactly the same.

Elizabeth repeated her question in Turkish. "*Kızım Christina nerede?*"

Zari fought the temptation to claw the other woman's eyes out. Time had not healed the pain. She'd been robbed of a life with her own Tiam. Still, she knew at any sign of hostility Elizabeth would shove her out and slam the door in her face. How many time has the door been slammed in her face over the years as she'd tried to get back her stolen child?

"I was sent here by your real daughter," Zari answered in English.

The blue eyes widened, and she took a step forward. Zari refused to flinch and stood her ground.

"What the fuck is this about? Who are you?"

"Zari. Zari Rahman. I worked for you for two years in Ankara."

Recognition registered, and the mask fell away from Elizabeth's face. Zari caught a glimpse of unexpected vulnerability behind the blue eyes.

"You...what are you doing here?"

"I've been living in Istanbul for thirty years." Each word was heavy with her angst. Each word carried the weight of the suffering Elizabeth had inflicted on her.

People were coming down the hall toward them, and Elizabeth backed into her room and motioned to her to enter. Zari followed and heard the door click shut behind her.

"I can't believe this. Everything is happening all at once. Christina found Patricia, but you probably know that." She didn't wait for a response and went across the room. She poured herself a drink. "Did Mrs. Nicholls tell you I'm here? We can't let Christina know about... about our arrangement. If you want more money, I'll arrange for it. Whatever you want. But my Christina can't find out what we did."

The dam was broken. Anger clawed its way up into Zari's throat. "What *we* did? *Our* arrangement?"

"Yes, our arrangement."

"Have you lost your mind? You stole my child, and you ran away."

"To give her a good life! A much better life than you could have ever given her."

"That is theft. Kidnapping." Zari hissed. "I was left to chase after you with the clothes on my back and a sick baby in my arms."

"That's not true." The drink sloshed in the glass as Elizabeth spun to face her. "I left you money. Mrs. Nicholls was to manage everything."

"I wasn't even paid the wages you owed me."

"There had to have been some mistake, though I don't know how Patricia could have managed to screw that up. She had her instructions. But we can remedy that right now." She walked toward the desk and reached for her purse.

"Stop. Your money means *nothing* to me. You left a sick and fragile child behind. Your own daughter!"

"I left enough money to pay for Christina's hospital bills and...and for her funeral arrangements."

"Funeral?" Anger flared into cold fury. How could a mother be so heartless as to care for a corpse more than the child when she was alive?

"I left enough to carry you through for quite a while," Elizabeth continued coolly, as if her arguments were perfectly logical. "And Mrs. Nicholls was to give you an excellent reference so that you could find work again when you were ready."

Zari forced herself to speak clearly. "The only thing I received from her was the news that you had left with my Tiam. And that she'd have me arrested if I told anyone about what you had done."

"You were an impulsive woman. Too emotional and hot headed. It was her job to stop you from doing anything stupid."

"*Stupid?* Loving my child and wanting to go and find her is stupid? To stop a thief from stealing my life and blood is stupid? But you, leaving your sick baby with a servant, a refugee, someone with no friends or connections is *not*? Doctors, medicine, hospital stays. Who was to take care of her?"

"What do you mean, the only thing you received? I don't understand this. I trusted Patricia to take care of my daughter's expenses to the end of her life...and after."

"And I put my trust in Allah. He saw to it that she would survive."

"Christina was very sick. She was dying. The doctors told me she wouldn't live to the end of the month."

"Well, she *did* live." Zari paused, allowing her words to sink in. "I renamed her Tiam...after the child you stole from me."

Elizabeth's hand shook as she put her drink down on a table. "With no help from Mrs. Nicholls?"

"With no help from you *or* your friend."

"What did you do?"

"I came to Istanbul to find you, but you were gone. It was only by the grace of Allah and good doctors and some kind and generous people that Tiam received the care she needed."

"But the hospital bills? How did you pay them?"

How pathetic that everything was about money. The crimes that she'd committed. The lives she'd destroyed. "I used everything that I'd saved. Then I got a job."

Elizabeth stared, taking in her words.

"I'll repay you. I'll repay you for everything you did. But how was she?" There was a catch in her voice. "Did she live to take her first step? Did she learn to string together words?"

"She took her first step walking toward *me*. Her favorite word was *maman*." Zari blinked back the tears welling up in her eyes as she remembered every milestone. And she mourned every milestone of her own child that she'd missed. "I raised the daughter you left behind as my own. I cared for her and loved her. I saw to it that she never suffered the horror of knowing that she had been abandoned, unwanted by her own mother."

"I'm sorry. I believed what they told me. I had no idea. I..." Elizabeth sat down on the nearest chair and buried her face in her hands.

Zari waited, remembering the day Christina showed up at her door. To find a child that she thought she'd lost made the ground swell and move beneath her feet. To hold her was to find a piece of heaven on earth.

Deep in her heart, she pitied Elizabeth and wondered at the twisted life that must have made her the person she was.

"For how long did you have her?" Elizabeth's face was wet with tears when she finally looked up. "How much longer did my baby live?"

"How much longer?" Zari repeated. "She is alive still. And she wants to see you."

PART X

_____

If you will speak the truth unmixed with lies,
Unmixed with false prevaricating words,
And faithfully point me toward the caves
Of the White Demon and his warrior chiefs—
And where Kavus is imprisoned—your reward
Shall be the kingdom of Mazandaran;
For I, myself, will place you on that throne.
But if you play me false—your worthless blood
Shall answer for the foul deception.
                                   —Ferdowsi

34

ELIZABETH

THEN

ELIZABETH HAD ONLY an hour left to get out of her apartment before Zari returned from her errands.

She went back and forth from the closet and the dresser drawers to the two suitcases open on the bed. All her clothes, everything she had in this apartment in Ankara, were disposable. For the most part, she was only taking what she'd need immediately. Still, she grabbed the leather jacket she'd had custom made for herself last month. A baby blanket was wrapped around antique pottery she'd bought in Cappadocia.

Patricia Nicholls stood in the bedroom doorway, keeping an eye on the toddlers watching TV behind her in the living room.

Elizabeth zipped one of the luggage bags closed. "The rent is paid to the end of next month. Zari can stay here to the last day. After she goes, donate all the furniture."

"And the hospital bills?" Patricia asked.

"This morning, I deposited what we agreed into your account. There's more than enough money to pay the final balance. There's money to cover funeral costs too."

The older woman crossed her arms over her chest and leaned against the doorjamb, her face turned away.

Elizabeth picked up her jewelry box. "And write a recommendation for Zari. A good one. And give her a generous severance." She dumped her gold into a padded bag. "When you talk to her, make sure she understands the consequences of making a fuss."

She looked around the room, trying to think of anything she might have forgotten. When she'd moved for her job in the past, she usually limited herself to one suitcase. But this time, she had a baby with her. And she was going back to the US for good. She zipped up the second suitcase.

"There has to be a better way of doing this," Patricia said in a tired voice.

"Well, there's *not*."

Elizabeth pushed past her, going to the next room to double check the diaper bag.

"Go outside?" Tiam's question made Elizabeth pause.

The two girls were next to each other on the floor watching some sing-along video. They were only six months apart in age, but Tiam had been walking and running around for nearly a year. The two-year-old picked her own clothes, fed herself, spoke and understood two languages. She was smart and healthy. A beautiful, happy child. Christina was sitting beside her, supported by pillows to help her remain in an upright position. She was still too weak to walk more than a couple of steps. She never made a peep unless she wanted to have something that Tiam was playing with.

When the doctors had discharged her from the hospital two days ago, their directions were clear. *Take her home and say your final goodbye.*

This morning, she could see Christina was already starved for air, struggling to breathe. Her daughter's eyes turned from the television to her. She knew. A toddler, not old enough to understand, not strong enough to survive, was judging her. Guilt dragged its sharp claws along Elizabeth's skin, and bitterness threatened to choke her. The universe was punishing her.

She had known for months what the eventual outcome would be, and it ripped her heart out. She did everything she could until she couldn't take it any longer. When it became clear that Christina's health was continuing to fail, she prepared herself for the inevitable. Still, she couldn't watch her child die.

"I go?" Tiam stood up.

"Yes. You go, my love," Elizabeth said to her. "Soon."

There wasn't enough air in the apartment for her to breathe. Back in the bedroom, she looked out the window for the car service. The driver wasn't here yet.

"I still think you should try to get visas for Zari and Tiam," Patricia said. "Take them both back with you to the US. You can afford it."

Her friend had no idea what Elizabeth could afford. Things weren't as they seemed.

"Do you think I haven't already looked into it?" She was angry that Patricia would bring this up again. She worked for the embassy. She knew the law, the red tape that was involved. "Zari is an undocumented Kurdish refugee. Tiam doesn't even have a birth certificate. They entered this country illegally. You know how our government works. They won't issue them visas."

Patricia's suggestion was impossible, and Elizabeth needed to get out. For two months, she'd been planning for this. When she applied for a US passport for Christina, she substituted Tiam's baby picture. No paper-pusher in any airport would question a mother and child. But it didn't hurt that she carried credentials connecting her to the US State Department.

Elizabeth had to do this, to go and live her life. At the age of forty-four, she was too old to get pregnant again. And even if she did, there was no saying if her next child would be born with the same disease. She'd thought everything through. She knew what she was doing. There was no other way.

"You and I don't work for the same people. You have far better connections. Someone must owe you a favor." Patricia wasn't giving up.

"No one is willing to stick their neck out to give papers to a Kurdish woman and her baby. No, it's not happening."

Her friend had no idea about Elizabeth's recent trouble. No one at the Agency wanted anything to do with her. She'd been privately reprimanded and "retired." Langley had frozen her bank accounts and confiscated nearly everything for the deals she'd made on her own. But the news was being kept under wraps. As far as her colleagues were concerned, her departure was voluntary. She was going back to the US to devote her attention to raising her daughter. The truth was that she was returning to US to start again, get a job, and find a way to raise a baby. A healthy baby.

She lined up her suitcases by the end of the bed.

"Then at least talk to Zari. She has no future in Ankara—nothing more than being someone's servant. You're a fairy godmother. You're giving Tiam a future that she could never have with her mother. Get her blessing and adopt the child."

"Adoption takes months, sometimes years. Besides, that woman has been working for me for nearly two years. I know her. She'll never agree."

"She's still a mother. My heart goes out to her."

"Your heart should go out to *me*. I've given you fifty thousand dollars. *Fifty thousand*," she repeated, pointing a finger at Patricia. "That is enough to pay the baby's expenses and give Zari a handout, and *still* leave plenty for you."

That money was nearly everything she had left. And she only had it because it was cash the Agency hadn't found.

The older woman looked at her feet.

"Are you backing out on me now at the last minute?"

"No," Patricia said feebly. "I need the money."

"Then help me. Put her jacket on."

Elizabeth rolled the suitcases to the front door of the apartment and dropped her purse and the diaper bag next to them. The intercom from the front door buzzed, and a momentary panic shot through her. She looked at the clock. It was too early for Zari to be back. She pressed the intercom. The car service had arrived.

She opened the apartment door and waited for the driver to come up and get her luggage. Her gaze fell on the children. As Patricia wrestled Tiam into the jacket, the excited toddler jumped up and down. Beside them, Christina sat quietly and watched her playmate.

"Do you want to know when...when it happens? Should I notify you?"

From the first day, waiting helplessly for the baby to take her first breath, Elizabeth had dreaded the thought of Christina's death. For eighteen months, that horrible feeling had never left her. Each doctor's visit was laced with disappointing news. The midnight trips to the emergency room, the pacing the corridors, the discussions with experts here and over the phone to the US never made a difference. The answer was always the same.

The prognosis is terminal. Respiratory and digestive failure is imminent. Patient survival is unlikely...

And then there was this last hospital stay.

It is time, Ms. Hall. There is nothing more to be done.

Elizabeth turned to her friend, still waiting for an answer. "No. Don't contact me. It's better that way."

The driver appeared at the door, and Elizabeth had him take her luggage downstairs. Once the man's footsteps died away, she crouched before her daughter.

"So this is it. The end. Can I have a hug?"

Christina didn't have the strength to raise her arms. Elizabeth picked up her daughter one last time but stopped as a breath hissed out of the small, congested lungs. The child stared at her from beneath long lashes. She had her large blue eyes, her soft skin, her quivering chin. Even in temperament, she was Elizabeth's daughter.

This was too much for her. It was too much for anyone. Something was dying inside her, and if she didn't go now, Elizabeth didn't know if she ever would. She thought of what she was leaving here—a dying child, a ruined career, an empty bank account. And she thought of what the future offered in America—a healthy baby and endless possibilities.

She straightened up, whispering, "Goodbye."

Turning away, she scooped Tiam into her arms and brushed a kiss on Patricia's cheek. "You do understand that I don't want to hear a word from you...ever again."

Without another glance backward, Elizabeth went out the door and down to the street.

35

ZARI

THEN

Z<small>ARI KNEW</small> something was wrong the moment she walked into the apartment. Elizabeth's friend was sitting in a rocking chair and watching the news, and the volume was too loud for the baby sleeping on her lap. Patricia Nicholls visited often, and she was always chatty and easy to talk to. But today she didn't look up. She said nothing in response to Zari's greeting.

"My Tiam is sleeping?"

Again she received no answer. Zari carried the groceries into the kitchen and put the bags on the counter. It struck her as odd that the woman barely acknowledged her presence. She was never like this.

The errands Elizabeth had given her today had taken her across Ankara to a distant neighborhood. She had to take three different buses to drop off two of her employer's winter coats at a specific dry cleaner. It was not the one they normally used. After that stop, Zari had a long list of things to buy at an American grocery store in the same neighborhood. She took packages of overpriced prepared foods and the cans of pumpkin, black beans, and cranberry jelly—whatever that was—out of the bags. This was a waste of time and money. The food she cooked on a daily basis for Elizabeth and herself and the girls didn't use these ingredients, and Zari knew her dinners were far healthier.

Leaving everything on the counter, she went to check on Tiam. Her baby was a light sleeper, and the television was too loud. The room she and Tiam shared opened off a hallway leading from the back of the kitchen.

The door was closed. She pushed it open slightly and peeked inside. There was no crib; she and her daughter shared the same bed. But the baby wasn't there. Zari went to Elizabeth's room. Her employer occasionally had the girls take their naps on her bed.

Looking in from the doorway, she saw immediately that Tiam wasn't there either. Zari's stomach clenched. Clothes were scattered carelessly on the chair and on the bed. Shoes lay where they'd been thrown, along a wall and in the corner by a window. Before she left to run her errands, Zari had made the bed and tidied the room. And Elizabeth wasn't a messy person. Everything had a place.

The closet door was open. Empty hangers dangled from the closet pole and lay on the floor. Elizabeth's jewelry box lay on its side next to the bed. Its drawers had been pulled out. Zari picked it up. The box was empty.

"Ms. Hall?" she called out, but no one answered.

She glanced at the closet again and paused, perplexed. Elizabeth stored her suitcases on the shelves. But they were both missing.

"Ms. Hall?" she called louder, hurrying through the hallways to the living room. "Tiam?"

The single stroller and the double stroller stood against the wall. Elizabeth never took the children out without them.

"Mrs. Nicholls, where is Ms. Hall. Where is Tiam?"

The older woman didn't answer. Her attention remained glued to the television screen. Zari's heart raced, and cold waves of fear washed down her spine.

Patricia Nicholls was divorced. She'd never had children of her own. Zari had heard Elizabeth say numerous times that she would never leave either of the girls alone with her. Her friend didn't know the first thing about what to do with a baby.

"Did something happen, ma'am?"

Babies got hurt all the time. Maybe Tiam fell and needed to be taken to the doctor. What if she choked on something? Bumped her head. Elizabeth kept her sleeping pills next to the bed. What if she took them? What if she'd been poisoned?

But what about the missing suitcases and the jewelry?

"Where is Ms. Hall?" she asked sharply. "Mrs. Nicholls, I need to speak with her."

The woman didn't look up. Zari switched off the television and stood in front of it, facing her.

"My daughter Tiam...where is she?"

Patricia glanced at the clock first before turning her attention to Zari. The baby woke up with a start at that very moment, wailing.

"Hush. Hush, little one. Come here."

She took her out of the woman's arms, caressed her back and whispered in her ear until the child dozed off on her shoulder.

"Ms. Hall. Tiam. Where are they?"

Mrs. Nicholls was again studying the clock on the wall. Something was seriously wrong. Zari's stomach lurched.

"For the love of Allah, you're killing me, ma'am. Please talk to me."

The woman finally looked at her. "I think you should sit down."

"I can't sit down. Where is my baby?"

"Do you know how lucky your child is? How *fortunate*?"

"I don't know. And I don't want you to tell me. But I do want you to tell me where Ms. Hall has gone and when is she coming back?"

"Do you know the Cinderella story?"

"Yes, it's a cartoon. Please answer me."

"It is a story of a girl rising from rags to riches."

"I don't care. I want my child." Panic drove her pitch higher every time she spoke. If it weren't for the baby in her arms, Zari was angry enough to shake the other woman. "Where is she? What has happened to her?"

Christina cried out again, and Zari rocked her from side to side. Her heart was ready to explode. She kept thinking of the missing suitcases and clothes, the empty jewelry box.

A horrible, horrible thought materialized in her brain, and a chasm opened before her.

Elizabeth spent more time with Tiam than with her own daughter. How many times had their conversation begun harmlessly only to turn into things that made Zari wonder if she was being teased or not?

Tiam likes me better than you.

Can she sleep in the bed with me tonight?

Can I have her?

How much to buy her?

We'll just swap the babies, Christina for Tiam. What do you say?

"No!" The anguished cry was directed at herself. Her imagination was running wild. This couldn't be happening.

"Elizabeth will give Tiam the best life any child could dream of. A privileged life. A good home. A good education. Money. There isn't a thing your daughter will be wanting for in her life. Do you know what other refugees in your situation would do for this opportunity? Do you know how lucky Tiam is?"

The blood ran out of her body, and Zari's vision wavered. She'd stepped into a nightmare.

"She can't just *take* my baby. She can't walk away with another woman's child."

"She's taking her to America."

Zari gaped at her in disbelief.

"America!" Patricia said again, as if it were *Jannah*. Paradise.

Blind panic seized her by the throat. She stumbled toward the phone. "I'll call the police. I'll report her. I'll tell them what she's doing. She's a thief. A criminal. They'll stop her."

Zari picked up the phone, but before she could dial, Patricia was beside her, wrenching the handset out of her grasp and slamming it down.

"You will *not* call anyone," she snapped. "You will not *tell* anyone. If you so much as breathe a word of this, she'll hand you over to the Turkish police."

"She *can't* steal my baby." Tears rushed down Zari's cheeks, as she tried to dial again.

Patricia tore the phone cord out of the wall. "Do not forget who you are. You are a bloody nobody. You don't exist. You have no rights whatsoever. Elizabeth will destroy you. And I'm not only talking about deportation. She'll have you charged with crimes. She'll say you're a thief. That *you* stole from her. It'll be her word against yours. No one will believe you. They'll put you in jail."

"But why?" Zari cried. "Why is she doing this? Didn't I serve her? Wasn't I honest? Didn't I take care of this child—*her* child—like she was my own?"

Christina's cries turned into gasps. Zari clapped the baby repeatedly on the back until she coughed and managed to catch her breath.

"You're being hysterical. I can't deal with you right now." Patricia walked away and picked up her purse from the chair. "I'll come back tomorrow after you've calmed down. We'll see what needs to be done then."

Zari stood in the middle of the living room, discarded, dismissed, forgotten. Tears blurred her vision as she watched the other woman go out the door. Christina made a soft sound, and Zari looked down at the innocent child in her arms.

We'll just swap the babies. Those words weren't spoken in jest. She meant them.

"And you, my love? What is going to happen to you?"

Zari tried to absorb the reality she was facing. Her precious child was gone. A woman she'd trusted had taken Tiam and run away. Tears ran down her cheeks. Only a monster could do such a thing. Only a twisted and heartless monster.

A thought came to her. She saw a printout this morning on the kitchen counter. A hotel reservation in Istanbul.

Her Tiam was there. She must be.

Zari had to go after her.

PART XI

"Take this," he said, "and if, by gracious heaven,
A daughter for your solace should be given,
Let it among her ringlets be displayed,
And joy and honor will await the maid."
—Ferdowsi

36

CHRISTINA

Iᴛ's cold and damp in my cell, and I've lost all sense of time. Maybe I've been here for hours, but I'm not sure. There's no way of knowing if Kyle and Elizabeth even realize I've gone missing.

Loud, angry voices reach me from the other room. Two men are arguing in Turkish. A third person is trying to interject, but he's having no success at all in calming the others.

The only thing I do know is that my arms are numb from the shoulder sockets down. I try to move them and flex the muscles, but pins and needles is the best response I can get. And regardless of how frequently I shift my weight on the rug, the sharp cramp in my hip won't go away. No one has checked on me since they dumped me here.

In every abduction film I've ever seen, the villains take a picture or a video and use it to get their ransom. Or they have the kidnap victim talk to their family on the phone. None of that has happened here. Maybe these men haven't watched the same movies.

Something crashes against the door, setting my already taut nerves on edge. It sounds like a thrown chair. One man's voice, loud and harsh, silences the others. He's right outside my door. It's obvious now that nothing has happened because they'd been waiting for the big boss to arrive. If this is the guy, he certainly doesn't sound happy.

A bolt is pulled back, scraping metal against metal. Pushing myself upright and sitting tall, I stare at the door, ready to face whoever is coming in. No begging for my life. No cowering or crying or carrying on. If they're going to kill me, they'll do it, and no amount of drama from me will make any difference. Once again, my tremendous expertise comes from a thousand police shows.

The door squeaks open, giving me a glimpse of the room. Two younger men are standing by a table, squabbling in low voices. Their hands are gesturing angrily in every direction, and one of them jerks a thumb toward my door just as it closes.

The tall man in the dark suit has a face I've come to recognize. His brows are drawn together, his lips are thinned. I should have known he'd be behind this. On the way to the airport, I thought he was going to kidnap me, but he didn't and asked about Tiam instead. And yesterday, he had been watching Elizabeth at the hotel. The puzzle pieces are starting to line up. The two out there, and whoever else was involved with grabbing me, must be his minions.

"We meet again." My voice catches, and I clear my throat.

He stares down at me. It's difficult to guess what's going on in his mind. Trapped like a fish in his net, I must be a sorry mess. My neck hurts, so I stop trying to look into his face.

I know he understands English. "Elizabeth won't do it. She won't make a deal for me."

There are two quick flashes in the room. He's taken a picture of me.

"I know who she is and who she used to work for," I continue. "And the same way that the US government says they won't negotiate with terrorists, she'll use the same excuse. She'll just tell you to keep me. You'll get nothing from her."

"She won't save her daughter's life?"

These are the first words he's spoken. I look up. "No, she won't."

"Then you die."

"Yes. I'll die."

"Maybe I should do it now?" He produces a knife. The blade is short, but it gleams in the dim light.

"Go ahead." The quicker, the better.

Death doesn't scare me. Events, good and bad, from the past few months come into my mind. Becoming pregnant. Experiencing the joy of finding my true family. Losing Jax. The car accident that should have taken my life, but instead stole my daughter from me.

"Any last wish? Maybe a message that I will pass on to your mother?"

Your mother.

Last night, it must have been a premonition. Before going to bed, I wrote an email to my lawyer and asked him to set up a will naming Tiam and Zari as my beneficiaries. Maybe an email is legally binding and maybe it isn't, but at least he knows my wishes. He has names he can pursue after I'm gone.

"Nothing, I see." He takes a step toward me.

His face is expressionless, but I'm not afraid. A memory comes back to me—the moment when I became conscious in the hospital after the car accident. I was drowning in the pettiness of everything I'd done wrong. And then, suddenly, my life wasn't about me, but about her. I was terrified for my baby. The bond between mother and child consumed me, and I knew how far I was willing to go, how much I was willing to sacrifice for her. I would have gladly died for her.

My life was not worth a single hair on my daughter's head, not worth a single scratch on her. It was during that awakening to what maternal love really was that I asked for my own mother. But it wasn't Elizabeth that I wanted. It was Zari.

"You know my friend Tiam. You asked me about her." Words tumble out. "My message isn't for Elizabeth Hall. It's for Zari, Tiam's mother."

I'm fighting back tears, but some of them must be escaping because I taste the saltiness on my lips.

"Please tell her I love her."

37
———

TIAM

EVERY MUSCLE in my chest strains with each breath. Tubes feed oxygen into my nose, and my body is connected to machines. Since they brought me to ICU, a calm has descended over my mind. I'm no longer afraid or sad or angry. I have no regrets about how I've taken care of my health. I did the best with what I was given. The road my life traveled on—rough and marked with deep ruts and potholes—is coming to an end, and I'm ready for whatever comes next.

"What should I do?" The woman's voice is close to me.

"Sit beside the bed. Hold her hand," Zari says quietly.

Soft, cold hands take hold of one of mine. Lips press against my skin, but I'm too exhausted to open my eyes.

My mind wanders back to the night at the rooftop terrace over-looking Hagia Sophia. A white-jacketed server meets me at the top of the stairs.

"*Hoş geldiniz. Buyurun hanım efendim, her yerde oturabilirsiniz,*" he says, telling me I can sit anywhere.

"*Sağolun.*" I thank him, and he disappears down the stairs.

The air is cool, and the clusters of chairs and benches are inviting. I spot Christina and stand still. She's listening to *adhan*. The call to prayer is coming from a dozen mosques in this section of the city.

They join together, creating an evocative call and return. Her eyes are closed, her face lifted to the sky. She looks beautiful, so serene.

If it weren't for my period, I would be praying in one of the mosques right now. Instead, I offer up my own silent words of devotion.

Christina opens her eyes and sees me. We both smile, and she begins to gather her things. We have so much to catch up on.

The torches on the rooftop flicker, and a shadow comes between us. The woman begins to complain to Christina before she even reaches her.

"I've been searching for you everywhere. I called you..."

As I begin to walk away, the thought comes to me. *Not now*. It is too difficult to introduce myself to my mother tonight.

I feel fingers entwine with mine. They're not letting me go away. I want to turn around, to walk down the stairs, toward Elizabeth as she continues talking. I see Christina's eyes meet mine and welcome me. She's encouraging me.

"There's someone here who would like to meet you."

The voice should belong to Christina, but it's Zari's warm tones that fill my ear. I'm not on that rooftop terrace.

"Christina...my child. Open your eyes. Please." An American accent.

Zari's voice weaves in with the other. "Call her Tiam. That is what she likes to be called."

I know who this woman is, holding my hand, calling out to me. For ten years, I've been waiting for this moment. But am I brave enough to face her?

My body is failing, but my mind is at peace. Inside, I've never felt stronger than I do now. I open my eyes.

"My baby. My daughter."

Elizabeth's face is crumbling. Her tears have streaked her cheeks with eyeliner and mascara. She presses her lips to our joined fingers, and I realize with some surprise that I have no emotions for this woman. Anger, rage, disappointment, and all the pain that churned within me when I learned she had abandoned me...it's all gone, vanished like the night in the face of the rising sun.

My gaze moves past her, searching for Zari. She's standing near the window, and our eyes meet. I don't want her to go away. When I take my last breath, she is the mother that I want to be looking at.

She presses a fist to her chest and flattens her palm against her heart. She grieves for me, and she loves me. She'll stay.

"I didn't know you survived. I just assumed...I trusted what those doctors told me. They told me to say goodbye to you. I couldn't bear to watch you die."

"For thirty-two years, I've lived." My words are little more than a whisper. "And I've been fortunate...loved by the finest mother Allah ever created."

"I can never hope for your forgiveness. I was a broken woman. I had no family left. You were my only hope, my last chance of having someone in my life. But you were dying on me, like everyone else. I allowed a selfish fantasy to obscure the reality." Tears tumble from her eyes. "But Christina—"

"Tiam. My mother named me Tiam."

"Tiam, if there's anything I can do now. Anything you want or need." She falters, fighting down a sob. "I'm going to find new doctors. Specialists. I'll fly them here. I'll find out who is the best anywhere."

"Nothing. I want nothing from you." My chest lifts, painfully, and falls. "Only to see you...tell you. I have survived in spite of you."

Elizabeth is weeping openly, and my eyes are drawn to Zari again. She gives me a nod, and I understand what she's encouraging me to do.

My judgment, my culture, and my religion all urge me to forgive. A verse from the Holy Quran comes to me. *Whosoever forgives and reconciles, his reward is upon Allah.* But it is difficult.

Elizabeth's head is resting on my bed. Her shoulders are quaking as she cries. She isn't the same woman I have watched and was intimidated by over the years. She's come undone. Her heart lies in my hand, as naked and vulnerable as a wounded swallow.

I draw our joined fingers to my chest. Her face lifts off the bed, and her reddened eyes gaze into mine.

"I forgive you, Mother," I say. "I forgive you."

38

ELIZABETH

ELIZABETH STOOD beside Zari in the waiting area of the ICU as the doctor told them what to expect.

"She has one day left, perhaps two."

She'd been introduced to the medical staff as a close friend of the family. A generous label, considering all that she'd done to them.

"Is there anything that can make a difference?" she asked. "The cost is absolutely of no consequence. Perhaps a different facility. Drugs that aren't available to her at this hospital. Is there anything at all?"

"I am afraid it is too late for any of it."

Thirty years ago, she'd researched cystic fibrosis thoroughly when they told her Christina was afflicted with it. She knew the progression of the disease and what the end was like. But she'd made a mistake in believing the doctors' prognosis. Sitting at her daughter's bedside today, seeing how fragile she was, and watching her battle for every breath, Elizabeth had believed them. But she was not ready to give up. Not this time.

"What about the possibility of a lung transplant?"

"She's been on the national waiting list. But even if a miracle happened at this very moment and a compatible organ became available, there is no guarantee that her body would accept it."

The intercom paged the doctor, and he hurried away. Guilt and grief were working in tandem to tear Elizabeth apart. Her eyes were so puffy that she could barely see out of them. Watching Tiam in the ICU forced her to measure each of her own breaths. For all of her life, she'd been active and had lived her life to the fullest, while her child struggled for every ounce of air. If she could only swap places with her.

She turned to Zari, standing quietly beside her. She was calm and at peace, as if she were looking over garden beds rather than these sterile hallways.

With no thought of how she might respond, Elizabeth pulled her into an embrace.

"I'm sorry, Zari. I'm sorry for what I did to our daughters. I'm sorry for what I did to you. My actions were vile. Nothing can ever excuse the wretched choice I made. I stole your baby. I left mine..." She faltered. "I left my child behind. And absolutely nothing I say or do can justify that."

Zari's body was stiff. She drew back.

"If it is forgiveness that you are after, you heard Tiam. I raised that young woman as my own, so how could I deny her words? How could I turn a face of stone to you? You did us all wrong. You shattered our lives. But I say the same thing. I forgive you."

Elizabeth held the woman's gaze, knowing in her heart that she could never repair the damage she did so many years ago. She didn't deserve their forgiveness.

"I have a searing pain in my heart," Elizabeth said. "I would rip open my own chest if it would help her breathe."

"To be a mother, you give them your heart. You give them your life. You give them your love. You must love your children as Allah loves you."

Two mothers raised daughters that were not their own. In her own way, Elizabeth tried to love the child she'd raised, but she'd never given Christina the unfettered, unconditional love that Zari had given Tiam. Every time Elizabeth felt a twinge of guilt about what she'd done, she would shower the child with gifts. Christina had been raised in a life of comfort. But Elizabeth had never given her enough affection. Her generosity didn't say, *I give you my heart. I give you my life. I give you my love.*

Tiam grew up surrounded by this loving warmth every day, but Christina had never felt it for the simple reason that Elizabeth didn't know how to give it.

But perhaps it wasn't too late.

"I'm going back to sit at my daughter's side," Zari told her before walking away.

Elizabeth's phone rang for the umpteenth time. She'd been ignoring it. Glancing at the screen, she saw that Kyle was trying to reach her again. She'd missed their dinner.

Her thoughts went to Christina. She should be told. She should be here. A new panic seized her. These two girls had to meet. Zari had to see her daughter and know that although she was losing one child, her other one was alive and doing well.

She dialed Christina's number, but it rang and then went to voicemail.

She texted her. *Please call me. It's urgent.*

Elizabeth paced along the hall. Monitors beeped on the walls behind the nurses' station. The intercom requests for physicians were frequent. She tried to imagine what it would have been like if she had taken her own baby back with her to Southern California thirty years ago.

There was no doubt in her mind that the medical care would have been better, more advanced. Maybe her daughter would have had a new lung by now. Maybe she wouldn't be lying in an ICU bed, fighting for her final breaths.

"Where are you, Christina? Answer the text." Elizabeth needed her here with them now.

The screen on her phone showed she had voicemail messages. Elizabeth pressed the play button.

The first one was from Kyle.

"Christina used a car service today. It's five o'clock, and she's still not back at the hotel. I tried to call her, but she doesn't answer. Do you know anything?"

The next message was from Kyle again.

"I put a call in to the car company. The driver isn't answering her cell phone either. They're checking the GPS services for a location on the car."

A new worry added to the anguish Elizabeth was already feeling. "Where are you, Christina," she murmured. "I need you."

There was a third message from Kyle. She listened to it.

"There's been an accident. The driver is hospitalized. Christina wasn't in the car. Police are involved. Call me."

"Shit. Shit. Shit." Elizabeth rushed down the hallway, past the double doors of the ICU. Waiting for the elevator, she called Kyle.

Thankfully, he answered immediately. "Where are you? Where have you been?"

"What's happening, Kyle? Where is she? Please tell me she's okay."

His long pause sent her stomach into a free fall. The elevator doors opened, but she wasn't strong enough to go in. She leaned back against the nearest wall.

"Talk to me, Kyle."

"The police think she's been kidnapped."

A fierce buzzing began in her ears, blunting Kyle's words. Pain hammered at her head and spread downward like hot pulsing poison. She wanted to curl up and disappear, but she couldn't. She forced herself to focus.

"Who would kidnap her? Why? For money? What do we have to do?"

"The police don't know anything yet. They're asking lots of questions. They want to talk to you. Where are you?"

She couldn't let police come to the hospital. She didn't want Zari to know. But she couldn't leave and go back to the hotel either. Her daughter was here. But what about Christina?

"Elizabeth, are you there?"

"I'm here. I'm thinking."

"It's possible that...well, that whatever is happening to Christina has something to do with you."

"If they want money, they can have whatever I have. I don't care. Give them the whole fucking company if that's what they want. We have to get Christina back."

"It might be more than money that they're after," he said.

"What else is there? What could they want?"

"Your name is on a kill list. I saw it myself. It's on the dark web."

Elizabeth's knees gave out, and she slid down the wall. Sitting on the floor, she buried her head in her hand. She thought she was clear of the past. When she wasn't named in the lawsuit filed by the Iraqi Kurds a couple of years ago, she'd assumed she was out of it. She was a fool to even hope for it. If Jax and Christina could find out her old connections to the weapon sales, so could others.

She knew what a kill list was. Assassins were available for hire, and foreign governments used them to get rid of their enemies, or those who spoke against their politics, by putting innocent people's names on the list. The US government had their own kill list and was famous for using drones and rockets to wipe out entire villages to get their target.

"Did you say any of this to the police?" she asked.

"No, not yet. But shouldn't our embassy be notified?"

She was well aware of how they would respond. Elizabeth was a nobody in their books. The embassy would hand the case to the local police, who would rush in and shoot the place up once they knew where the kidnappers were holding Christina.

"Elizabeth?"

"I'm thinking." A text notification showed on her phone. "I'm going to call you back, Kyle. I just got something from Christina."

Elizabeth ended the call and opened the text. Her hand immediately went to her mouth to stifle her cry. It was a picture of Christina, sitting on a dirty rug, her ankles bound, her hands behind her. Elizabeth enlarged the photo and studied her face. It looked like there was blood on one cheek.

She pushed to her feet and quickly typed her reply. *You bastards are going to die. I'm going to kill every...*

Elizabeth stopped and deleted her message. She had to be calm. She couldn't afford to piss them off. It would just fall back on Christina. Whoever was behind this, they were using her daughter's phone to communicate. Modern cell phones could be tracked. Three decades ago, she was a trained CIA operative. These assholes didn't know she was still as sharp as ever.

She typed a new message. *What do you want? What's your price?*

Elizabeth sent the message and waited. Staring at the screen, she knew someone was typing on the other end, but it felt like forever before the text came through.

Must meet.

They weren't asking for money. She thought of what Kyle said about the hit list with her name on it.

Where? she typed.

46 Sokak in Bahçelievler.

She stared in disbelief at the reply.

You remember.

"No. No. No. This is not happening," she muttered. She rubbed her aching temple. Bahçelievler was a neighborhood in Ankara. It was the area where she lived. And 46 Sokak was an address near there. She remembered too clearly. He was taunting her, making sure she knew who was behind Christina's kidnapping.

No kill list, no extorting money. Her daughter had been taken out of revenge.

You want me to go to Ankara?

The answer came through right away.

Forget that. Meet me on Karaköy Koprusu.

When?

Come now.

PART XII

—So Adam in his visioned Paradise
Saw but God's gifts, till taste of bitter truth
Taught him what earth's creation is in truth:—
Now, O stern angel, none can make relent
Your steely wrath, your sword of punishment.
— Ḥafeẓ

39

ELIZABETH

THEN

As ELIZABETH WALKED from the street to the courtyard of their Ankara apartment complex, she saw the new facilities man for the first time and realized what all the talk was about.

Her building was occupied, for the most part, by American and British government employees and their families. The women living here knew each other, and many of them got together once a week for coffee, tea, and gossip. This past week, the room buzzed with discussion of the gorgeous guy who'd been hired to work the grounds and to see to any painting or plumbing or odd jobs that needed doing.

Elizabeth stopped by the line of mailboxes, close enough to get a good look at him.

He was hard at work digging, and longish hair fell over his face. The new tree with its burlap-covered ball sat beside the hole. His back muscles flexed, showing through the sweat-soaked shirt. She admired the shape of his powerful ass as he leaned at the waist to wrestle the tree into its new home. It was unfortunate that men in this part of the world didn't work shirtless, or even wear shorts in public.

Elizabeth waited until he was done packing dirt around the tree before she approached.

"*As-salamu 'alaykum*," she said in greeting.

He pushed the lock of hair out of his face, and she knew with certainty what all the fuss was about. He was young. Twenty-some-thing, she guessed. And from the hazel-colored eyes to the strong jaw and the sharp lines of his cheekbones, he might have easily been the best-looking guy she'd seen in Ankara.

"Good afternoon, ma'am," he answered in English.

"Elizabeth Hall." She extended a hand toward him. His were dirty, but she didn't care.

Instead of accepting the handshake, however, he pressed a palm to his chest and politely bowed in respect.

"Yahya Rahman."

"Welcome to Bahçelievler."

"Thank you."

"Where are you from?"

He hesitated to answer and eyed the tools at his feet. Elizabeth had a good idea what the problem might be. Most of the hired help in their neighborhood, especially those doing menial jobs and manual labor, were in the country illegally. She tried to put his mind at ease.

"Everyone around here is from somewhere else. And no one goes around checking papers."

"If you say, ma'am." He motioned toward the building. "You must excuse me, please. My next job is waiting."

She wasn't ready to let him go. "You live on the premises, don't you?"

"Yes, ma'am. Very generous of the building manager."

"You can call me Miss Hall. Or Elizabeth."

"Thank you, ma'am."

He was a stubborn one, she thought. "Do you have family in Ankara, Yahya?"

"Not in Ankara. But I'm hoping that will soon change."

"Getting married?"

"I am married already. And I hope my wife will join me."

The hint of a smile on his full lips made him look both sexy and irresistible.

"What is your wife's name?"

"Zari, ma'am."

"Will you please stop calling me *ma'am*?" she asked sharply. "I understand you are doing it out of respect, but I'm not a hundred years old."

"I'm sorry, Miss Hall."

"Better." She nodded her approval. "Where is your wife now?"

"Qalat Dizah."

She'd guessed right. He was a refugee, an illegal from Iraqi Kurdistan. Elizabeth knew what was happening in Qalat Dizah and in the rest of Kurdistan. It was a rarity for couples to reunite once they were separated.

"I work for the US Embassy here. I live in apartment 2A." From experience, she knew that people like Yahya got excited when she mentioned her credentials, thinking they might have made an important connection. "After you clean up, come and see me. We can talk more."

"My next job is waiting, Miss Hall."

She admired his wide shoulders and long legs as he walked away. Maybe he wouldn't show up today, or tomorrow, or even this week, but she'd get him up to her place soon enough.

ELIZABETH LOVED YOUNGER MEN. They were uncomplicated, energetic, willing to learn, and eager to please. Their expectations rarely went beyond the physical. And she was an expert at bringing their fantasies to life.

Yahya proved to be a tough nut to crack, however. Elizabeth met him first in September, and her seduction of him required three months of playful effort. She learned he enjoyed pastries, so she always picked up something from the bakery on her way home. And she bought him gifts—a sweater, a jacket, gloves for the coming winter.

Having him where she wanted him, however, required numerous calls for repairs in her apartment, and with every visit, she chipped away at the walls of his decorum. When he changed the light on the ceiling, she held his legs instead of the ladder. When he unclogged her sink, she leaned over his shoulder in the small bathroom, brushing her breasts against him. She was forty-one, but she had the tight, conditioned body of a woman half her age. She always drew his eye by wearing shorts and a tank top with no bra.

Yahya was a virile young man with a wife who might never arrive in Ankara. It was only a matter of time before he gave in. They were separated in age by eighteen years, but what did she care? She was looking for good sex, not a meaningful relationship.

About two months after they began sleeping together, Elizabeth noticed the change in her body—sore and sensitive breasts, queasiness at the smell of coffee, an increased sex drive.

Yahya always rolled on a condom before they had sex. But there were a few times that she recalled not giving him enough time. She'd become pregnant three times in her thirties, each one ending in a miscarriage in the first trimester. Her gynecologist in Ankara said it was due to a chromosomal abnormality in the fetus. There was something wrong with the baby to start with. Better that way, she told herself.

Once she turned forty, she'd given up hope of ever being a mother. But here she was, pregnant. She confirmed it with her doctor.

The thought of being a single mother thrilled her. She had money, a good job, and no family left who would lay guilt on her for being unmarried. Friends and colleagues would provide her with a support group. It would all work out fine. A child would complete her life.

Elizabeth's only problem was Yahya. He'd know the child was his the moment the news got out.

When she became pregnant before, the other men ran and never looked back. But it wouldn't be the case with him. Yahya was protective, honorable. He was the alpha-type male who'd enjoy the idea of having staked a claim on her. Elizabeth guessed he'd push his way into her life and make himself a pain in the ass. She couldn't allow it, professionally or personally.

Having him fired wouldn't work. Everyone at the complex adored him. Reporting him to the Turkish police about his lack of papers wasn't enough either. They regularly sent people to camps, only to have them return a month or so later.

Elizabeth needed something more permanent.

The idea came to her on a steel-gray morning at the end of February. She was sitting in her silk robe by the window and spotted Yahya walking across the frosty courtyard to the street. She knew where he was going. Five days a week he went to exercise before work. A small gym operated in their neighborhood of Bahçelievler. Not much more than a hole in the wall, it was popular with the Kurds.

Later that day, Elizabeth made a phone call to the anti-terrorism attaché at the embassy.

The next morning, as he came out of the gym at 46 Sokak, Yahya Rahman was taken into custody and wrestled into an unmarked van. No one at the complex knew where he'd gone or what happened to him. He was here working one day and had vanished the next. Disappeared.

And Elizabeth happily began making plans for her baby.

40

ELIZABETH

NOW

TAKING a taxi to the ferry landings, Elizabeth paid the driver and got out. From the pier, a wide walkway led up onto the *Karaköy Koprusu*, the Galata Bridge, one of the major landmarks in Istanbul. The two-level structure spanned the Golden Horn, and she glanced at the water, gleaming and black and covered with shimmering lights from the bridge.

Much had changed since the last time Elizabeth stood in this spot. The old bridge had burned and been replaced with this new one. As she walked along the pier, she could see the lower level of the bridge with its brilliantly lit bars and restaurants. The upper level was busy with car and tram traffic, and local fishermen along the railing, casting into the waters below.

The beat of the city itself was far different from what she recalled. As the crowds wandered along the walkways of both levels, the sounds of Turkish pop and techno music mingled with the horns of the ferries and the cries of the vendors.

She paused and looked around her. Istanbul was a city that cherished the old as much as the new, and Elizabeth realized she too had changed. Suddenly, she'd been awakened. In her seventies, she was seeing the world with new eyes and new understanding.

God knows she'd made mistakes, terrible ones—in her personal life and in her career. But worst of all, in the way she'd destroyed other people's lives. The young Kurdish girl in the alley called her *Shaitan*. Devil. She'd spoken the truth.

Her crimes were deep and far-reaching. She'd profited at the expense of innocent lives. And now, once the sale of Externus went through, she'd be very rich. But what was the good of all that money when her heart threatened to implode with guilt and grief? For so many years, she'd been able to curtain off that part of her life, but no longer. The walls had come crashing down.

Christina. Tiam. She was about to lose them both, and the probability of it was crushing her. Children should not die before the parent or because of the sins of the parent. She pinched the bridge of her nose as tears threatened to fall. She couldn't let her weakness show. She had to face Yahya with a clear mind. He wanted to hurt her, but she needed to make him understand what was at stake.

"*Mısır?*" A young vendor pushed a cob of grilled corn in front of her face, breaking into her thoughts.

"*Yok, sağol.* No, thank you." She shook her head and reentered the current of people moving onto the bridge.

Elizabeth thought about the history of the Galata Bridge. Traditionally, Turks would gather on the upper level to demonstrate and express their political differences, often violently. On the lower level, people gathered in the restaurants to discuss the same topics in a more civilized fashion, over a glass or two of *raki*.

He didn't say where exactly they were to meet tonight, but she guessed he would be waiting for her on top.

Once she was on the bridge, the smell of the sea filled her senses. The breeze was picking up. Elizabeth moved steadily along the wide walkway. The metallic clacking of a passing tram occasionally competed with the heavy growl of slow-moving traffic. As she walked, she maneuvered past men and women casting their fishing lines over the railing.

There was no sign of Yahya yet, but she guessed he was already watching her. He was probably making sure she was alone, and that no authorities were standing in the wings, ready to pounce. Not quite halfway across, she leaned against the railing and watched the ferry-boats coming and going from the pier.

Elizabeth's phone rang, and her heart gave a sharp kick. She turned her back to the river and looked at the screen. Kyle was trying to reach her. She let it go to voice mail. At the whine and revving of a motorcycle engine, she looked up as its helmeted driver weaved between cars on the roadway.

A little girl, no more than four or five years old, ran into her. Another one, not much older, was in close pursuit. They were wearing exactly the same jackets and looked like sisters. A Turkish woman called to them from a few feet along the railing, and they ran back to her.

Elizabeth's mind flickered back thirty years to two others.

"Sister." Tiam liked to pat Christina on the head or the hand.

Zari corrected her. "No, Tiam. She is your friend."

"No, Maman. Kız kardeşi. Sister."

Elizabeth wondered if, even then, Tiam instinctively knew she shared a blood connection with Christina.

Three men passed her, carrying fishing equipment and speaking Kurdish.

Before she ever decided to remove Yahya from her life, she'd warned him not to mix with the PKK, the militant and political Kurdish group. They were very active in Ankara at the time, and depending on the fickleness of Washington, the organization went back and forth from ally to enemy numerous times. Perhaps it was her ego, wanting him to know how connected she was, but Elizabeth had told him how easy it was to make people disappear forever.

Yahya had texted the address of the gym in Ankara where she'd had him taken into custody. He was making sure Elizabeth under-stood that he knew she was responsible. She worked for the US government, whose operatives had picked him up.

Back then, very much like now, there was no trial for men and women who were detained by US agents. A phone call was enough—a vague mention of an unconfirmed back channel hint of a terrorist connection—and a person would disappear into a CIA ghost prison. Elizabeth had done that to Yahya. She'd lied and used her influence to make him vanish from her life forever. But somehow he'd survived. And sometime after she left the country, he'd been released. After whatever he'd been involved with since then, he was now capable of kidnapping.

The image of Christina—bound, bloodied, and alone on that filthy floor—burned into Elizabeth's brain, and she clenched her fists to keep from screaming.

Yahya's grudge was deep and fierce and deadly. This was not about some Kurdish or Iraqi group putting her name on a kill list. His business was personal. He wanted revenge.

After seeing him at the hotel, she knew what he looked like now. She studied the crowd on the bridge. He was not among the people who were passing by her—the fishermen, the sightseers, the fun-seekers.

She thought about the message Yahya sent her. He'd texted her from Christina's number. She read the exchange again and then typed in a message.

I'm here.

The reply was immediate. *I know.*

Of course, he knew. Elizabeth stepped away from the railing and searched for him among the faces around her. She moved to the edge of the roadway and scanned the sidewalk across the lanes of traffic. Another motorcycle weaving through the crawling traffic swung close to the curb, causing her to back away.

She quickly typed a response. *Please talk to me before you kill me.*

After a pause, he answered. *As you talked to me before they took me in Ankara?*

She couldn't blame him, but she had to try. *I'm not begging for my life. I'm begging for Christina's.*

"For your daughter."

Elizabeth jumped back. Her heart was in her throat. She hadn't seen him approach, but here he was, looming over her.

In the years since Ankara, the lanky youth had matured into a muscular man. His arms hung confidently at his sides. If he was armed, she guessed the weapon was inside the jacket of his dark suit. But he probably didn't need anything more than his bare hands to break her neck or throw her over the side of this bridge. She looked into his face, searching for any sign of the gentleness that once resided there. All she saw were the cold, empty eyes of a man who had seen the world for what it was, hard and ruthless and lethal. And he had survived.

"You did not send your dogs. You came yourself."

"And I came alone," she told him.

He held out Christina's phone to her. "I think they are tracking this. No?"

She took the phone and stared at it as if the device could somehow tell her where she could find her daughter. "It's possible the Turkish police are doing it, but I don't think they move that fast. They know she was kidnapped. But I haven't spoken to them or to anyone else since you texted me."

"I should believe you, Elizabeth?" He glanced up at the dark sky above them. "Maybe Blackhawk helicopters will be landing on the bridge at any moment."

He was mocking her. And he was clearly unafraid.

"Is she alive, Yahya? Is Christina okay?" she asked. "Please tell me that you haven't hurt her. Please."

"Stop. Such fine acting is wasted on me. Do not pretend that you care for anyone but yourself. I know you better."

"I came here in good faith. I'm willing to do whatever you say. I'll pay whatever you want. I'm a wealthy woman. Tell me your price, and you'll have it. But please let her go."

"I am not after your money. I never was."

"I know. I know. But Christina is innocent. She's nothing like me. You can't punish her because of what I've done to you."

"You know the saying, *a life for a life, an eye for an eye, a nose for a nose, an ear for an ear, a tooth for a tooth.*" With each word he inched closer, crowding Elizabeth and backing her up until she bumped against the metal railing. His hand delved into a pocket. "I have no use for your money. And killing you fast is not punishment enough. I want you to suffer as you made—"

"Please, Yahya." No matter how long she had, no matter what torture he had planned for her, Elizabeth had one thing she absolutely needed to tell him. "Do what you have to do to me. But please don't hurt your own daughter."

"My daughter?" he asked, his shadowy face expressionless.

Thirty-two years ago, no one knew the identity of the father of her child. Not even Patricia Nicholls. Elizabeth had been successful in keeping her relationship with Yahya secret. And when he went missing, no one suspected that she had anything to do with it.

"Yes. Your daughter. I was pregnant when you went away."

"Went away?" He scowled fiercely. "People go away to see their family, to find work. You had me arrested. You told them to make me disappear."

"I'm sorry, Yahya. I knew I was carrying your child. Our child. What you say is true. I didn't want to be tied to you. I only thought of myself and what I wanted for *my* future." She expected him to come at her any second. His silence was ominous. "A month after you were arrested, Zari came to Ankara with Tiam, your baby. She came looking for you. She had nowhere to go. For once, I decided to do the right thing. I hired her and gave her a place to live."

She stared at where his hand had disappeared in his pocket. He could be holding a weapon that would end her life right here. People walking on the bridge went past them. No one so much as looked their way. If he decided to toss her over the railing now, she doubted anyone would be able to stop him. But there was more that she needed to say.

"Christina—our child—was born in September. From the very beginning, she was sick. She had cystic fibrosis. For eighteen months, I did the best I could. And then the doctors told me she was dying, that there was nothing more to be done for her."

Whatever he thought of her now, she was about to make it so much worse. But what was worse than evil?

"At that time, my life was a disaster. Because of other things I'd done, I had to leave my job in Ankara. And my child was dying. I was distraught. I...I took Zari's child. Your child. Tiam. I justified it in my own mind. I told myself I was giving her a better life. I took your Tiam and gave her Christina's name. I left Turkey and went to America and didn't come back for thirty years...until now."

Elizabeth felt exhausted, as if she'd run a marathon. But there was no sense of accomplishment in saying these things. This was nothing to be proud of. It was simply an admission of her guilt. Only shame. She'd confessed her sins, but she knew there could be no forgiveness. Not from Yahya.

He continued to stand silently. A cold, unreadable mask stretched tightly across his face.

"Christina and Tiam. Two girls, six months apart in age. They're both yours, both your daughters. You took the daughter Zari carried and gave birth to...the child I stole." Her voice shook. "Today Zari came to the hotel to tell me that Tiam was in ICU. I never knew that my real daughter had survived. The doctors say that she's dying. And this time it's true. She is dying."

Elizabeth's hands couldn't keep up with the tears tumbling down her cheeks.

"Her wish—her unbelievable wish—was to see me. The mother who abandoned her. She wanted to see me."

Elizabeth chin sank to her chest. She didn't deserve Tiam's words of forgiveness. God help her, she absolutely didn't deserve them.

Fighting back overwhelming grief, she forced herself to look up at Yahya's face.

"Do what you want with me, but please...please don't harm your own child. I beg you. Let Christina go."

He looked away from her, and time stood still. She stared at the clenched muscles of his face, at the long white scar along his jaw, at his hard profile. And she feared Christina was already hurt. Perhaps already dead.

Elizabeth had raised her, loved her as well as she could, treated her the only way she knew how. The way her own parents had treated her. Christina's words came back to her now.

Why can't you love me?

I'm your daughter. Why don't you trust me?

Tell me, Mother. Please tell me that you love me.

She had pushed aside and ignored Christina's words over and over again as the whining complaints of a spoiled daughter. But when was the last time Elizabeth had been truly and honestly affectionate toward her? When had she accepted her, not been critical of her, showed her that she was proud of the woman she'd become? It was too late for such thoughts. Far too late. She was about to lose them both. Elizabeth touched Yahya's arm. "I'm begging you. Tell me that Christina is okay."

He shook off her touch but turned his gaze to her. "Go."

"Go where?"

"Go to the hospital. To Tiam."

She grabbed hold of his jacket. "But what about Christina? I can't go anywhere until I know she's safe."

His glare was fierce and unbending, his tone sharp and punishing. "You say she is *my* daughter. Yes?"

"Yes, she's Zari's daughter...and yours."

"Then go," he snapped. "I will take care of my own."

Pulling himself free of her, he strode off, and Elizabeth stared in stunned silence.

41

CHRISTINA

AN HOUR EARLIER

THE HELPLESS AGONY of waiting for the executioner to cut my throat sharpens as he crouches down and stares into my face. His knee pushes against my legs. His size dominates the space, and the knife in his hand is terrifying.

"What did you say?" he asks, his voice low and threatening.

"I said, please tell Zari that I love her."

"How do you know her?"

"She's my...my friend. I've been to their apartment. Hers and Tiam's."

"When you came to Istanbul in April and June. I know."

It's my turn to be surprised, and I hazard a glance at his face. The night he drove me to the airport to pick up Kyle obviously wasn't the first time we met.

"How do you know so much about Zari and Tiam?"

"It is not for you to ask questions," he growls.

"Why not?" I snap, letting my anger and frustration show. How much worse could things get? When they dragged me out of the car, I assumed I was dead anyway. "You already know I've been to their apartment. And not only been there, but that I stayed with them for two weeks in June. So why are you asking stuff that you already know?"

He takes hold of the zip-ties binding my ankles and pulls my legs out straight. The blade flashes in the light of the bulb, and I flinch as he leans toward me. But then, with a quick motion, he cuts the ties at my ankles, and my legs are free.

"Now tell the truth," he orders. "Who are you?"

He's giving an inch, but I'm far from out of the woods.

"And don't give me more *bullshit* about internet. How do you know Tiam? Why Elizabeth Hall's daughter is a friend to Zari Rahman and her daughter?"

Fuck it. What do I have to lose by telling the truth? That's the question I've been asking myself since they dumped me in this room. I know I won't be putting Tiam and Zari in danger with this man. He's clearly being protective of them.

"You do not talk, and I go out there and let those animals come in. They can convince you to speak."

"Are they tougher than you?" I can hear the sarcasm in my own voice. "Are they supposed to be scarier than you?"

He stands up and takes a step toward the door.

"Wait," I say quickly. "This past April was actually a reunion between me and Tiam and Zari. A reunion that was thirty years overdue."

He stares down at me. His face is twisted in a dubious frown.

I doubt that he wants to hear the long story of how Tiam and I found each other. Or how I knew for my entire life there was something wrong with me. Or how I always felt there was a piece of me missing, but never guessed that it was because I was separated from my mother at such a young age. So I give him the abridged story of two mothers and two daughters, of a baby abduction, and how Tiam and I connected.

"I didn't lie to you in the car. It really was the internet that threw us together. Once I found her, I met with her and Zari. In April, and again in June."

He stands as silent as a statue, watching me.

"That's the reason," I continue, "why I don't think Elizabeth will be too enthusiastic about handing herself over to you in exchange for me...if that's what you think is going to happen. I'm not her daughter."

It's uncomfortable tilting my head up, trying to gauge his mood.

"This is true? All of it?"

My legs are tingling and need some blood flowing into them. I try to stand, but with my hands still zip-tied behind me, it's difficult to find my balance right away.

He grabs me by the arm and helps me up. The knife flashes in his hand.

"It's true. Why would I make up a story that's so complicated?"

He looks at me for an eternity, as if he's searching my face for confirmation of what I've told him. My life has been hanging in the balance since this morning, but something about him strikes a familiar chord in me. I can't explain it, but it's as if our relationship has changed. I feel calmer, and I'm not surprised when he finally turns me around and cuts the ties binding my wrists.

Pain and relief battle for dominance as a deep breath whooshes out of my lungs. My shoulders and arms are burning as I try to move them.

He goes to the door and listens to the conversation on the other side. Something about the way he's standing catches me off guard. It's the angle and tilt of his chin as he focuses. Kyle teases me that I do the same thing.

A thought is forming, but I can't believe it. "Who are you?"

He turns his eyes toward me. His gaze is intense, and the brow is creased. Shit. It's the same expression I get whenever I'm angry or stressed about things.

"We are walking out of here, but you must do what I say."

"What do you want me to do?"

He gestures to me, and I go to him.

"Stand here and wait. I must speak to them first, and then we go."

"Just like that?" I ask, finding this turn of events a little unreal.

He puts a hand on my shoulder and looks into my eyes. "You must trust me."

My heart melts. My eyes are the same as his. We have the same cleft in our chins.

"What is your name?" I ask softly.

"Does it matter?"

"It matters."

"I am Yahya Rahman."

I blink several times, but a tear escapes and tumbles down my cheek. He's the reason why I started doing all the genetic tests. Without the motivation to find this man, I might never have met Tiam. Or Zari. I would never have come home. Finding him completes my search.

"I trust you."

He opens the door and slips through, closes it behind him and immediately begins shouting at the two men. They're speaking Turkish. Actually, two are speaking and one is shouting. I have no trouble distinguishing my father's voice from the other two. He's chewing them up like a movie drill sergeant.

I still can't believe it. My father. Yahya left Kurdistan before I was born. The way Zari spoke of him, Tiam always imagined he must be dead. But here he was, alive in Istanbul and keeping track of his family.

I jump back when the door opens. Yahya holds out a hand to me.

"We are going. Do not look at their faces. There can be no retribution for their stupidity. Not from police."

"Of course."

He takes hold of my arm. I lower my chin and stare at the floor as he leads me through the outer room. A few steps along the way, he shoves my purse into my arms, and I clutch it against my chest.

"*Bize borçlusun,*" a man's voice calls out.

"*Para iadem nedeniyle yaşamanıza izin verildi,*" Yahya answers.

"What did he say?" I ask when we're beyond the room and passing through a dark hallway. The door to the street is straight ahead. I still can't believe I'm walking out of here alive.

"They think I owe them something," he tells me. "They think they are very smart, but they are stupid. They took you to get money from Elizabeth."

"That wasn't *your* plan?"

His glare is my answer. And that explains the shouting and furniture throwing I heard when he first arrived.

"What about the robbery in Elizabeth's room when we first arrived in Istanbul?" I have to know.

"I did not want her to come and go. They did the job as I told them. I wanted her passport and identification. They kept her money and jewels."

"What did you tell them now?"

"I told them they are lucky that I let them live."

Yahya's confidence and toughness are striking and obvious. He has the quality of a Tony Soprano. I still have no idea, however, if he's a gangster or an assassin or simply an airport driver who moonlights as a kidnapper. Whatever he does, I'm just happy he's my father.

He pushes me through a steel door, and we step out to a side street that is little more than an alley. Night has descended, but a streetlight illuminates a motorcycle parked near the door. Not far away, where the alley opens out a little, a half dozen kids are kicking a soccer ball, oblivious to the kind of business going on in their neighborhood. At least, I hope they're oblivious to it.

"This way."

I follow him down the end of the alley to a wider street. Around the corner, he waves toward an old, battered Mercedes parked under a red and white sign depicting a tow truck. He opens the passenger door and I climb in.

My adrenaline has been pumping in high gear since the moment those men dragged me out of the town car, but I'm finally able to take a deep breath.

"What happened to the driver of my car?" I ask, almost afraid to hear the answer.

He shrugs. "She is fine. Frightened, I am certain, but fine. She is probably safe in her house with the doors locked right now."

I'm relieved. "Can you take me back to the hotel? Or to Zari and Tiam's?"

"No. Not yet. Give me your mobile."

I look in my bag, and find my cell. There are dozens of missed calls and messages.

"What do you want it for?"

"To reach Elizabeth. She must meet with me."

I thought we were done with that kidnapping business. "She won't come. She's not going to put her life in danger for me. Why would you want to meet with her, anyway?"

"We have unfinished business."

After what I told him about Elizabeth swapping babies, I have a bad feeling. "Please, I don't want her to be hurt. She raised me."

"I will not hurt her." His hand reaches out, waiting for me to hand over the phone. "Trust me."

42

ELIZABETH

NOW

ONCE YAHYA DISAPPEARED into the crowd, the city gradually filtered back into Elizabeth's consciousness. The traffic, the conversations of fishermen, the smells from the restaurants below, the ferry horns, the lights on the boats and in the hills of the city. She was alive, free. She breathed a deep sigh of relief and stared for a while at the brightly lit skyline of old Istanbul.

She had to trust what he said about Christina. He wouldn't hurt her, now that he knew she was his daughter.

Elizabeth turned her attention to Tiam. She needed to access the resources that were available back in California. The doctor she and Zari spoke with said a day or two was all that they could hope for. She needed to act now. Perhaps that was enough time to fly Tiam to the US or bring someone in who knew what they were doing.

Her friend Sheila from the tennis club was on the advisory board of the School of Medicine at UCLA. She was affiliated with multiple hospitals in LA. She'd know who to call, what to do, how to expedite what needed to be done. She looked at her phone and her heart sank. None of her old contacts were on this phone.

Kyle could find the number for her. She started dialing his cell as she moved to the raised curb separating the sidewalk from the bus lane. Taxis crawled along, and she lifted her hand to signal for one.

Kyle answered and his sharp tone conveyed his urgency. "Finally! You were supposed to call me back. Did Christina contact you?"

In the corner of her eye, Elizabeth saw a motorcycle carrying two men weave between the cabs and roar along the curb.

"She'll be okay."

Elizabeth froze as she saw the rider draw a pistol from his leather jacket. The gunmetal gleamed in the light from the streetlamp.

"What do you mean okay? Where is she? Have you seen her?"

The phone dropped out of her hand in her rush to back up. She stumbled as she turned away. The pistol barked, and a searing blast exploded in her head, knocking her to the concrete sidewalk. Elizabeth rolled onto her back, and the light above her grew so bright that she closed her eyes. Shouts and cries rang out, and as the motorcycle roared off, footsteps pounded toward her.

43

CHRISTINA

NOW

SITTING ALONE IN THE MERCEDES, I can see the ferryboats docked at the pier. They're brilliantly lit for their trips back and forth across the Bosphorus, between the old city and the Asian side of Istanbul. It occurs to me that these boats are always going somewhere, constantly moving, but only briefly touching the distant shore. For their entire working existence, they blast their horns, throw their wakes, announce their arrival and departure and travel, but in the end they are destined always to return home.

"Like all of us," I think out loud.

Yahya's instructions to me were to keep the doors locked and wait until he gets back. He still has my phone, and I saw him walk in the direction of the Galata Bridge. He showed me some of the texts he exchanged with Elizabeth. They're to meet on the bridge, but I have my doubts about her actually being there.

Different scenarios are running in my head. My mother could have sent Kyle to talk to him and see what Yahya wants for my return. Or she'd send the police and have him arrested. Or even worse, she'd get the consulate involved, who in turn would get their security people involved. In two of the three, Yahya gets locked up or killed, and that terrifies me.

I don't have any confidence that she'll come herself, not to save me. And I don't know how Yahya intends to settle their *unfinished business*, as he called it. Is he after money? He said to me he won't hurt her. I do trust him, but I'm worried he doesn't know exactly what he's dealing with when it comes to Elizabeth and her connections.

He's my father. Zari's husband. I think of my real mother, and how Tiam told me there's never been any other man in her life. She thinks Zari is still in love with him. Their wedding picture, the only photo she has of the two of them, is set up like a shrine in the bedroom. Twice before, when I had stayed at the apartment, I looked at the image of the smiling young man standing next to the beautiful bride. And now that I've met Yahya, I have no doubt that he is the man in that photo.

I wonder if Zari knows he's alive. If she does know it, what I can't fathom is why he hasn't been part of their lives for all these years. I have so many questions.

When I reunited with my mother, she held me and Tiam in her embrace, and the three of us stood in their apartment and sobbed for what felt like hours. Today, when I learned Yahya's name, we skipped over my entire fantasy about the moment when I'd finally meet him. But to know him, and for both of us to recognize what we are to each other, is enough. I've finally met my father, and I don't want to lose him.

Time is dragging by too slowly. He's been gone for a while. He took the car keys with him, so I have no way of knowing how long. Half an hour? An hour? I'm getting restless, and my worry is growing with each passing minute.

Trying to distract myself, I turn my attention to the pier. A ferry that has been carving a wide arc across the Golden Horn in now gliding slowly and smoothly toward the dock. People are on deck, crowding around two openings in the railing where the gangplanks will be placed.

A policeman on a motorcycle passes the car, startling me. Yahya parked the old Mercedes under another tow zone sign, but the cop doesn't give me a second glance. As he rides off, I look back toward the bridge. Something must have happened. Anxiety is gnawing away at me. And then I see him.

He's working his way through the crowds on the pier. Beyond him, the arriving ferry sounds its horn. Yahya stands a head taller than most of the people around him, and from what I can see, he is unharmed.

Relief floods through me, and I step out of the car as he approaches. "What happened?"

"She came."

"Alone?"

Yahya nods and glances back at the bridge.

"I can't believe it," I murmur.

"She cares about you."

Today has certainly been a day for revelations. For thirty years, Elizabeth has played the role of mother to me. I suppose she's done it the only way she knows. Despite any complaint I might have, however, she showed up for me tonight. For *me*.

I wonder if I should go there and find her.

"Did you tell her that I'm safe?"

"She knows."

Before I can ask him any more questions, he goes around the car to the driver's side. "I must go to the hospital. You should come with me."

"Why?" My stomach drops. "Who's in the hospital?"

"Tiam. She is not doing well."

Before I can say anything else, a loud crack echoes across the water. It sounds like a large firecracker to me, but Yahya utters something angrily and starts running back toward the bridge. I reach inside the car, grab my bag, and hurry after him.

The crowds on the pier have stopped moving. There is a commotion on the bridge, and the sound of shouting rises above the hum of the ferryboats' engines. On the upper level, people are running, and I can barely keep up with Yahya. Traffic is at a standstill, but in the distance, I hear sirens.

All I can think of is Elizabeth. Kyle told me her name is on a kill list. There has to be a price tag attached. My kidnappers wanted money. Would they go after my mother? I'm hoping the thoughts burning in my brain are nothing more than panic and conjecture.

It takes only a few minutes to reach a large knot of people crowding the sidewalk on the bridge, and I struggle to get closer.

"Let me get through," I cry out as I shove against the wall of bodies. "Please!"

Suddenly, Yahya appears, reaching toward me through the onlookers. He takes my hand and pulls me through.

"They shot Elizabeth," he says in my ear. "She is alive."

I hear the words, but my mind is slow to comprehend. No one wants to move or make room for us to pass, but he bulls his way forward, and I follow in his wake until we reach the center of the circle.

Nausea slithers through me at the sight of blood on the sidewalk. A uniformed policeman is crouching beside the body. The shoes, the slacks, and the purse lying in the dark red pool belong to Elizabeth. I'm vaguely aware of an ambulance coming to a screeching stop somewhere nearby. The lights are flashing.

Finally, the truth hits me. I try to go to her, but a police officer blocks my way.

"*Aile*," Yahya shouts into his face. "*Kızı.*"

The officer drops his hand and allows me to pass. My ears are ringing, and tears blur my vision. My throat is squeezed shut as I kneel next to Elizabeth. Her head lies in a pool of blood. Her eyes are open, but I don't think she sees me. I grab her hand.

Two EMTs appear, and I'm shoved aside as they start to work on her.

"*Kimsin sen?*" someone asks me. I don't know what they're saying. A hand tries to pull me away.

"No," I cry out. "Let me stay. I'm her daughter. Her daughter. She's my mother."

Elizabeth's eyes focus on my face and her hand moves. I grasp her bloody fingers in my own again.

"You're safe," she murmurs.

The crowd parts and a gurney rolls up beside her.

"Hospital. You go with her," a policeman tells me in broken English. He motions where I should stand as they maneuver my mother onto the stretcher.

I search the faces of the crowd and find Yahya. His eyes meet mine. He holds something out to me, and I hurry over to take it from him. It's my phone.

He holds my hand for a second, gesturing with his eyes toward Elizabeth. "Not me."

"I know."

They're moving Elizabeth into the ambulance, and I run over and climb in. An EMT is pressing a bandage against the back of her head, at the base of her skull. The grey blanket they covered her with is already dark with her blood. Everyone is speaking Turkish, and the urgency of their tone tells me how badly she's doing. Calls are being made, and I assume they're notifying the hospital to prepare. Elizabeth seems to be drifting in and out of consciousness.

"You're going to make it," I tell her. "You *will* make it."

Her eyes focus on mine and her lips move. I bring my ear closer.

"Do the right thing."

I don't understand what she means. Elizabeth's *right thing* has always been different from mine.

"For your sister."

"My sister?" I look into her face and touch an escaping teardrop.

"Tiam...you...sisters."

The first thing that comes to my mind is that sometime today, after I'd gone missing, Elizabeth must have finally met Tiam. But Yahya told me Tiam was already in the hospital.

"Did you meet her? Tiam? Your daughter?"

"Listen."

"I'm here, Mother."

"Sister...your sister...Tiam."

Elizabeth isn't aware of the fact that I've known the truth for the past six months. "I know Tiam. She's like a sister to me. I've met Zari too. She told me what happened in Ankara."

She closes her eyes and squeezes my hand. When she turns her gaze on me again, more tears escape.

Her words are slurring. "You...Tiam...same father."

I stare at her as my brain struggles with what she's telling me. Yahya's words come back to me about the unfinished business.

"Do the right thing for Tiam," Elizabeth says and closes her eyes.

PART XIII

Do me justice, You who are the glory of the just,
Who are the throne, and I the lintel of Your door.
But, in sober truth, where are throne and doorway?
Where are "We" and "I"? There, where our Beloved is!
— Rumi

44

ZARI

THE TOUCH on Zari's shoulder was comforting and familiar. Hospital hours passed slowly, but Emine came up to the ICU every hour to check on her and Tiam. There was nothing more to be done for her daughter but wait and pray. And pray she did. Zari believed in God and in miracles. At the same time, she feared having exhausted her pleas heavenward. Still, she wasn't giving up.

"Someone out there wants to speak to you," her friend said quietly.

Elizabeth left the hospital some time ago, and Zari assumed that she'd returned. "Tell her she can come back in."

"I think you should speak to him yourself."

The doctors had been both kind and efficient in letting her know what was happening at every step. For some time now, Tiam had been drifting in and out of consciousness, so Zari reluctantly let go of her daughter's hand and followed her dearest friend out.

In the hallway, Emine gestured to one of the consulting rooms. Over the years, Zari had learned that the doctors preferred to relay the worst news in the privacy of those rooms. But what could be more crushing than what she already knew? Zari braced herself and her steps dragged as she went in.

The light shone brightly overhead. He was standing against the far wall.

"Yahya?" Her hand clutched the back of a chair for support.

In all the years of knowing he was around, this was the first time the two had been in such close proximity, had stood in the same room. She looked into his handsome face and his troubled eyes. He always found out whenever Tiam was hospitalized, and Zari knew of his presence through the accounts that were settled and the flowers that would appear. She guessed Emine had something to do with him being here tonight.

"I had to come."

"Of course."

He ran a hand behind his neck as if he were in pain. Zari wished she'd been brave enough to tell him the truth about the girls long before this moment. She could read the suffering in his furrowed brow and his clenched jaw.

"I'd like to ask your permission to see my daughter...before she's gone."

"Of course you can see her. But..." She had to free herself. Zari had accepted his generosity for a very long time, but she didn't want his grief to be misplaced. "But I need to tell you. She's not your child, Yahya. Tiam is—"

"Elizabeth Hall's daughter. I know."

Stunned, Zari struggled to find her voice. For years, Emine had been in contact with Yahya, but she didn't know this secret about Tiam. How he'd discovered the truth was a mystery to her.

"I spoke to Elizabeth tonight. Tiam is also *my* daughter."

As his words registered, Zari's legs wobbled, and she sank to the edge of the nearest chair. She stared with unseeing eyes at the white walls, trying to comprehend all that those few words conveyed. Their past was crumbling around her, piece by piece.

She'd believed the promises they had made to each other in Qalat Dizah before he had to leave. The letters they exchanged had been full of hope. Their love was stronger than the ravages of war. When she left their home amid the screaming percussion of falling rockets and bombs, it was the thought of reuniting with her husband that gave strength to her steps. While giving birth to their daughter in the home of strangers, the thought of being with him again was the single thing that fortified her.

But his devotion didn't match hers. His love for her lacked substance. He'd betrayed the vows they'd taken.

"I was a stupid and gullible young man back then, alone and lost and undeserving of you and your love."

Zari listened to his words, but she couldn't bring herself to look into his face. She was angry, wounded, bleeding. Many times during these past thirty years, she'd imagined him married to someone else and having a separate family. But she found it difficult to grasp this admission. Certainly, he must have loved her still at that time.

"I can make excuses and say Elizabeth seduced me, but then I'd be a coward," he continued. "I must take responsibility for my part in it. I always had the choice of walking away. She couldn't force me. I had made a solemn promise to you. We'd exchanged vows. But all I can say is I never thought hard enough about consequences."

"There are always consequences."

When Zari arrived in Ankara, Elizabeth was already pregnant. She was so generous, giving Zari—a stranger—a job in spite of having no references. At the time, she'd thought it was miraculous, but everything made sense now.

"I thought you were incorruptible, and I believed Elizabeth to be generous. Foolish me!"

"I paid a hard price for my disloyalty," he told her.

As was right, Zari thought. More than a three decades had passed, and she still hurt. How could he do that to her?

"When she was finished with me, Elizabeth had me arrested. I didn't know until tonight, but it was because she had become pregnant with my child. She wanted me removed from her life."

Zari focused on his face. Standing before her was a strong and dangerous man, and yet he couldn't bring himself to look at her. It was easy and right to lay blame, but she had fallen victim to Elizabeth's evil herself.

"What did they do to you? Where did they take you?"

"The Americans moved me a few times before handing me over to the Turks. I was taken to the military prison on Imrali Island and remained there for over a year.

When they finally realized I was a nobody and that I knew nothing of any value, I was transferred to Ulucanlar Prison in Ankara."

Zari knew about both of those places. Kurdish people talked about the nightmare of overcrowding, of hunger strikes, of the torture and the beatings that existed in Turkish prisons, but those two were among the worst.

"Did they torture you?" she asked.

Yahya's eyes met Zari's, and his face hardened. "I don't want you to think about the things that happened to me. I don't deserve your sympathy."

"My pain is mine. You can't dictate how I feel."

He paused and then nodded. "I was foolish and weak, Zari. I deserved what I got. I learned a grave lesson from it."

Hot, wild anger erupted and raced through her. Elizabeth did this to him. She did it callously—just as when she stole her daughter—without any thought of the damage she was inflicting on so many lives. She destroyed everything she touched. A few hours ago, Zari stood in this hospital and told her that she'd forgiven her. Now she prayed to Allah to help her, for all the rage was back, pumping fire through her veins.

"Long ago, the Yahya Rahman you married disappeared," he told her. "But I am also no longer the foolish young man who lost his way in Ankara."

"You certainly are *not*."

"I regret all I did to you, all the disappointment I have caused, all the pain my broken vows have inflicted on you."

What they had between them was long gone. She'd come to terms with that the first time Emine told her that Yahya was in Istanbul. But Zari also knew that broken faith was difficult to mend.

"I don't expect forgiveness. I don't deserve it. That is for you alone to give."

The moments of happiness they had shared were behind them. They had traveled separate paths and become different people.

"Tonight, I've come here with one purpose."

Zari stood up slowly. She understood. "You're here to meet and to say goodbye to your daughter. Come with me."

45

CHRISTINA

FOR OVER SIX HOURS, I've been pacing in the hospital waiting area. I'm already climbing the walls. An administrator has been checking on me occasionally, but so far the only thing I've been told is that my mother is still in surgery.

In the distance an elevator dings, and a moment later Kyle comes down the corridor. He's only been gone from my side for a few minutes, and when I tell him there's been nothing new, he puts a cup of coffee in my hand and leads me to the chairs lining one wall of the waiting room.

"The meetings with the buyers have been postponed indefinitely. I also called and spoke to Elizabeth's lawyer."

Kyle arrived at the American Hospital in the Taksim neighborhood a short time after Elizabeth had been wheeled into the operating room, and he's been more than supportive.

This has all been a nightmare. She lost consciousness while I was with her in the ambulance, and it was clear the EMTs were doing everything they could to keep her alive en route to the hospital. Since she went into surgery, the wait has been excruciating.

A couple of hours ago, I told Kyle everything about my family, so he knows all about Tiam and Zari and Yahya and me. He already knew about what Elizabeth did years ago working for the US government, but now he's fully aware of her actions in Ankara. Most of all, he knows that—since she's not actually my birth mother—I feel unqualified to make any unilateral decisions regarding her health, her life.

Since I've been here, I've spoken to Zari on the phone too. I was relieved to hear that Yahya is there with her. It's strange that Elizabeth and Tiam, a mother and daughter, are both struggling to stay alive in hospitals only twenty minutes apart.

"Elizabeth's lawyer told me that they revisited her will when Jax died two months ago," Kyle tells me. "She also has a living will on file with him. He emailed it to me while we were on the phone."

"Is it valid here?"

"He is checking, but he was fairly certain Turkey recognizes its validity. In this case, you're informing these physicians of her wishes regarding end-of-life medical care."

"End of life." I shake my head stubbornly. "She's going to live."

He rubs my back and gathers me against him, and I take tremendous comfort in knowing I'm not alone in this. I think back to the days after Autumn's death and how I rejected Kyle, pushing him away, making him feel unwelcome. Somehow, deep down, I held him responsible simply because he wasn't ready to have a child. The truth is, I'd betrayed his trust and used him, and he'd been trying to do his best to deal with it.

"It won't be easy, but you have to be prepared." He brushes a kiss on my forehead. "How is Tiam? Did you talk to your mother again?"

I look at my phone, but there are no messages and no new calls.

"Once Elizabeth is out of surgery, I want to go over there." My voice breaks. "That is, if my sister is still alive."

He holds my face in his hands and looks into my eyes. "Maybe you should go now. What can you do here?"

"I'm torn between here and there. Between who I am now and who I was at birth. It's so hard to know who needs me most—this mother who raised me or the one who brought me into this world. My heart is in pieces, and I feel like an outsider in both places. I can't decide where I really belong."

He presses my face against his chest, and the tears I've been holding back break free. I'm lost. I'm truly lost.

But I'm not alone. Sharing this knowledge of the truth has brought the two of us closer. I know he'll stay beside me and help me for as long as it takes to get through what lies ahead.

An administrator appears, and I wipe my face.

"If you could follow me, the doctor can speak to you now."

Kyle holds onto my hand. In a small room near the nurses' station, a man dressed in scrubs and a younger woman wearing a name badge are waiting for us.

After the door is closed, the doctor begins to speak, but I don't hear anything after his first words.

PART XIV

Once more, O happy hill and peaceful plain,
Once more, O kindly meadow, laugh with glee:
Now is all earth's old nature young again.
O hold you dear the flowers, that through Spring's door
Enter your garden: ere you may no more
Behold them, love them who live but for thee.
Greet them, ere they through Autumn's gate depart:
Since for your pleasuring, God made them be,
Gaze on them gladly,—on me too, sweet heart,
Who for your sake alone live; give me one
Welcome, once smile on me, ere I be gone.
                                   — Ḥafeẓ

EPILOGUE

CHRISTINA

Two Months Later

FROM THE OBSERVATION deck of the Galata Tower, the view of the city after last night's dusting of early snow is more than breathtaking, it's magical. It's nearly noon, and in the light of a brilliant November sun, Istanbul is a glistening, jewel-encrusted treasure.

My gaze travels from the mouth of the Bosphorus far to the south, all the way to the great Blue Mosque, the Hagia Sofia, and the Suleymaniye Mosque, which sit proudly atop the hills to the west of the sparkling Golden Horn.

Two months ago, I felt lost, but no longer. Brushing away a tear, I breathe in the cold clear air and fight back feelings that still threaten to overwhelm me. I think about those difficult moments in the hospital and the confusion of that entire week following Elizabeth's shooting. But out of those hard, chaotic moments emerged irrevocable change in all our lives.

Do the right thing for Tiam.

Those were the words that stayed with me during the times of greatest difficulty. Decisions had to be made. Elizabeth's heart was beating when they took her into surgery, but she never regained consciousness. The bullet that entered her brain had done too much damage. She was declared brain-dead almost immediately, but the doctors kept her on mechanical support and continued for hours in the futile effort to save her.

I don't remember a great deal from that meeting with the surgeon. The value of Kyle's presence beside me was immeasurable. He stayed by me and talked to me and checked the legal aspects of what needed to be done while I considered the immediate future.

Do the right thing...

Elizabeth had opted to be an organ donor years ago, but that was only important to me and not to the doctors involved. Regardless of the lies coloring our family's past, on record I was her next of kin, the decision maker. Once I put her medical team in contact with Tiam's, the assessment started. Elizabeth and my sister had the same blood and tissue types, and that made the chance of rejection less likely.

The most miraculous thing for me as we waited through those two long days before all the tests cleared was that Tiam fought to stay alive. It was as if she somehow sensed that the mother who'd abandoned her thirty years ago had returned offering the very possibility of life.

The police never arrested the men responsible for shooting Elizabeth. No suspicion ever fell on Yahya.

He wants to be part of our lives, but as far as his relationship with Zari, the decision is hers. Tiam tells me they see each other occasionally. And the couple of times that she's espied them together, they're more like a couple on first date than two people who share a thirty year history.

I spoke to Patricia Nicholls once after Elizabeth died. She's a very lonely woman, and her health is failing. I got the sense that she felt overpowered by my mother when they were friends in Ankara. Patricia claimed that she meant to help with the baby and the hospital bills and all, but Zari disappeared and Patricia never saw them again.

My eyes are drawn to a pair of trams that are passing each other on the Galata Bridge far below me. The crowds on the bridge are moving briskly in the cool breeze coming off the water. A vendor has a handcart almost on the exact spot where Elizabeth was gunned down. From here, it looks like he's selling bunches of flowers. Life goes on.

I think of Autumn all the time. She changed me, and she will forever be part of me. Every time I see a mother and daughter walking down a lane, I think of the void in my heart. Every infant's laughter and cries, every affectionate exchange between parent and child, brings back the memory of those few precious days we had.

Wiping the moisture from my cheeks, I look around and see the beautiful hijabi woman approaching along the tower's metal railing. Tiam. I turn to her and enfold her in my arms. To hold her, knowing we're truly sisters, is a gift that I had never expected in life. The steroids she takes to make sure she doesn't reject Elizabeth's lungs have helped her gain some weight. She looks vibrant and alive, and her cheeks glow from the effect of the cold air.

"How was the doctor's appointment?"

"Everything is good." She hooks her arm in mine, and we stand together with the city beneath us. "I can go back to work next month."

"Back to work?"

Money is a bone of contention between us. Externus was sold, and Elizabeth's estate is substantial, but neither of us wants her wealth. An idea that we've been pursuing involves using the funds to establish an education and training center for refugees in Istanbul. With my business and computer background, and Tiam's knowledge of the culture and local resources, we believe we may have found a worthy use for the inheritance.

"Is this Sunday still good for you to go to the Sufi lodge and watch the Whirling Dervishes?" she asks. I take note that she's blushing slightly.

Tiam and Kemal Osman, the handsome pharmacist, did know each other through their university connection, and I'm quite proud of myself for getting them to meet over coffee and pastries last week.

"Yes, it is. But I refuse to act as a chaperone for you two," I tell her. "Also, Kyle is flying in on Friday."

Tiam's blue eyes are mischievous when they meet mine. "How long is he staying this time?"

"For the weekend."

"Why don't you bring him too?"

"I'll ask him."

My relationship with Kyle right now is complicated. He accepted the job in Japan, but he's involved in sales and marketing, and he says he doesn't have to live there full-time. Since Elizabeth's death, I've been going back and forth between LA and Istanbul, settling her estate. And every time I've come to Turkey, he's turned up here. To visit, he says, or to check on me.

Unfortunately, it took Elizabeth's death for me to take a good look at who I was before, and to take responsibility for my actions. What I did to Kyle was wrong, but he's still interested in trying to give our relationship another try. I'm not ruling out the possibility. Long distance relations are difficult to maintain, but we're walking into it with our eyes open. We've both learned from the mistakes of the past.

For my whole life, I've never been the person I thought I was. I was actually a broken reflection from a mirror shattered long ago in an apartment in Ankara. But these days, I'm finding myself, piece by piece, and gluing the fragments back in place. And as I look at the smiling profile of the sister who said, *I am you. And you are me,* I know where I belong. I like the reflection I see between the cracks in that mirror.

Another woman in a headscarf comes out to the observation deck. When Zari sees us, her eyes light up with happiness. She moves with the grace of a woman who carried her unborn baby through rocket barrages and rugged mountains. She is a woman who dedicated herself to raising a sick child that was thrust upon her. She built a life on a lasting foundation of love. She opens her arms as she reaches us.

"*Kızlarım*. My daughters. My life."

And as the three of us embrace, I know we're home.

Thank you for taking the time to read *When the Mirror Cracks*. If you enjoyed it, please consider telling your friends or posting a short review. Word of mouth is an author's best friend...and much appreciated.

Hope you'll page down and take a look at the other novels that we've written under the pen names Jan Coffey and May McGoldrick.

Enjoy!

AUTHOR'S NOTE

Stories come to us in bits and pieces, and as writers we try to weave them into a seamless tale. In case of *When the Mirror Cracks*, the fate of refugees in the world has always been important to Nikoo. Because of her own experience as an immigrant, the issues of identity and inclusion often play a critical role in the creation of our characters. It was true in this novel, as well. Then, we concocted a story involving the mystery of two children changing places, the definition of mother-hood, and the damaging effects of privilege. We added to the mix Kurdistan, a place and culture with which Nikoo has a family connec-tion, and set the action in Istanbul, a vast city brimming with history and beauty.

And in putting together our stories, we make use of a cast of experts.

We are so grateful for the people in our lives who support us and sustain us with their love and knowledge and wisdom. We want to thank the following people for their contributions:

To Cyrus McGoldrick and Sarosh Arif, who helped us with their knowledge of Istanbul, their language translations, their story input, and their sensitivity.

To Sam McGoldrick, who deftly steered us with his skills and insights with regard to story structure and character development.

To Olivia Zeff, who helped us with her expertise in the psychology and trauma of separation and child development.

To Jeff McGoldrick, who contributed with his professional knowledge in the area of emergency response team work.

To Isabel Ngo, a member of the Tessera Editorial group, for her editing and perceptive reading of the manuscript.

To our talented and generous cover designer, David Provolo.

To our wonderful beta-readers, whose honesty and encouragement made this story better.

And to Nikoo's Kurdish family, for their love and support.

Thank you for reading our story. If you enjoyed it, leave an online review and help us spread the word.

www.MayMcGoldrick.com
www.JanCoffey.com
NikooandJim@gmail.com

THE JANUS EFFECT

PEACE AND WAR, FRIEND AND FOE, LIFE AND DEATH... A
PERILOUS JOURNEY HOME!

AN IRAQI KURDISH scientist has been wrongly held in a CIA "black
site" for over five years. Now, as cases of unexplained deaths—marked
by rapid decomposition—are cropping up across the U.S., Homeland
Security is willing to bend any rule to find the source of the deadly
infection, even if it means resurrecting a "dead" Iraqi biochemist.
Fahimah's sister risked her life trying to destroy the super-microbe
that causes the flesh-eating disease. Fahimah tried, too, but landed in
prison.

Austyn Newman was sent to gain the cooperation of the scientist.
Arriving in Afghanistan, he recognizes that the CIA has been holding
the wrong sister all these years. They need her, but how will he gain
her trust?

With time running out, Austyn must help Fahimah find her way
through war-ravaged Iraq and Kurdistan...for the answer lies at the
end of her journey home.

Winner: Connecticut Press Club Award— Best Book of the Year

ALSO BY JAN COFFEY & MAY MCGOLDRICK

Romantic Suspense & Mystery

Trust Me Once

Twice Burned

Triple Threat

Fourth Victim

Five in a Row

Silent Waters

Cross Wired

The Janus Effect

The Puppet Master

Blind Eye

Road Kill

Mercy (novella)

Young Adult

Tropical Kiss

Aquarian

NOVELS BY MAY McGOLDRICK

16th Century Highlander Novels

A Midsummer Wedding *(novella)*

The Thistle and the Rose

Macpherson Brothers Trilogy

Angel of Skye (Book 1)

Heart of Gold (Book 2)

Beauty of the Mist (Book 3)

Macpherson Trilogy (Box Set)

The Intended

Flame

Tess and the Highlander

Highland Treasure Trilogy

The Dreamer (Book 1)

The Enchantress (Book 2)

The Firebrand (Book 3)

Highland Treasure Trilogy Box Set

Scottish Relic Trilogy

Much Ado About Highlanders (Book 1)

Taming the Highlander (Book 2)

Tempest in the Highlands (Book 3)

Scottish Relic Trilogy Box Set

Arsenic and Old Armor

18th Century Novels

Secret Vows

The Promise (Pennington Family)

The Rebel

Secret Vows Box Set

Scottish Dream Trilogy (Pennington Family)

Borrowed Dreams (Book 1)

Captured Dreams (Book 2)

Dreams of Destiny (Book 3)

Scottish Dream Trilogy Box Set

Regency and 19th Century Novels

Pennington Regency-Era Series

Romancing the Scot

It Happened in the Highlands

Sweet Home Highland Christmas *(novella)*

Sleepless in Scotland

Dearest Millie *(novella)*

How to Ditch a Duke *(novella)*

Royal Highlander Series

Highland Crown

Highland Jewel

Highland Sword

Ghost of the Thames

Contemporary Romance

Thanksgiving in Connecticut

Made in Heaven

NOVELS BY NICK JAMES

Caleb Marlowe Westerns

Outlaw Country

Nonfiction

Marriage of Minds: Collaborative Fiction Writing

Step Write Up: Writing Exercises for 21st Century

ABOUT THE AUTHOR

USA Today Bestselling Authors Nikoo and Jim McGoldrick have crafted over fifty fast-paced, conflict-filled historical and contemporary novels and two works of nonfiction under the pseudonyms May McGoldrick and Jan Coffey. Beginning in 2021, they will be adding the pen name Nick James and writing historical Westerns

These popular and prolific authors write suspense, mystery, historical romance, and young adult novels. They are four-time Rita Award Finalists and the winners of numerous awards for their writing, including the Daphne DeMaurier Award for Excellence, the *Romantic Times Magazine* Reviewers' Choice Award, three NJRW Golden Leaf Awards, two Holt Medallions, and the Connecticut Press Club Award for Best Fiction. Their work is included in the Popular Culture Library collection of the National Museum of Scotland.

facebook.com/JanCoffeyAuthor
twitter.com/jancoffey
instagram.com/jancoffeyauthor
bookbub.com/authors/jan-coffey

CPSIA information can be obtained
at www.ICGtesting.com
Printed in the USA
BVHW031155200820
586906BV00001B/21

9 780984 156733